MUM ON A MISSION

CARMEN REID

B

Boldwood

First published in 2005 as *Up All Night*. This edition published in Great Britain in 2025 by Boldwood Books Ltd.

Copyright © Carmen Reid, 2005

Cover Design by JD Smith Design Ltd

Cover Images: Shutterstock

Every effort has been made to obtain the necessary permissions with reference to copyright material, both illustrative and quoted. We apologise for any omissions in this respect and will be pleased to make the appropriate acknowledgements in any future edition.

A CIP catalogue record for this book is available from the British Library.

Paperback ISBN 978-1-83751-722-0

Large Print ISBN 978-1-83751-721-3

Hardback ISBN 978-1-83751-720-6

Trade Paperback ISBN 978-1-80656-042-4

Ebook ISBN 978-1-83751-723-7

Kindle ISBN 978-1-83751-724-4

Audio CD ISBN 978-1-83751-715-2

MP3 CD ISBN 978-1-83751-716-9

Digital audio download ISBN 978-1-83751-717-6

This book is printed on certified sustainable paper. Boldwood Books is dedicated to putting sustainability at the heart of our business. For more information please visit https://www.boldwoodbooks.com/about-us/sustainability/

Boldwood Books Ltd, 23 Bowerdean Street, London, SW6 3TN

www.boldwoodbooks.com

FOREWORD

It's amazing to realise that this is the 20th anniversary edition of a book first published in 2005 with the title *Up All Night*. At the time, it was my fourth novel in four years, and I was living in a whirlwind of writing and promoting books, alongside having two very small children. When I say it was a busy time, I'm not exaggerating!

I've really enjoyed re-reading and re-editing this new addition, which we are going to re-launch as *Mum on a Mission*. It's made me think back to my busy young-mum life and also to the years I put in as a very earnest newspaper journalist.

Twenty years ago, I was very into 'alternative' healthcare and worried a lot about my babies and medicines and vaccines and all the other things new mums obsess over. So, one of the original plotlines of this story reflected this.

But over the years, I have had my fair share of medical dramas; and my daughter is now studying medicine, so my attitude to the medical profession has definitely changed. Don't get me wrong, I am all for healthy eating and daily exercise. I still treat minor ailments with edible remedies like lemon, garlic and yoghurt, and I love a quirky Instagram health tip. But when you're seriously ill, or bleeding out, or you've broken a bone, or you're living through a pandemic (!) or your loved ones are ill, then doctors with *years and years* of study and training are in a better position to help you than some random on the internet.

I've tweaked journalist Jo's story in line with my much greater respect for the medical profession. But I hope we continue to have serious health reporters just like her, who are prepared to delve deep and work out what's really going on.

This is all making it sound too serious! Yes, this story has its serious moments, but I hope you'll mainly come to it for the humour, light-heartedness, fun and the slices of 'mum life' that I do love to write about!

1

MONDAY: 10.35 A.M.

The massage had not begun well. The towel had fallen off, leaving Jo stark naked on the bed for several painfully long seconds. Oil had run into her freshly washed hair and her masseur seemed to have some sort of indigestion situation going on, which involved small but faintly smelly garlic burps.

The mobile in her bag had rung twice, which she'd tried to ignore, shrugging off images of today's babysitter – her mother – desperately trying to contact her because the girls had choked/drowned/been abducted.

But now, despite the annoying tinkly music in the background, she was finally settling down into this and relaxing. The masseur was circling his thumbs firmly down the sides of her spine, unwinding the tension that had built up since she'd returned from the half-term holiday week. For those six glorious days, newspaper journalist Jo had managed to avoid all newspapers, most news bulletins and phone conversations with her divorce lawyer, Hugo. But she was now back in London, back in reach of the news desk, and already she felt bombarded, although technically she had one last day of holiday left.

The massage was fanning out over her neck and shoulders and she sank gratefully into the mattress trying not to think about the list of things she had to do today: more presents were needed for Mel, her older daughter's birthday and she had run out of ideas; then Hugo would have to be called;

her mother 'wanted to talk'; a mountain range, no, make that, the Himalayas of laundry was waiting for her back at home, not to mention last week's entire set of newspapers that she would have to plough through so when she walked into the newsroom at 9 a.m. tomorrow morning she would have some inkling of what to write about this week.

Oh... that was good. The masseur had leaned right over her so that he could elbow his way into the mass of tension knots at the base of her neck. He was pressing down and it was painfully blissful.

Then there was a tap on the door.

The masseur straightened up, went to answer it.

'Sorry to interrupt but is Jo Randall in here?' the woman at the door asked. 'There's someone on the phone, says it's urgent.'

'Oh no!' she blurted. Then, clutching her towel, Jo sprang from the table and made for the shop's front desk. See?! She should never have ignored those mobile calls; it had obviously been her mother... the girls *had* choked/drowned/been abducted and it was all her fault. She should be at home on the last day of her holiday, not here, listening to muzak, indulging in a tolerable massage.

Hair sticking up in a towelling band, ignoring stares from the other customers, she jogged to the salon's front desk and took the call.

'Hello, Jo here,' she barked into the phone.

To the strained interest of the few people milling about the reception, whoever the somewhat crazed but energetic-looking woman (slim but with bum, broad shoulders and chunky calves – surely once a hockey champ) was talking to, didn't seem to be making her very happy.

'Look, I don't want you to take this the wrong way, Rod,' she snapped into the receiver, with a softened Northern accent, at the number three news editor manning the desk on Monday: 'But I am trying to have a bloody day off here.' She paused to listen to the response, then went on: 'Well, you're right, that is bad. But there's not much I can do about it on a Monday morning, is there?' She answered her question herself: 'No! I'm not going all the way up to Warrington. The daily papers will be all over it and by the time we come out on Sunday, this will be old news, dead as a doornail. Look, don't cry—' This caused heads to swivel in her direction. For good-ness' sake, she was only joking, you didn't get to be one of the top Sunday newspaper reporters in the country unless you always gave as good as you got. 'Rod, I'll see you tomorrow, OK?' she added, almost quite nicely, but then with another blast of annoyance, she remembered to ask: 'And how did you know I was here? I see. Well, I'll have to kill him. Until tomorrow morning I am still officially on holiday. So, goodbye.'

She slammed the phone down and stomped back to the treatment room where she managed a quite charming smile for the masseur, considering.

'I realise I'm presenting you with a challenge here, but I *need* to relax,' she told him. 'I want to get my shoulders down from round my ears before I start work again tomorrow. Now another thing...' Jo leaned over to look at his name badge, 'Jamie. I've got some mints in my handbag. They'll help with the garlic indigestion thing you've got going on there.'

Jo felt as if Bella had been watching her carefully for the past hour, scanning for signs that she really was as OK as she kept insisting that she was.

Five months after the separation is a dangerous time, Bella had told her twice this evening and said she knew from supporting other women through similar marriage meltdowns, which is why she'd had to respond to Jo's message:

> Flat as a fart, please say you'll come round later.

It was only three weeks or so since the night Bella had driven over to Jo's new home unannounced one evening because she hadn't liked the way Jo wasn't answering her calls or responding to her messages. This never happened, it was an accepted part of Jo's job to always to be contactable: she even had a pager to clip on if she found herself in an area with a bad phone signal. So, Bella had gone to investigate and pulling up at the newly bought 'railway cottage' – i.e. miniscule terraced red-brick house – she'd found the curtains drawn but chinks of light coming from the front room. She'd rapped on the door, rung the bell and after a few minutes with no reply, she'd shouted into the letterbox: 'It's me, so stop hiding and let me in. I'm not going away. I'll annoy you all night if I have to.' Finally, Jo had come to the door with puffy eyes and a streaming nose swathed in a grubby white dressing gown.

Bella, known in various London circles as the tough-as-nails boss of her own computing consultancy, knew she was a slightly unlikely angel of mercy. Nevertheless, she'd put comforting arms around her friend and demanded to know what was wrong.

Jo had led her into the sitting room where all the telltale signs of heartbreak were in place: a generous scattering of crumpled tissues, a blanket on the sofa, three empty mugs, plus a plate stacked with white toast, dripping butter and what looked suspiciously like Marmite. The TV freeze-framed on the funeral scene in *Steel Magnolias*.

'What's the matter?' Bella had asked.

'What's the matter?!' Jo had repeated, sounding incredulous, flinging herself onto the sofa: 'I'm going to be divorced. I'm going to be a single mother. I'm going to damage my children for life. I'm going to struggle to pay the mortgage even on this horrible little house... and' – choked-back sob – 'I'm never going to celebrate my twenty-fifth wedding anniversary.' Desperate snivel. 'Who's going to watch Mel's ballet shows with me? And Nettie's first day at school... Will I even get to take her? Or will it fall on a Simon day? And... and—' Jo's voice had disintegrated into a wail, 'I'm practically *forty*!' Then she'd dived for the tissue box that Bella had thoughtfully held out to her.

'You're thirty-five,' Bella had reminded her, starting with the obvious. 'That's not "practically forty".'

Bella then let Jo cry on the shoulder of her designer suit for a few moments before asking crisply: 'Do you seriously want to be married to Simon for twenty-five years? If you do, why not just pick up the phone and tell him? Go on, it's over there. That's just another fifteen years of Simon to go.'

These words of wisdom had Jo slowly shaking her head. 'Jo,' Bella had put an arm round her friend's shoulder. 'You've done the right thing, for many reasons. I could reel off a whole list of reasons, but the most important one, the one you should keep right in the forefront of your mind, is that you don't love him enough and he doesn't love you enough. And everyone deserves better than that.'

'But *why* doesn't he?' Jo had asked, dissolving into a fresh burst of tears.

'This is the first time I've seen you cry,' Bella had told her, sounding almost surprised. 'You've been so together about bringing your marriage to a close. It was *your* decision,' she reminded Jo, as she held her close. 'You always pretend you're tough as old boots.'

'No... I'm not really,' Jo had admitted, 'Very sensitive on the inside.'

'That's probably what makes you so good at your job,' Bella had said.

'Of course I'm better off without Simon. I know it,' Jo had replied, before blowing her nose forcefully. 'It's just the idea... I always wanted to be happily married, part of a family, for years and years.'

'You are part of a family,' Bella had reminded her. 'It's a modern family, it's normal. It's just not a Walt Disney, 1950s family.'

'You're a Disney family!' Jo had accused her. 'With your husband and your 2.2 children. And you're happy.'

'I earn three times more than Don, that's hardly Disney,' had been Bella's reply, along with: 'And he's much older than me, which might not be so sexy in ten years' time and we've had plenty of problems. We have at least one Mount Etna scale row every month on top of the one I blame on PMT. Don claims I'm in a bad mood the whole time because I'm so busy. Sex is something he has to schedule into my diary weeks in advance and anyway, we've only been married for five years or so. And I've told him when he hits fifty-five, that's it, I'm trading him in for a toyboy.'

This outburst had at least made Jo smile.

'What are you doing?' Bella had asked gently.

'Wallowing,' had been Jo's answer.

'*Steel Magnolias* and Marmite?' Bella had pulled a face.

'I know, I know. And I don't even like Marmite.'

'You have to stop eating like this.' Bella had picked up the plate, 'Five extra pounds and a yeast overgrowth are not going to help. I'm going to pour you a drink and then you're allowed one of my "emergency" cigarettes.'

'So, liver failure and lung cancer are better, are they?' Jo had countered.

'Tea, then?' Bella had suggested, trying to sound enthusiastic at the prospect of tea.

'God no,' Jo protested. 'I've had about eighteen cups of tea already. Go into the kitchen and open a bottle of wine.'

Once Jo was tucked up under a blanket on the sofa, wine glass in hand, the trigger for this wave of divorce grief had emerged. She'd confided to Bella that Simon hadn't moved into his new flat alone: an old 'family friend' had moved in with him.

'Gwen!' Jo had exclaimed, still hardly able to believe it. 'You've met her, haven't you? I'm sure you have. She's...' and Jo had paused, wondering how she would have described Gwen in the past. Now only the words 'pathetic, needy, selfish and completely inconsiderate' came to mind.

'He swears nothing was going on between them until a few weeks ago,' she'd told Bella. 'But then why is she *moving in* with him so soon? She's lived alone for years. She's older than him! Sensible... court shoes, white blouses, string of pearls type. It's as if he's moved in with a younger, slimmer version of his mother!'

'Don't worry,' Bella had said as she'd left a comforted Jo later that night: 'You've got your children, your new house and you've got your job.'

'Yup and that's enough,' Jo had replied. 'Don't know how I coped with a husband as well.'

* * *

Tonight, here in the kitchen of the home she'd been in for barely two months, Bella had told Jo that she was looking much more 'together'. Divorce phase one: weight gain, saggy grey tracksuit and un-dyed hair seemed to be over. The house sale was behind her, along with the dreaded house clearance – when every shred of Dr Simon Dundas had been taken out, wept over, boxed up, chucked, or, in the case of exceptionally emotional items, stored. And now Jo was ready to emerge anew from the rubble of her ten-year marriage. The week away with her daughters had done her good. The colour was back in her cheeks, the downward turn her mouth had adopted lately seemed to have lifted and there was new hair: shortish, high-lighted, feathery and flattering, not too post-break-up drastic.

'So, you're looking great. Holiday must have been relaxing, then?' Bella asked.

'Yeah, we had a great time – beachy, but bracing,' Jo said as she spooned chicken salad onto their plates. 'But I'd hardly got back to London before it all kicked off again: work harassing me, phone calls from the dreaded Hugo Hemburrow...' Jo rolled her eyes.

'Is there still a lot to sort out?' Bella liked to keep a watchful eye on friends' divorces, to make certain they weren't being ripped off. Hugo Hemburrow, family law expert, came with her personal recommendation.

'The pension,' Jo replied. 'We're having a good old fight about Simon's NHS pension. Hugo thinks I should be entitled to half of it, when the day comes.'

'And what does Simon think?' Bella asked.

'I think the words "stick it" and "you know where" formed a large part of the conversation. We may have to settle for a portion.'

'A portion is good.'

'I think a portion will be fine.'

'How is this affecting post-marital relations, though?' Bella asked. 'It can't be very easy having to see him twice a week, discuss the children and everything.'

'We're both trying very hard,' Jo managed, as generously as she could. 'We don't ever talk about the finances ourselves. We let the lawyers deal with that. We just stick strictly to the children, make polite conversation and try to keep it as friendly as possible. 'Jo bit back the long list of complaints she would like to have added about her ex-husband, the man who was rapidly turning into the cliché of a divorced dad. He was overdoing the hair *tint*, he'd upped the gym routine, grown a goatee, bought a swanky riverside bachelor pad, moved in his *doting* girlfriend, after about five *minutes* of dating, and even got himself a red BMW convertible that Jo knew he could barely make the repayments on, even though he was one of London's top colon consultants. Oh yes, as she'd always loved to tell people – what Simon didn't know about shit wasn't worth knowing.

* * *

He took care of their daughters for three days every week: Thursday, Friday and Saturday. In her opinion, he didn't do nearly as good a job of looking after them as she did, of course. He forgot their homework, he didn't make packed lunches, he lost socks, pants, hats and scarves, let them have far too much screen time, relied on Gwen to do the cooking – but Jo was determined not to whine about any of it. On the plus side, he picked the girls up promptly from after-school club on Thursdays and Fridays and he spent all his Saturdays with them. These were things he'd never done regularly during their married life. So, Jo could see that shared care was the best way forward for them all.

On Sunday morning, seven-year-old Mel and three-year-old Annette came back to her so they were together for the best part of her two days off – Sundays and Mondays – and then her less frantic workdays, Tuesdays and Wednesdays. Jo now had three nights a week to herself, which was still a strange novelty. No one had warned her how silent her home would be without the girls, how desolate the little pink bedroom would feel, especially if last thing at night she went in to check on them as usual, forgetting that they weren't there.

She coped with those nights in another way now, staying in the office late. Then going out to renew a long-forgotten acquaintance with select nightclubs, the cocktail menu, the dawn taxi home and, for the past few weeks, she had been falling into bed with a young man that she didn't know very well.

It wasn't exactly healthy behaviour, but after ten years of marriage to a doctor, a little unhealthiness was an understandable reaction.

'Let's not talk about Simon any more,' Bella decided. 'I think you should tell me much more about Marcus. The new boyfriend...'

'No, he's not a boyfriend.' Jo held up the wine bottle. 'You want some more?' she asked her friend.

Bella shook her head: 'Well, what is he then?'

'He's a date...' Jo tried.

But Bella wasn't going to be put off: 'He's more than that! Please at least tell me that he's a fantastic shag.'

'He's a gift,' was Jo's response and she couldn't help smiling. Because it still seemed too ridiculous. To be neck high in all this 'D-I-V-O-R-C-E' crap – she couldn't think about it without breaking into Tammy Wynette – and yet to be granted the wonderful, distracting *gift*, there really wasn't any better word, of Marcus: funny, scruffy, carefree, significantly younger, unstoppably physical, distractingly physical. Marcus, who could single-handedly remind her of the meaning of the phrase 'can't keep their hands off each other', who was unashamed about the three great loves of his life: cooking, eating and having fun in bed. Yes, he could whip up a hollandaise just as easily as he could whip off his clothes. Or hers, for that matter.

'Look at you, you're blushing,' Bella teased. 'If your readers could see you now, the hard woman of Fleet Street, all smitten kitten for a handsome young chef.'

'Ha ha.'

'When do I get to meet him?'

'I've no idea.' Jo took a sip of her drink. 'I've no idea what I'm doing with him—'

'I think the rest of us know though,' Bella interrupted.

'It won't last,' Jo insisted. 'The chef. Very soon he'll melt away into the night... like ice cream. Mint chocolate chip, his favourite...' she gave a laugh.

'He's obviously doing you good,' Bella told her. 'You're losing that "fresh out of marriage" look, edging more towards "boy bait". I like the day dress thing you have going on here. You never wore dresses before, did you?'

'Oh God, am I so obvious?' Jo asked, anxious about the new make-up and the shirtdress. 'Should I just get a badge saying "I've dumped my husband" and be done with it?' she asked.

'No. No. You're fine. What am I saying? You're gorgeous!' Bella soothed her.

'I'm slightly worried that Marcus is...' Jo looked up and met her friend's eyes. 'Bella, am I not doing what divorced men are supposed to do? I'm being totally mid-life crisis predictable.'

'It's a natural reaction,' Bella assured her. 'Simon got all sensible and boring. Your sex life withered on a stick and this is what happens when you're set free. Anyway, Marcus isn't *that* young,' Bella reminded her. 'You're rejuvenating!'

'Bella!'

'Like in those Swiss beauty clinics where they inject you with sheep embryo. You've got yourself a cheap and much more fun-filled version of that.'

'Please!'

'Oh don't be shy about him,' Bella added. 'He's in his twenties, isn't he?'

'Twenty-six.'

'Not even ten years younger than you!' Bella exclaimed.

The phone began to ring. Jo took a glance at her watch and uttered the word: 'Arse.'

'What is it?' was Bella's response.

'It's work.' Jo put her glass down. 'Again.'

'How do you know?' Bella asked.

Jo didn't answer, just shook her head and picked up the offending receiver. 'Jo Randall,' she said as crisply as she could manage.

'Hi, Jo, Declan here,' came an Irish voice on the other end of the line, as if she hadn't already guessed. By 9.50 p.m., her newspaper's doggedly efficient night news editor would have had the first editions of tomorrow's papers for about seventeen minutes, just long enough to speed-read every single one and start harassing reporters, even though it was only Monday night, still a full five days away from the next edition of their paper.

'Just thought you'd want to know before the morning,' Declan went on. 'The *Mirror* has a fifteenth case of whooping cough confirmed, in a new area, so it's starting to look like an epidemic.'

'Hello, Declan,' Jo pretended to gush. 'Lovely to hear from you too. What about: "How are you? Did you have a good holiday? How are the girls?"'

'Yeah, yeah, whatever. Glad you're back. Your department's crap without you,' was all the graciousness Declan could manage.

'Charming. Look, fifteen cases of whooping cough is not an epidemic,' she reined him in. 'I've already had a conversation about whooping cough cases with Rod and my verdict is, we'll be over it like a rash in the morning, OK?'

'Just thought you should know soon as,' Declan said.

'Much appreciated,' she managed, although it totally wasn't. She bade him goodnight, replaced the receiver and turned back to her friend.

'Nothing urgent,' Jo explained. 'Where were we?' Jo brought her attention back to Bella and for about the twentieth time that evening, wondered how her friend managed to keep it so together. There she was, raven hair pinned up in one of those effortlessly stylish things she did, sophisticated brown and butter button-through summer dress, making the most of the honey tan her usually Snow White complexion had taken on. Personal trainer-perfect stomach. Breezy, cheerful and funny, despite working relentlessly.

'Where were we?' Bella repeated, a smile breaking over her face. 'We were deep in all the usual overworked women in the 21st century shit. How tired we are, how busy we are, how overworked and underpaid we are, our latest totally neurotic worries about our children, how our men never clean the sink—'

'Your nanny cleans the sink,' Jo broke in.

'She does, God bless her,' was Bella's reply.

'Anyway, we weren't talking about all that.'

'No,' said Bella, 'we weren't, because it's Monday, so I'm not too tired or overworked yet.'

'Or underpaid,' Jo couldn't help adding.

'No. Things are going well, at the moment, touch wood.' Bella looked around momentarily for something to touch. 'But it almost makes me worried when things are going well. I think I prefer to be dealing with a crisis and looking forward to the good times.'

'Oh, don't get all anxious,' Jo told her. 'Enjoy. You've got very good times ahead.'

'There are no women in computing!' Bella said in outrage. 'The whole techie world is a glamour-free zone. It's full of ugly geeks who couldn't wow a conference if you employed Daniel Craig's tailor and Tom Hardy's hairdresser.'

'I'm telling you,' she said and drained her glass, 'the techie world is mine for the taking. But anyway, you were about to tell me more about the chef.' Bella's eyebrow arched in a sly and teasing way: 'The handsome, talented, outrageously good in bed young chef. Weren't you?' Bella reached over to top up Jo's glass.

'Oh, wait—' Jo's eyes fixed on the telly, she felt for the remote and turned up the sound.

They caught the very end of the report: '— in the light of this news, the Chief Medical Officer is urging parents who have not yet had their children protected with the new Quintet vaccine to come forward as soon as possible.' The bulletin cut to tonight's footage of the Chief Medical Officer, on the steps of his building, telling the nation: 'Quintet is the best way to protect your child against whooping cough and four other illnesses. All our research indicates that this injection is totally safe.'

'Must be another kid in hospital with whooping cough,' Jo said.

She turned to Bella: 'Have your boys had the new vaccine yet?'

'Quintet?' Bella asked.

'Yeah.'

'Well... you know Don.' Jo did know Don, very well. She'd known Don, the news editor on her paper's daily sister title, for about two years longer than she'd known his wife. He was sound. Very good at his job. Straight. Honest. An honourable man in a messed-up business. Also, an inescapably attractive man. Hearts had broken right across London when word got out that Don had finally met his match and was marching her to the registry office before she could get away.

'Don is pretty straightforward about doctors,' Bella told her. 'Not one tiny bit alternative. I'm not either, really. Hell, I even work for some of the drug companies. So, the boys are up-to-date with all their injections and Don's keen to let them have Quintet as an added precaution against this outbreak. Why?' Bella wanted to know, 'Do you know something?'

'Well, you know me. I always want to be the sensible face of health reporting and I've done plenty of stories on anti-vaccine conspiracies and scares and they have all turned out to be false, so I've sort of turned into the pro-vaccine voice,' Jo replied. 'Unfortunate, really,' she added, 'Because I would love to be the journalist to break a really good story about Evil Big Pharma. That would put my name in lights.'

'Do you want your name in lights?' Bella wondered.

'Well... I am a journalist. We're always after the big story *and* the fame...' But was that true, Jo wondered. 'Oh, I don't know,' she said, 'I still feel a bit undervalued by my paper maybe. And... even though we're divorced, I would like to show Simon that sometimes my job is as important as his.'

'Ah...' Bella said. 'Try not to think about Simon too much. You're no longer defined by Simon, or your job, or your kids. And if you're undervalued, you need to look for another job with a Big Fat Pay Cheque.'

'Wise words,' Jo told her.

'Anyway, this whooping cough is bad,' Bella went back to their original conversation. 'The children in hospital are really ill.'

'Yeah, we need to get our kids the new vaccine. Keep them extra safe,' Jo said, but then she couldn't help thinking that nothing in life was totally safe. Not even lying fast asleep in your own bed. She'd once done a story about a couple who'd been crushed to death by their chimney, which had fallen through the roof on top of them in the middle of the night. But that was the problem with news reporting. You spent most of your life thinking and writing about the bad stuff.

The phone rang and her heart shrank a little at the thought that it might be Simon, sitting in bed with Gwen – euwwwww – thinking of some aspect of her parenting he had to criticise before falling asleep. 'Jo Randall,' she said into the receiver.

'Hello, Jo Randall. Can I come and see you later, Jo Randall?' That mix of teasing and sincere, confident and unsure, sexy and funny – it was *him*.

'Oh... hello there.' Something about the way she said it caused Bella's eyebrow to shoot up comically.

'I'm... er... there's someone here. A friend.'

Bella stood up, slid her feet into her mules, picked up her handbag and shook her head to indicate that she was out of there.

'Well, actually, she's not staying much longer,' Jo went on.

'Why? Am I not allowed to meet your friends? Are you embarrassed about me?' Big tease in the voice now.

'No, no, don't be silly...' She felt all wrong-footed now. 'You'd like her. It's just...' *Well, face it, Jo*, she acknowledged, *Marcus hasn't been allowed to meet your friends, your parents, your children or anyone else because you don't want to admit to his existence. You don't want to admit to being freshly separated and already involved in a casual fling, sleeping with a twenty-something chef. That headline would write itself...*

My romps with five times a night chef!
    'He's my tasty dish of the day,' says Greenwich mum, Jo Randall, 35.

Noooo, stop it! Was her brain going to boil her life down into the worst kind of tabloid headlines forever?

'I won't be finished here till after eleven. Is that going to be too late?' he asked.

It was too late. She had work tomorrow, but then again, she didn't have to do the girls' packed lunches and the school/nursery run because her mother would be here in the morning.

Her mother...! If Marcus could be gone before her mother arrived, then maybe it was possible.

She heard his breath rise and fall down the line. Knew how much she would like to hear that breath rise and fall over her. Against her ear, against her neck.

She hadn't seen him for ten days and it felt like longer.

'You'll have to leave early,' she warned him.

'But can I stay up late?' he asked. The tease.

'I'll see you later, then.' Jo caught Bella's eye and suddenly couldn't keep the smirk from her face.

Once she'd hung up, Bella flicked open her mobile and called a cab.

'You don't have to go just yet,' Jo insisted. 'He's not coming for another hour or so.'

'Aha, I do so have to go. Look at you...' Bella gave a nod in Jo's direction. 'You look lovely to me, my darling, but let's face it, you've got to shower, shave everything, change, change again, do your hair, then mess everything up a little, as if you haven't tried, as if you've just been hanging about all evening looking gorgeous.'

Jo laughed at her. 'I do not,' she said. 'Well... maybe a bit... What shall I wear?' she asked, immediately wishing she could strip the dress from Bella's back because it would be perfect. 'Everything's in the wash from our holiday.'

'A miniskirt and frilly pants,' Bella suggested. 'Don't think he'll notice much else after that.'

'A miniskirt! I haven't worn a miniskirt since...' *Since when? School?!*

'You've got great legs,' Bella advised her, swinging her soft, jangling suede bag over her shoulder. 'Have fun.'

Once Jo had closed the front door on her friend, she flew round the house, clearing the kitchen, making the bed, throwing dirty laundry into the basket, then ransacking the remains of her wardrobe. She headed to the bathroom for the makeover, ignoring her ringing phone as soon as she saw it was Simon.

3

STILL MONDAY: 11.35 P.M.

When Jo opened the front door, there he was on her doorstep, stepping out of the luminous dark of an unusually warm May evening.

'Hey,' Marcus said, slow and easy smile spreading.

'Hey,' she said back, meeting his eyes, relieved to see he was just as good-looking as she remembered. Because there was always that risk: she'd worried she might come back from her break, see him again and wonder what on earth she'd been thinking.

'Here we are,' he said, still on the doorstep, still smiling, trying not to let the smile run away into a nervous laugh.

'Are you going to come in?'

'Yup,' and the nervous laugh escaped, but he stepped into the little hall and they moved in to kiss hello.

And once they started to kiss, the nervy newness and the awkwardness fell away. It was as if they'd moved into the right gear or their native language. This was the easy part, the familiar territory. His wavy shoulder-length hair fell around her face, his fingers linked round her waist and he shut the door behind him with his foot.

Jo's hands were on the skin of his back, warm and slightly damp to the touch after his bike ride over. She ran her hand round, brushed it against the fuzzy warmth of his stomach, then up to his chest. She could just pull off his T-shirt. He wouldn't care. He wouldn't care if she undid his jeans and pulled them off either, he was happy and unselfconscious naked. At one with himself, comfortable in his skin and grounded. It made her feel like a mass of complications but was part of his irresistible attraction.

She eased the T-shirt up to his shoulders, running her fingers across their smooth, muscular roundness, then tugged the top over his head and met his smile before they were kissing again.

Want pulsing through her, she could feel her heart race, hear her breathing switch to shallow.

She loved the kissing. He had a small, precise tongue and he tasted dry, salty, but with a hint of sweet too. His curtain of hair smelled slightly of caramelised onions, cigarette smoke and fresh bread. This was Marcus: always delicious, good enough to eat.

She slid her hands into the back pockets of his jeans, squeezing at the solidity of him. He moved slowly, feet planted firmly to the ground, rooted. His hands pulling her into him, into the push coming from the crotch of his jeans.

'Missed you,' he said, breaking from the kiss to smile at her.

'Me too,' she said back. She pressed her face against the warmth of his neck and couldn't resist sliding her nose down his skin to the fold of his armpit. The smell of his sweat had a strange effect on her. It didn't matter that he was nine years younger than her, that they didn't have much in common, that, if she was honest, she found many things about him intensely irritating, there was a magical something – hormones? Pheromones? – whatever chemical ingredient it was that governed the laws of attraction, he was her perfect match.

She didn't think she'd ever been so giddily moved by anyone. She ran her tongue against him, bit gently into his shoulder, heard him undo his belt buckle, and closed her eyes. His hands moved in under her dress and she felt herself slipping into an unfocused, breathless place. When she opened her eyes again, she registered the framed photo on the wall opposite of her girls crouching in the snow, building a snowman. It had a sobering effect. Her children were upstairs, she couldn't just get naked in the hallway with someone they'd never even met.

'Shower?' she asked and when Marcus nodded, she took him by the hand up the small set of stairs into the cramped white and pale blue bathroom. Jo had moved into this mini-house with various grandiose decorating schemes, but so far, all she'd had the time or energy to do was slap hideous Barbie-trademarked glitter-pink paint over the girls' bedroom walls. All the other rooms in the house were slightly shabby, but calmingly ordinary. When you'd spent years trying somehow, all at once, to have a brilliant career, be a wonderful mother, a good wife, chef, housekeeper and interior designer, it was a huge relief to let standards plummet.

Behind the security of the locked bathroom door, Marcus and Jo undressed each other quickly, kissing, touching, tripping in the tangle of clothes, hurrying into the liberation of the shower where they could lather up and slide against each other.

Did anything else matter more than Marcus? Yes, of course, but not in this moment when he was leaning back against the shower tiles, eyes half closed, water splashing down, his fingers moving against her, inside her, his other hand guiding hers urgently over his soapy, swollen hard-on. No, nothing else mattered. She ran a nail over his nipple and watched him come.

* * *

Afterwards, they lay on her bed together, Marcus naked, apart from his woven leather bracelets, damp hair spilling out over the pillow beside her, one hand companionably on his crotch, the other holding a cigarette. Jo was much shyer – she had stretch marks, tummy bumps, cellulite, history – so she'd put on a silk slip, one Simon had given her years ago, but virtually unworn, then lay down, then got up again to open the window and let the smoke out, then got back onto the bed, where with her head on Marcus's chest, they talked and joked comfortably together.

When he was halfway through his cigarette, she began what she knew perfectly well was her ridiculous smoking dance. She took it from his fingers and had a drag, then she decided, yes, she would have a cigarette of her own. She lit it, took four puffs, felt her lungs contract and her head spin and quickly stubbed it out on the outside windowsill. Then she fanned the air and sprayed perfume.

'I can't just *smoke*, you know,' she told him. 'This is the one thing in life which does exactly what it says on the packet...' She waved the cigarette box at him. 'Kills you! Not to mention gives you wrinkles, bad breath, yellow teeth. Nothing about it is good.' She took the cigarette from his hand again and put it between her lips.

'Calm down!' was his response to this.

After another drag, Jo handed it back to him and started looking in her bedside table for her vitamin pills to counteract the effect of the smoke.

Smoking! She knew perfectly well she was only smoking again to annoy Simon, and to pretend she wasn't that old, to deny that she thought about death much more than she had done a few years ago. Smoking could only be done with true enjoyment when you were young, when death was a far-off country you wondered if you'd ever visit.

But she now worried at least three times a day about what it was that would finish her off: a sudden heart attack, a slow cancer, the tragedy of a late-night car accident. Horrible, horrible. She popped two vitamin pills as Marcus slid his hand over her breast.

* * *

Marcus had been sleeping with Jo for several weeks now, but she suspected he'd been watching her with interest for some time before that.

She was a once-a-week, or at the very least once-a-fortnight, regular at the cosy but fashionable restaurant where he worked. Not that chefs and diners ever usually met. Chefs were relegated to the hot metal creative sweatshop at the back, diners pampered in the intimate leather booths at the front.

But, once she'd had several glasses of white wine (he knew now she never touched red in public because she thought she was too clumsy) and her soup or oysters, fish and salad then pudding – always chocolate of some sort – Jo liked to go to the back courtyard, not the front of house, and smoke a cigarette. This was where they had met, in the grubby courtyard, down by the bins, with the kitchen doors flung open to let out the heat, chefs and sous-chefs coming and going to blast their lungs with strong cigarettes whenever they got a chance.

Jo liked to sit on the wall and gossip with whoever was around, make mock complaints about the food, moan about how boring her dining companion was and confess that she was out with them 'just for work'. She always wanted to know if anyone famous had been in that week and what did they eat? Who were they with? Who was dating whom? It was a new restaurant at a fashionable address, had only been open for half a year and all the cool, important people ate there. She had soon realised that Marcus had started watching out for her, sneaking glimpses of her through the serving hatch when she was in. Her and the ever-changing rota of people she brought to the restaurant. The occasional face he recognised from the papers.

'You're smart,' he told her on one cigarette break, 'you remind me of Bond girls. Not the ones in the bikinis that get killed,' he'd added quickly over her laughter, 'but the clever ones that carry guns and know how to scramble up walls and deactivate nuclear devices.'

'Yup, that's me,' she'd joked. Pointing at her battered bag, she'd added: 'Tape recorder, notebooks, nuclear codes.'

Jo had seen him noticing that she didn't wear a wedding ring. She still had the mark where one had been. Her fourth finger was slightly narrower below the knuckle.

Then, one night she'd turned up at the restaurant in a knockout outfit: tight grey pinstriped skirt, even tighter matching sleeveless waistcoat. She'd taken her smoke break mid-meal and she'd been too cold to sit in her usual spot on the wall, so she'd come and stood beside him in the warmth of the kitchen door. 'Did you make the monkfish and mango?' she'd asked.

'Did you eat it?' he'd asked back.

'No! Way too retro,' she'd told him. 'It was so back to the Nineties.'

He'd smiled. 'Who are you with tonight?'

'Ah. Someone important who doesn't want to give me the story, hence the need for full-on temptress wear—' She'd gestured to her waistcoat and skirt.

'Is it working?' he'd asked.

'I'll meet you back here after dessert and let you know.' Jo had winked, causing him to dare the question: 'So, are you married then?' with a shrug supposed to show how casual he felt about it.

Her answer, which she gave with an unflinching look, had been the flirtatious challenge: 'Why, do you want to ask me for a date?'

'You'd be lucky,' he'd managed in reply, still sounding cool, but feeling far from it.

'I'm separated,' was her reply.

'Sorry,' he'd said. But their eyes were locked together and it was hard to ignore the mutual attraction.

'Don't be,' she'd said. 'I'm better off without him.' She'd broken eye contact at that, drawn in one last lungful from her cigarette, then flicked the butt high over the wall and out into the street on the other side. 'So,' she'd turned to face him, head a little to the side, hair brushing her bare shoulder, 'where shall we go afterwards?'

'Huh?' he'd asked, not understanding.

'On our date,' she'd said.

* * *

Jo had waited in the restaurant till closing time when he'd taken her to the cramped bar the kitchen staff went to after hours for beer and vodka shots. 'Don't you have to go home?' he'd wanted to know. 'Don't you have kids?'

'They're with their dad,' she'd explained, buying yet another round of drinks, paying cash from her battered brown wallet, which was overstuffed with receipts and scraps of paper.

'Anyway,' she'd told him later, 'I don't like going home when I'm the only one there. I'd rather stay out.'

So, they went to someone else's flat and drank more. 'Don't you ever get drunk?' he'd asked her, leaning too heavily on her bare shoulders, until she'd just turned and kissed him, full on, mouth to mouth, sliding her hands straight into his cargos, as if she did this kind of thing all the time.

'No,' she'd replied after the kiss. 'I'm very practised at pretending I'm drinking just as much as everyone else. I think I should take you home,' she'd said against his ear. 'Where do you live? I'll get us a cab.'

They had snogged in the taxi all the way back to his flat, Jo running her hands over his soft hair, softer skin, feeling breathless, dizzy at the thought of getting him bare, solid and real against her.

But she'd had to help him out of the back of the cab, then she'd had to get his keys out of his pocket, unlock the door for him and get him up the stairs.

Once they were in his flat, he was still trying to kiss her but he could hardly stand up and she could see that for tonight he was a lost cause. 'Too many shots. You made me nervous,' he'd mumbled as she'd helped him out of his shoes and jacket, then put him into his unruly tangle of a bed, complete with the kind of grimy, flowery sheets she hadn't encountered since uni. After another deep kiss, his eyes had closed and he'd immediately fallen into a heavy, drunken sleep.

She'd searched for the kettle and tea bags in his kitchenette and made herself a mug of tea. Sitting on the sofa with the hot drink, she'd wondered what on earth she was doing. Getting someone many years your junior rolling drunk then taking them home was the kind of behaviour middle-aged men got into trouble for. Was she having some sort of early mid-life crisis?

She'd called another cab then taken several minutes to decide what to write in the farewell note that she intended to put on the counter beside the kettle.

'Sorry, I bought you a vodka too many.' No. Too sinister.

'This wasn't what I'd planned.' No... even more sinister.

What to write? *'See you again'*? *'Give me a call'*? She'd gone for the noncommittal:

Goodnight, Jo x

and her mobile number.

Before she left, she went through to his room. To check he was OK, she told herself, but really to have another look. Marcus was curled up on his side, snoring slightly. His closed fist was up beside his face on the pillow and she saw the faded sweatband on his left wrist. There were two brown leather ties and a beaded one on the same wrist. It looked carefree and young – it reminded her of a long time ago, and she'd felt a glimmer of guilt. She didn't belong here, intruding on his sleep and his privacy.

So, she'd slung her bag over her shoulder, closed the door on his flat and decided to wait for her taxi downstairs.

4

TUESDAY: 9.18 A.M.

'Morning, Jo. Good holiday?'

'Yup.' Jo's face broke into a smile. 'When do I get another one?'

'Oh, in a couple of years, if you're good,' came the reply from news editor, Jeff, who was already in full swing. His number two, Mike Madell, was wading through the full set of papers and magazines spilling across the desk. His number three, Rod Butcher, was reading one of the stories that arrived every minute on the screen in front of him.

But they all took a moment to wave, nod or say hello as she passed the desk. Jeff looked as if he was about to say more, but his phone rang. He picked it up, answered, listened and then made the finger-waving gesture that she knew meant 'Busy now, speak in a minute.'

Fine, she thought. She wasn't together enough for the first newsgathering chat of the day. She needed to sit at her desk, drink tea, switch on the computer and psych herself up for the hours ahead.

Her mother had arrived at her house at 8.15 a.m. prompt but looking tired, Jo thought.

'Everything OK?' Jo had asked her, over the breakfast *mêlée*. In the morning rush, Jo had managed to spill orange juice into the rattan seat of her kitchen chair. How in the hell were you supposed to clean that? Those 'rustic country kitchen' photospreads had omitted that detail.

'Everything's fine, Jo, and just leave that,' her mother had insisted. 'I'll sort it out when the girls are dressed.' Jo read reproach into that comment. Mel had to leave the house by twenty to nine at the very latest, or she would be late for school, but there she was down on the kitchen floor with Annette, playing dolls. There were ratty-haired Barbies everywhere Jo stepped. Grubby, ripped evening dresses revealed their anatomy-defying moulded plastic chests, and their bright blonde tresses were all snarled and snagged. This was heroin Hollywood Barbie. A whole new look.

'Mum,' Mel looked up. 'I've got a new joke.'

Jo didn't have time, she really didn't, she still had to put on her suit, her lipstick, fly round the house for all the other essential bits and pieces, but... the sweet little heart-shaped face looking up at her. Daddy's dark gold hair falling below her shoulders, Daddy's sparkling eyes and shapely eyebrows...

Quickly Jo sat down on one of the orange-juice-free kitchen chairs.

'OK, let's hear it.'

Mel sprang up and stood on one side of her. Annette, not wanting to be left out, rushed to the other.

'I got a joke too,' Nettie announced.

'Oh, good. Two jokes,' Jo smiled at them.

'Knock knock,' Mel began.

'Who's there?' Jo obliged.

'Alec.'

'Alec who?'

'Alec to pick my nose,' came Mel's triumphant punch line.

'Yuck!' Jo said but still managed to drum up a hearty laugh. 'And now you have to get dressed. Upstairs, quick, quick, or you'll be late.'

'My one!' Nettie reminded her in outrage. 'You have to listen to my joke.' There was hardly anything Nettie asked for which Jo could refuse, because her youngest daughter was as insistent and stubborn as she was gorgeous.

'Of course.' Jo fixed on the improbably blue eyes and tiny pink lips. 'You tell me.' She wondered what was coming now, because Nettie's grasp of the joke, as a concept, was still pretty sketchy.

'Knock knock,' Nettie said, leaning back on her heels and sticking out her tummy.

'Who's there?'

'Nose.'

'Nose who?'

'I like my nose.'

Jo laughed, 'Very funny. I like your nose too.' She landed a kiss on it, then scooped Nettie up into her arms.

'I don't want Granny,' Nettie said into her ear, 'I want you.'

'I know,' was Jo's reply. 'I want you. I want you and Mel all day long. I miss you,' she said, stroking the velvety head. 'But you know what, I'm going to be home early tonight, so what shall we do when I'm back?'

'Have supper in front of the TV?' Nettie asked hopefully. It was enough to make Jo weep. You painted with your children, you baked, you talked, you read them stories, you took them out, you dressed up, you played games, you went with them to the park, wind, rain or shine, but if you ever asked what their idea of heaven was, it was eating toast in front of the TV.

'Maybe,' she said carefully, not wanting to upset or promise anything she didn't mean. 'What are you going to do with Granny?'

She looked over at her mother, hoping this would be a good moment to do the handover. It was best for everyone if it went smoothly; nothing worse than leaving the house with the sound of outraged sobs ringing in your ears.

'Shall we collect all the bread crusts from the plates?' Her mother took Annette from Jo's arms and held her up, although her daughter looked far too big for a carry against her mother's delicate frame. 'We'll put them in a bag and then take them out to the ducks, shall we?'

'Mummy doesn't let us feed the ducks,' Nettie replied. 'She says it gives them a sore tummy.'

'No, it's fine, honestly, it's fine to feed the ducks with Granny,' Jo said quickly. There wasn't time to give the environmentally friendly duck-feeding explanation and anyway, she didn't like to criticise anything her mother did with the girls. God knows, quite enough unintended criticisms surfaced without her even trying. She was extremely grateful for her parents' part in the childcare: she loved that her daughters were so close to their grandparents and all other concerns about how her parents looked after them were secondary to this.

'You collect the bread crusts,' Jo said, 'I'll round up Mel.'

As she'd expected, Mel was still in her pyjamas, reading a book on her bed. She'd got distracted somewhere between the kitchen and her wardrobe.

'Mel! Get changed!' Jo urged her, exasperated at the look of surprise on her daughter's face. 'School! Remember?!'

Just before Jo headed out of her front door, she planted big kisses on her daughters' cheeks and squeezed them tightly. 'Have fun,' she urged them both. 'See you soon.'

Then she gave her mother a peck on the cheek too. 'No lifting,' she warned her. 'Not even if she screams! I don't want to have to pay your chiropractor bills.'

'Don't be cheeky,' was her mother's response.

And Jo left, glad that her daughters were with her mum, glad also that her mum seemed to be forgiving her at least slightly for leaving her husband.

That was undoubtedly the good thing about Simon's decision to move Gwen in with him: it had switched her parents' sympathy right back in her favour. Before that, her loving, but nonetheless old-fashioned Lancashire parents hadn't been shy to voice their disapproval.

'No marriage is perfect,' her mother had told her. 'Everyone goes through these phases. You've got to stick with it, for the children. Every child needs two parents.'

'They'll have two parents,' Jo had argued back. 'We'll be two parents who aren't at each other's throats all the time. We're both still here for them, totally committed, 100 per cent. We're only living a mile apart and the girls will spend three nights a week with Simon.'

This information had tipped her mother over the edge: 'You're going to let your daughters live somewhere else for half the week? *What kind of mother are you?*'

No pretending that hadn't hurt.

'A practical one,' she'd flung back. 'I work late those nights anyway, and if they weren't with their dad, they'd be with a childminder.'

'You know we'd—'

But Jo broke her off: 'No. It's a very kind offer, it really is and I appreciate everything you do for us, but Simon wants to do this. It's a surprise to me, quite frankly, but he's their dad and we have to give him the chance.'

Still, no opportunity was missed to make her feel she was behaving selfishly, even recklessly.

Until news of Gwen broke and at last, the sniping by her parents had stopped.

'Do you think anything was going on between Simon and this woman— before— you know?' her dad had ventured.

'No,' Jo had told him, 'I'm sure of it. I think Simon has just panicked.'

But clearly, they'd formed their own opinion and now it was full guns blazing for Simon. 'He's looking a lot older, I thought,' her mother had managed to get in just this morning. 'And the little beard is awful. Do you think he dyes it?'

* * *

Anyway, back to the carnage of unopened envelopes on her desk and the computer declaring:

You have 1,781 new emails.

And probably only two would be interesting. See. She started scrolling down: Free downloads, upgrade your software... and all the press releases: medical breakthroughs, new medicines, launch invitations, boring... oh, Friends of the Earth announce new campaign manager appointment, stark warning re: seabird population decline... there were at least twenty different releases from Tony Jarvis, the Green Party press officer. She called him and got through to his voicemail. 'Tony, answering machine?! You're supposed to be running a by-election campaign. Get up, get to your desk. Give me a call. It's Jo Randall by the way, back in the office.'

She started to rip through the pile of envelopes on the desk, putting almost every letter straight into the paper recycling bin as soon as she'd read it. Old news, last week's press releases, the odd story suggestion, none of them interesting. Bin, bin, bin.

It was almost 10 a.m. and the entire staff of her Health and Environment department, all two of them, would be in soon. Dominique would be five minutes early, almost exactly, Aidan would be ten minutes late, almost exactly.

The TV suspended in the corner of the room closest to her desk caught her attention, another Health Minister's press conference. She got up and went to stand underneath it, looking up at the screen, arms folded. 'Ask him a bloody question, why don't you?' she muttered when the minister had finished his statement and was met with silence from the room. 'Bloody TV dollies,' she hissed.

'So, are we getting stuck right into this then?' Jeff was up beside her, bringing a blast of coffee, Old Spice and fresh cigarette smoke. His steely below-the-collar hair was combed back and still damp. Allegedly, he worked out for an hour in the company gym before getting to his desk at 8 a.m., but Jo didn't know if she believed this. He was a broad and beefy man, whose thick leather belt was doing an impressive job of holding him at bay.

'Aha,' she said, not wanting to get drawn into the specifics just yet. There was still an hour to go before the first news conference of the week. Still time for her – head of a whole section – to draw up her 'list', which on Tuesday would be merely a list of possibles, potentials, ideas and ideals that would bear hardly any resemblance to the stories her department would have in the paper by Sunday.

'How's it been?' she asked Jeff, noticing his immaculately ironed pink shirt, slightly open at the neck despite the knitted navy tie. She wondered idly when he ironed. He was always here or in the pub across the road. Maybe his wife ironed... maybe they sent out to the dry cleaners.

There was a comfortable familiarity in standing beside Jeff, scanning the TV news and contemplating the week ahead. He'd been at the paper for years and years. Longer than the editor, most of the reporters, longer than her, of course, and she'd been here five years – *good grief*, five years. 'It's been a fabulous fortnight,' he said, which meant exactly the opposite. 'All that nonsense about the Labour MP and his lap dancer: totally made up. I don't think she'd ever met the guy. Spikey had to up his Valium dose after that fiasco.'

Jo smiled. Spikey was office code for their strange, unpredictable, tantrum-prone editor, firmly believed to be at the mercy of the vast range of pharmaceuticals rumoured to be stashed around his huge office with its view of the Thames.

'Then Declan's wife has left him. Met someone else.'

'No!'

Jeff nodded, adding: 'Shouldn't have kept him as night news editor for so long. Poor sod. Might as well keep him on nights now, though. Otherwise he'll be straight off the wagon.'

'How thoughtful of you,' she teased. 'And how's my department been behaving?' She'd just seen Dominique enter the newsroom, but she was still well out of earshot.

'Well, they cocked up their electric car investigation, the lawyers are dealing with that. Don't think it'll be too bad.'

'I have no idea why they went ahead with that. We were going to do it this week, when I was back.'

'Because they're two over-ambitious little dickheads,' was Jeff's verdict.

'Why did you run it?' she asked.

'They didn't have anything else. I was busy at the start of the week. Forgot I was babysitting. Then, come Thursday, that was all they had.'

'Anything else I should know?'

'Yup.' He told her the latest unprintable, outrageous rumour about the Prime Minister currently doing the rounds.

'Oh, rubbish!' she declared. 'Where's that supposed to have come from?'

'The coppers at Downing Street.' Then, 'Savannah Tyler?' Jeff asked without a pause. 'Where are we with Savannah Tyler?'

Aha, so they were still on the trail of the elusive environmentalist set to become Britain's first Green MP.

'Still trying,' Jo replied. 'I've only been in for ten minutes.'

'Are we going to get her?' Jeff wanted to know. 'Spikey is very keen. Think he's in love with her or something.'

'If she does a profile piece, she's doing it with us. Tony Jarvis has promised.'

'Well, make him sign it in blood. You've got thirty minutes left to come up with a list,' he smiled. 'Put Savannah Tyler at the top of it.'

Jo turned back to her section, where Dominique was already on the phone. 'Yes, yes, I understand,' she was saying into the receiver. 'But if you have a complaint, you need to put it in writing... an email or message will do. Yes... I'll give you the details.'

The women smiled and nodded their hellos at each other.

Dominique looked stunning, Jo couldn't help noticing – her micro-braids wound up in a monumental bun, a gorgeous white, orange and cherry-red dress showing off her slim figure and conker-brown skin. As

Dominique put her phone down, Jo's mobile began to ring. 'Hell,' she said with a smile then: 'Jo Randall,' into the receiver.

'Jo. You know I want to talk to you about Mel's school.' Bloody Simon. She could feel her heart rate leaping up.

'Simon,' she tried not to shout. 'You have talked to me about it and you know how I feel. You know how Mel feels about it too. She's been through enough change, Simon. She's not moving school.'

'But she's at a rubbish school, Jo. I want you to at least come and look at the one round the corner from my flat. I'm in a much better catchment than you.'

Oh yes, she thought, *yes, just get your little dig in about how much richer than me, how much better than me, you are, Dr Freaking Simon.* 'Simon, I'm in conference until twelve. I will phone you then and talk about it.'

'I'm busy later,' he snapped back. 'There is absolutely no reason why you, me and Mel shouldn't at least go and look at that school. They have a place available but it won't be open forever.'

'Simon. Please don't do this. She has friends, she enjoys school. We can think ahead for secondary school, or next year even. But there's no need to rush into this.' Jo kept her voice steady, was determined she wasn't going to plead.

'It's a much better school,' he insisted, 'Much nicer. Much safer.'

'Give me some time to think about it,' she said.

'Be sure you do.' He hung up abruptly.

And her phone rang again.

'What have you got for the list?' she asked Dominique, catching sight of Aidan sloping into the office. A full twenty minutes late today.

'Ask Aidan too,' she told Dominique before answering her call.

Their ideas, scribbled onto a bit of notebook paper and tossed back to her, weren't too bad:

A full whooping cough outbreak investigation.
A fresh look at wind power.
How Green are the top Royals?
Story idea. A backgrounder/interview with Savannah Tyler.

(Yes, thanks team, I've only been trying to get this for two months now.)

A report pulled off the internet:

cabbage and broccoli protect against Alzheimer's.

She was sure she'd heard that before. Several other minor health stories...

She was reading their list, not listening too closely to the cold caller trying to interest her in an issue which didn't sound at all interesting. 'Hmmm... could you send me an email and we'll give that some consideration?' Jo was telling the voice.

As soon as she was off the phone, she had to have it out with her 'department' about last week's electric car cock-up. She opened a copy of last Sunday's paper and smoothed the offending double-page article out in front of them.

'Hello, Aidan, maybe the solar power's run out on your watch or something, but ten o'clock is the time I'd like you in, please. Now,' she moved on quickly, 'you both know the lawyers are involved with this...' They nodded, looking sulky and embarrassed. 'Jeff's already told me about it. It was too ambitious, OK? I mean it's good to be ambitious, have a bold plan, that's what we try and do every week, but you're not ready for solo flights like this just yet. OK?'

'Aidan had a contact who gave us information he assured me we could trust,' came Dominique's excuse.

'But can I remind you, I still wanted to wait until Jo was back,' Aidan added frostily. Aidan slipped off his cord jacket and hung it over the back of his chair, then ran his fingers through his black hair. Jo realised she'd been watching him for slightly too long. Desperate divorcee. She turned her attention back to the offending article.

Like Dominique, Aidan was around the twenty-three-year-old mark. Jo had been landed with them both eight months ago.

'We're promoting you from chief health reporter and giving you your own department,' Spikey had called her into his office to announce. 'Health and Environment. You'll head it up, get a budget. Lots of great stories coming out of that area. I want us to be breaking them.'

For about half a day, Jo had been elated, thrilled with her dizzy new prospects. She'd wondered who to bring onto her team. Then Jeff had informed her that more trainees than usual had been taken on by the company this year and the executives were scratching their heads about what to do with them all. So, she was getting two trainees to look after herself.

Two trainees were not the same as a new department. Two trainees were not a promotion. Two trainees were a pain in the butt as all their work had to be checked even more carefully than her own.

Still, they were improving under her watchful eye. Yes, they were charming little rats who'd sell their souls for a front page exclusive but that meant that one day soon she was going to have a cracking team.

'OK, whooping cough. Obviously, we're going to be all over that like a rash. I'm hearing that the children had been vaccinated. But we need to be careful. We do not want to cause any kind of vaccination panic, so we need to find out the facts and report responsibly.' She had a large database to tap on the subject of vaccinations: scientists, doctors and ordinary parents. 'Aidan, I want you to stick like glue to the government side of this,' she instructed him, 'I want to know everything they know about the outbreak, every line they're giving us. Dominique, you need to find out all you can about the infected children, where they are, how they were exposed, how they're doing. The other suggestions,' she glanced through the scribbled list of ideas again: 'there's a few things here we'll follow up. But I'll let you know what grabs them at conference.'

'D'you want me to chase the Savannah Tyler interview? I've got a bit of an in with the Green Party,' said Aidan. *No, she did not want him chasing the talk she'd been sweating to get herself!*

'We would love to do Savannah,' she heard herself telling him in a calm and friendly way. 'I'm pressing the official buttons very hard. If you can tactfully explore other avenues to strengthen our case, without irritating or putting anyone off, then you're welcome. But you are not, under any circumstances, allowed to irritate Tony Jarvis, OK? He's very important to us. Right, I have to speak to Jeff—' she glanced at her watch '— about five minutes ago.'

Her desk phone sprang to life again.

'Someone get that, take a message.'

She turned and walked off to the sound of Dominique saying in a totally syrupy and ingratiating way: 'Oh, hi, Tony, no, I'm afraid she's just gone into conference. Can I help at all?' which is not the same as '*can I take a message?*' is it? No, it's journo speak for '*If you've got a story, tell me, so I can pinch it right off my department head's desk.*'

Anyway, first brief Jeff... then conference.

* * *

Spikey, real name Paul Skinner, was not nicknamed Spikey because he was prickly, although he was, nor because he frequently 'spiked' ideas, ditching them at the last possible moment and causing reporters to flurry around in desperate search of replacement exclusives, although he did that too. He'd earned the nickname because of his rumoured fondness for spiking his endless supply of coffees with all manner of mood-enhancers. He had a little metal box of alleged sweeteners that he click-clicked into his drinks with alarming regularity. He was constantly sniffing and numerous people were willing to testify in the pub to having walked in on him unexpectedly to find him dusting powder off his desk or putting little envelopes hurriedly back into drawers.

His drugs may well have been legal. He was probably taking Prozac, beta blockers, Valium even. Jo knew she would have to if she had his job. But the rumours continued to flourish. And to be honest, his random moods, tantrums and ideas were like those of a man in the grip of a drug addiction. It made perfect sense. It also made perfect sense for one of the country's best-selling Sunday newspapers to be run by a drug addict. He was needy, unpredictable, obsessive, moody, paranoid, demanded impossibly high standards, had few loyalties, was out to get everybody equally. So, he made a great editor.

She understood editors and news editors so much better since she'd had children. They were like big toddlers; they wanted what someone else had *now*! They would scream and scream until they got it and once you gave it to them, they didn't want it any more.

So, you had to stand firm. Maintain clear boundaries. Tell them what they could have, when, and not let them down. You never, ever made promises you couldn't keep. And just occasionally, you could reward them with a lovely surprise.

So here they were, once again, the editor, his department heads and several senior reporters together on a Tuesday morning, to spend a little time reviewing last week's cock-ups, but mainly to turn over a fresh new leaf and talk about how fabulous this week's edition was going to be. Of course, by Saturday's conference, the list of explanations, compromises and lost opportunities would be long and frustrating and Spikey's temper would be frayed.

But this was Tuesday. Nothing but clear skies ahead. Yeah, clear skies and a bitter Oxford by-election campaign.

When it was her turn to present her ideas for the week, Jo went through whooping cough in depth and then the wind farm idea. Aidan and Dominique would be good at that. The 'How Green are the Royals' idea was also floated.

Everyone listened, but she'd barely finished before Spikey wanted to know how it was 'progressing' on the Savannah front.

'If she's going to do a talk, she's going with us. But at the moment, she's determined not to do a personal profile piece. Says it detracts from her message.' Loud guffaws from the eight men in the room at this. Smiles from the two other women.

You could understand Savannah's point. She was fighting for election in Oxford next week. And according to the pollsters, she was on course to become Britain's first Green Party MP. Unfortunately for Savannah, she wasn't just a committed environmentalist with a serious scientific research background, someone who'd made regular research trips to the Arctic, someone who'd re-energised a woolly political party and was on the brink of making history and getting herself into Westminster, she was also thirty-something, single, female, and, perhaps worst of all, unusually attractive.

To say that newspaper editors were falling over themselves to get 'up close and personal' with this new politician-to-be was an understatement. But Savannah, unlike any other politician on the face of the earth, was shy of the press. She was willing to do TV interviews about policy matters, she was willing to take part in television and radio debates and she'd written several guest articles about her areas of concern. But at the slightest whiff of a personal question, she was off.

'I was not invited here to talk about myself,' she could say in a particularly chilly way, making it clear that one more question would cause her to unhook her microphone and vanish, as had already happened on one telly breakfast show.

There were numerous journalists digging about, trying to do 'backgrounders' on her. But as yet, nothing had come to light. The Green Party had closed ranks; her friends, the few that had been unearthed, did likewise.

Although Savannah was English, she'd been born and educated abroad, so there was no birth certificate, no childhood pals or college lovers to track down and no one had even found out where her family lived.

'She's very serious,' Tony Jarvis, the Green Party press officer, had warned Jo. 'This is not about her, not about some big ego trip. This is about the planet.'

'But doesn't she know how many extra votes she'll pick up by revealing her true self to the voters?' Jo had countered. 'I think she's wonderful. I wish every politician was like her, stuffed with integrity and excellent intentions. I need to tell the country about her.'

'So do,' Tony had replied. 'We've got info on all the stuff she supports, all the policies she wants to see introduced—'

'Tony, that's not what I mean.'

Yet another conversation leading nowhere.

'Is it about time to send you up there?' Spikey asked Jo now, his short hair on end. 'You know, go knock on her door, get whatever you can. Or do we still have any faith in negotiations? I don't need to tell you that Jason would like Politics to be all over her and Vince wants News to take over.'

No, he did not need to tell her. It didn't matter what story she was covering, both the political editor, Jason Caruth, and chief reporter, Vince Maguire, thought they could do it better.

'Give me two days. Then yes, I agree' – although she totally did not – 'we'll have to go and face her up.' She already knew what the outcome of that was going to be. A slammed door in her face and many good stories from Tony Jarvis no longer coming her way. 'We'll have someone on standby in Oxford on Saturday, unless we hear otherwise,' Vince said, making a big show of writing himself a note about it. He looked even paler, puffier and sweatier than usual this morning, must have had a late night 'meeting contacts' yesterday. He ran his fingers over his buzz cut and she wished he would take off his dark tweed jacket because the sheen on his podgy face was just creepy.

'Thanks for the vote of confidence, Vincent,' she heard herself hiss, which was petty and unprofessional, but so was he.

'OK, the light relief,' Spikey said and turned to his showbiz and fashion people. 'What have you got for me?' Martina Jarvis and Tilly London smiled and glanced over their notes. Showbiz editor, Martina, went first and reeled off a host of starry names, which elicited much nodding and scribbling from Spikey, then she paused for effect, pushed her short blonde hair behind her ear and held up a photograph, which showed a very unexpected celebrity couple canoodling in microscopic swimwear on the beach, unexpected because both the actor and the singer were married... to other people.

'Thought you might like to see this as well.'

'Oh yes,' was Spikey's response. 'We like that. But how much is it going to cost us?'

'All of this week's Showbiz budget,' she warned him. 'But I think it's worth it.'

'Totally exclusive – not even a rumour of it in the other papers before Sunday?'

'Totally... Well, I thought maybe I'd leak a hint of it for Saturday just to excite some interest and recoup a bit of my money.'

'Good idea.'

'Is that a genuine pap picture, or did the happy couple pose for it?' Vince wanted to know. 'I mean it's such a clear shot, you'd think they were in on it.'

Martina just raised an eyebrow: 'Don't think that matters to us, does it?'

'Doesn't he have a big film opening in about a week's time, which the reviewers have said is pants?' Vince asked.

'Didn't know you had such a conscience, Vince,' Martina defended herself.

'I don't have a conscience,' was Vince's reply, 'I just like news and advertising to be separate.'

'OK, that's enough. Martina will ask the snapper more about it,' Spikey said, to bring the spat to an end. 'Tilly, what's in this week? What's out?'

Jo's friend, Tilly, fifty-something, smart as a whip, eccentric, glamorous, pure, undiluted fashionista, leaned back in her chair and said: 'Oh, like you care, Paul! It's Tuesday morning, I've not even had time for a cigarette yet, if I decide on something today, it'll be out of fashion by Sunday. It's May, spring's turning to summer, expect a double-page spread of skinny girls in tight tops and tiny skirts, but then that's what I give you all year long.'

'The warm snap's over, though, heavy rain forecast,' Jeff warned.

'Shut up, Jeff,' Tilly replied. 'Do I need your advice? What you know about fashion could be written in capitals on the back of a molecule. Anyway, rain, no problem, we'll do miniskirts and see-through macs. Everything dark is out, everything light is in. That's all you need to know.'

Which perhaps explained why Tilly was dressed head to toe in complicated white items but these were tame compared with what the other women in her department wore: belt-sized skirts, crop tops and the kind of heels you wouldn't exactly be able to sprint about London in. Not that fashion writers did much sprinting – unless it was opening day of the Miu Miu sale. 'Right, go away everyone and get me something decent for the front page,' was Spikey's final remark. Class was dismissed for another day.

* * *

Jo headed for the bathroom, not because she needed to go, but because this was where she and Tilly liked to hold their private post-conference meetings and Jo, back from holiday, had to catch up with at least the most important elements of a weeks' worth of office gossip.

'You know about Declan, of course?' was Tilly's opener.

'Yes, the wife is off.'

'With another woman,' Tilly added.

'Oh, ouch, that's harsh.'

'Yeah, and the wife's been commissioned to write a piece about it for *Marie Claire*.'

'No!'

'Oh yes, Mrs Declan comes out in the July issue.'

'That's terrible.'

'Hilarious. And Vince has finally worn Binah down. They left together on Friday night.'

'Eeeugh, no, how could she?'

'She's run out, she's done everyone else,' was Tilly's verdict.

'Not everyone.'

'No, to my knowledge Spikey and Jeff are just about the only men left standing.'

'Aidan?'

'Oh God, no. Her car, his second week.'

'Why didn't I know that?'

'We didn't want to spoil your little crush,' Tilly said, scrunching her grey-white bob up in the mirror. She took off her dramatic lilac-framed glasses and began to polish them.

'Oh, please!' was Jo's response. 'Anyway, how's your department?'

'All good. But I'm fitting a new lock to the clothes cupboard. Another designer dress loaned to us has walked away. Causes me such a bloody headache. If anyone is going to steal expensive clothes from this office, it's going to be me, on an occasional and acceptable level, so I can't tolerate any further pilfering. There are going to be lots of high street spreads for the next few months while I suffer designer penance.'

'And your love life?' Jo asked.

'Still bonking the banker... with the help of the little blue pills.' Tilly replied.

'Him or you?' Jo snorted.

'Both of us, of course. He's taking me to Mauritius, so I'll stick around for that, but then – who knows? Still seeing the Little Chef?' Tilly asked. 'Bet he doesn't need Viagra. Bet he does a nice breakfast too. You'll have to watch your waistline. Mind you, I'm sure you're working it all off together.'

'Thank you, Tilly. Love you too. I'm not seeing him, I'm just dabbling,' Jo said. 'I'm Bridget Jones in reverse,' she added, putting on a fresh coat of lipstick in front of the mirror. 'I've spent over a decade of my life with one man and now I want to be single. Well, single-ish. Uncommitted.'

'The grass is always greener,' Tilly reminded her, then couldn't help herself from adding: 'Jo, that's an awful shade on you. Ageing. You need light pink or apricot.'

'Thank you, bitch-friend.'

'Bridget Jones in reverse!' Tilly laughed, 'You could finally be starting a fashionable new trend, Jo. Yes, darling, you, in your sensible shoes,' Tilly said, casting a despairing look at the offending pumps.

'I have to leave the office, you know, walk places, go on the Tube,' Jo reminded her, 'I can't totter about in stilettos.'

Jo peered critically at the lipstick. Bloody Tilly, she was always right. It was too dark. She did need pinky apricot. Hell. And this was the most expensive lipstick she'd ever bought.

* * *

Back at her desk, Jo left another message for Tony, who was now 'tied up in a meeting', she briefed Aidan and Dominique about the wind farm investigation and began with the thing she really wanted to get stuck into – whooping cough. She clicked into her email basket and looked at the messages that had arrived in the forty minutes she'd been away.

There was the one from Jayne, the leader of a support group for parents who believed their children had been damaged by vaccines.

Jo, how are you? Called last week, but you were away. Need to speak to you. Do not want parents with vulnerable kids to rush for Quintet. Can provide your paper with latest US research etc. Lots of angry parents wanting to speak to you.
Jayne

Jo opened her address book and dialled Jayne's office number. 'So, what's the latest?' she asked when their friendly preamble was over.

'OK. US researchers have found a link between a hereditary condition – admittedly rare – and susceptibility to the kind of problems we're seeing in some of our children.'

Jo liked the way she said 'our'. Every one of the children Jayne knew about was 'our'. Yes, she had a child herself, but she fought just as hard for everyone else's kids.

'If people know they have this condition running in their family, they must not, on any account, let their child have a vaccination, especially one that's new to market, until a full risk assessment is done.'

'Does the government know about this?'

'Of course the government knows. They have the US research, plus we've told them, we've sent the Department of Health all the papers, all the contact details of the scientists. But they're "considering all the evidence", apparently. They're quite happy to let other children be harmed, while they consider. They're prepared to wait for hell to freeze over before they act.'

'OK, calm,' Jo soothed, but then asked: 'Should I have my daughter vaccinated against this whooping cough outbreak?' Not particularly professional, but she and Jayne had discussed this several times already. 'Should I let her have Quintet?'

'How old is she now?' Jayne asked.

'Three years and two months.' Jo's eyes moved to the little silver-framed photo of her girls on her desk. It was a year old now: Mel laughing hysterically as her two-year-old sister, chubby and pretty as a doll, waved hands clad in giant oven gloves – she should get an updated snap, although it was lovely to remember them like this too.

'If there's no issues around blood clotting in the family, there shouldn't be any reason to worry for you, Jo. I'm not anti-vaccine, I always tell people that. I just believe that the facts need to be available, so that any possible harms are avoided. And this outbreak is nasty,' she added, 'The children are getting very ill...'

'And it sounds like some of them had already been vaccinated... so I don't know what's going on. Maybe this is some kind of new strain and we do need the newest vaccines to protect them,' Jo added. Dominique was holding a piece of paper up in front of her nose.

Tony Jarvis on line 2

was scribbled across it.

'Jayne, I have to go, sorry, another call. Why don't you send me that info over? I'll see if I can do something with it. Also, I'd like to do some fresh interviews. Some parents who've joined you recently. Don't suppose you've got anyone who's contacted you about a bad reaction to Quintet yet, have you?'

She was doing the 'just one second' wave to Dominique.

'I was just coming to that,' Jayne said. 'I had parents on the line yesterday. IVF twins. They're only two years old and they had Quintet the week it was introduced – one boy had a paediatric stroke days later.'

'Good grief.' There was nothing but sympathy in Jo's voice, but she couldn't help her story muscles from flexing. IVF twins.

My Vaccine Heartbreak by Mum of Twins

This could be really good.

'Could you ask them if they'd like to talk to me about it? I'll call you later. OK. You're a star, Jayne, really. Bye, darling.'

'Bye.'

'Tony,' Jo clicked to line two.

They did the hellos, how are yous, how was your holiday thing. Then he went straight into: 'Someone who may well be the first Green MP to get into Westminster wants to do a talk.'

'Oh yesssss!' She couldn't stop the grin.

'Talented, committed, good-looking, passionate... with a great story to tell—'

'Yesssssssss! I'm going to stand up and shout this to Jeff, if you don't mind.'

'He's called Finlay Logan,' Tony went on quickly, before she could do that. 'He's standing for election in Glasgow and you'll love him.'

'Er... he?? Finlay Logan?... Glasgow?! No, no, no! No Tony!' She was annoyed now, not least because Aidan and Dominique's eyes had swivelled to her when she'd uttered the first excited 'yes'. 'Look, Tone, you and I, we go way back, we have history, I came and covered Green Party meetings when only two hippies and their dog turned up. Don't take the mickey. I can't profile everyone who's scraped together a deposit and got themselves nominated.'

'Jo. There's another by-election in Glasgow next month. The hope is he'll achieve an even better result than Savannah.'

'So, I'll give you the number of our Scottish desk, they can do Finlay. I want Savannah.'

'The Scottish papers have done him. We want him to go national now.'

Then Jo had an idea: 'I'll do him with Savannah,' she said. 'The Green Team... the Green duo set to storm into Westminster. How about that?'

Tony paused. He was obviously imagining headlines along the lines of:

Double Green whammy, Green Dream Team

while Jo pictured the huge:

Savannah Talks – exclusive!

With a tiny insert about Finlay.
'I like that, Jo. Why didn't we think of it before?' Tony asked.
'Because you're a bunch of amateurs,' she teased.
'I'm meeting Savannah tomorrow, I'll put this to her. OK? Meanwhile, you look up Finlay. You'll like him and he's single,' Tony added cheekily.
'Thanks, yes, thanks, Tone, when I run out of men to date in London, I will come straight to you for advice.'
'You do that.'
'Bye.'
'Wind farms—' She shooed her trainees' glances back to their screens. 'Got anything good for me on wind farms yet?'

5

TUESDAY: 8.15 P.M.

'Do you think we can get a kitten? Josie has a kitten. Could I get a kitten for my birthday? Pleeeeeeeease,' Mel made a last bid to further the conversation and keep her mother in the bedroom for just a tiny bit longer. Jo had done suppertime and bath-time with her girls, then stories, snuggles and now it really was bedtime. And the kitten conversation – it was one she didn't want to have. Not again.

Her children really should have a pet. Of course they should, that was how children were supposed to learn about love, care, sex and death, wasn't it? From pets. Not from the TV.

And other friends had reported the transforming power of pets. Suddenly their tinies had forgotten all about the collected set of Thomas the Tank Engine and his overpriced plastic friends, the latest Disney release and all sorts of previously pressing requirements and they had played – yes, just played – for hours on end, with their new pet.

So why was it she couldn't commit to a cat? She didn't have good cat experiences. She recalled animals that landed heavily on your lap, were soft and purring until they dug their claws in, sinking them in even further when you yelped. Then there was cat litter, cat food, the all-pervasive cat hair, the inconvenience of not being able to go away whenever they wanted to... but then, how often did they do that? Was it just that she couldn't bear to take on responsibility for one more thing? That a kitten was too much?

One tiny cat life was going to tip the load? Or was she just being too control-freaky? A cat could look after itself more or less, couldn't it? It would just come to them for food or company when it wanted to, wasn't that the point with cats?

'A kitten... I wish for a kitten,' Annette said with a great, theatrically deep sigh from her pink pillow.

'Poor Nettie,' Mel sympathised. 'She doesn't even have a school guinea pig to cuddle like me.'

That was so typically sweet of Mel. It never failed to move Jo how close her daughters were. Mel was protective and caring of Nettie and really didn't take too much advantage of the fact that Nettie worshipped her and would gladly be slave to her every whim.

Jo had expected all sorts of bad reactions to the marital split: tantrums, bed-wetting and bad behaviour. But so far, the girls seemed to be taking it as well as could be expected. Mel was maybe quieter; Nettie was clingy and hated to say goodbye when Jo left them with Simon. But she hoped it would settle down. The children had had to move house and they now spent every week in two new homes and two new bedrooms. Understandably, they were disrupted, a little bit at sea with it all.

'I'll think about the kitten, OK?' Jo hovered at the door of their bedroom. A pink paradise, a tribute to Princess Barbie and her many cloned minions. 'You're always thinking about it,' Mel groaned. 'That's just what Daddy says as well.'

Little stab in the side at the mention of Daddy. She was slightly surprised Daddy hadn't caved and bought the kitten to win popularity points. She went over and kissed her girls again, burying her nose in their warm skin. Annette's fat fold of cheek, it was hard to resist giving it a gentle nibble... Mel's silk-soft, creamy face.

'Night, night,' she told them.

She would go and watch the news... no, she would just do a few things around the house. Then she'd watch the news – oh and she'd phone her mother. Her mother was worrying her. Whenever Jo went to her parents' little house, it seemed to be more and more empty. Her mother had discovered Facebook marketplace and instead of buying more household goodies, the way she would once have done, she was selling everything that wasn't nailed down. Anything that wasn't sold was stored away in those bizarre, shrunken packages – Vacu-sacks.

'I'm clearing out, getting rid of my clutter,' was her mother's explanation. 'I'm having a good old spring clean.'

But really, it had gone way beyond that. The sofa cushions had gone, Jo had noticed on the last visit and the rug that had once been underneath the coffee table.

'Where are the cushions?' she'd asked.

'Oh, I sold them. Didn't need them any more. Just got in the way, and the rug too.'

'Where did you sell them, Facebook?' Jo had asked, incredulously.

Her mother had nodded.

'What did you get for them? Was it worth it, you know, by the time you'd paid for postage?' Jo couldn't help asking.

'Four pounds apiece. That's probably more than I paid for them. There's no telling what will do well on Marketplace. There's lots of lonely old souls sitting up at night spending too much money on things they don't really need.' This said with a mixture of sympathy and disapproval. The bed linen, duvets, towels, pretty well everything left in the house after the Facebook clearances had been shrink-wrapped and put into the cupboards. 'I think your mum would like to Vacu-sack me,' her dad had joked. 'Put me in a big plastic bag, shrink me down with the vacuum cleaner then put me out of sight at the top of the wardrobe for a season or two.'

It was as if her mother was moving house, tying up loose ends, preparing for some sort of change, but nothing was on the cards. This was their retirement home. They'd taken the bold decision five years ago to uproot from the small town in Lancashire where they'd lived all their lives, where Jo and her younger brother, Matt, had grown up, and move to a quiet London suburb, so they could be close to her and the girls. No further moves were planned – so what was all the selling off and the shrink-wrapping about?

Jo's attention went back to the news: more whooping cough cases, and among them, children who had been vaccinated. She would get Nettie vaccinated. Surely that was the sensible thing to do? But it was just so new this injection... why did her child have to be in the first wave? And was it working? What was the drug company saying about children who'd been vaccinated who were still catching whooping cough? She would have to chase that line up in the morning. Jo poured out another third of a glass of wine. How many 'thirds of a glass' was it that she'd drunk this evening? Oh dear... somehow, two-*thirds* of the bottle seemed to have disappeared.

Her mobile rang from behind the wine bottle. 'Jo Randall,' she said when she picked up, without looking at the screen because she was certain it was Declan wanting to share his thoughts on the News at Ten bulletin. Poor old Declan. Going home to a lonely flat... wife finally fed up with the fact that every single night of her husband's working week was taken up with the paper.

'Jo, are you organising the new whooping cough vaccine for the girls, or am I?'

Oh... it wasn't Declan, it was Simon sounding all clipped and brisk.

'Do you think Mel should have it too? She's all up-to-date. It's only Nettie who is due—' Jo began.

'New strains need the latest vaccines,' Simon said. 'It's perfectly safe for both girls to have it. Extra protection against this nasty outbreak.'

Her head knew this. It really did. The part that made her hesitate was that she had interviewed parents with tears in their eyes, with utter conviction in their hearts that their children had been fine, had been totally well, totally normal, until they'd had a vaccination.

'Anyone in your family have thrombophilia?' she asked him now, changing tack.

'Why?' She heard the hostility in his voice.

'Anyone with the thrombophilia gene shouldn't have a combination vaccination because they run a greater risk of the complications associated with this type of immunisation.'

'Oh, they do, do they? And on which internet scare site did you unearth that little nugget?' he spat.

She told him exactly where the information came from. Facts, glorious facts: even Simon could be stopped in his tracks with enough confidently delivered information. She just wished she had a barrage of statistics at her fingertips that she could dump it all over him right now, prove to him that he did not know everything there was to know about health, just because he was a hospital consultant. *Especially* because he was an arrogant, narrow-minded hospital consultant.

It was ridiculous, having to prepare for a conversation with the father of your children as if you were preparing for a debate. But the tail end of their marriage had been like one long session in the House of Commons. *'With all due respect, would the right honourable wanker stop giving the girls so many snacks in between meals?'*

'Would my nagging colleague kindly refrain from criticising every aspect of the profession I work for, especially in her weekly rag?'

'As my pompous partner has explained, he is a being far superior to any other that has ever walked the face of the earth...'

'Moving the debate on, shall we hear the evidence from the opposition as to who does most of the housework in the Randall–Dundas home?'

'Are we ready to vote now? Which way will our friends go in the aftermath of the divorce? Gwen obviously through the Simon door on the left, Bella votes for Jo—.'

Simon had always believed he was so much more important than her. Ultimately, that was why their marriage had fallen on its knees. It had been fine years ago when she was a nurse, when she'd supposedly known her place. It was still OK when she became a local newspaper reporter and the mother of his children. He'd still been able to categorise this and work with it. But when they'd moved to London for his glorious career and she'd achieved the national newspaper job, the glorious career of her own – that's when his world view had fallen apart. He'd been threatened... jealous... or maybe just confused. He'd belittled her, put her down in front of their families and friends.

'Jo's one of those bloody journalists,' was how he used to introduce her at parties with a roll of his eyes.

He'd not been able to let go of the idea that he was so much cleverer, smarter, better educated than her. And wasn't that really what they were arguing about now? Who knew better, who had the most information about this?

'No one in my family has thrombophilia,' he answered briskly. 'It's extremely rare. So are bad reactions to both Quintet and any other vaccine.'

'I will book them both in, OK?' Jo told him firmly.

He gave an exasperated sigh, but didn't start up again with objections.

'All right, but as soon as you can. ASAP,' he added for emphasis. 'And

I'm going to book us in for a tour of the school. You need to at least see what else is on offer.'

'Simon! I've already told you... Oh, never mind!'

* * *

Once she'd hung up on the man-formerly-known-as-her-husband, she knew just what would be more comforting than another glass of wine, or even a bar of chocolate. She dialled Marcus's mobile number.

'Hello there,' he answered and she could hear the grin on his face.

'Hello. You busy?'

'I'm very busy. I'm the busiest person in the entire kitchen, but I deserve a cigarette break right now.'

'It's OK, I can phone you back,' she insisted.

'No. No, keep talking, I'm walking to the back door. How are you?'

'I'm fine.'

'Fine?' he asked and she could hear the click of his cigarette lighter and the deep first breath of smoke. 'Fine sounds a bit boring. Are you up? Are you down? Are you missing me? Are you wanting a late-night visit?'

Little surge of desire as she heard those words.

'No, not tonight. It's been a long day.'

'I could make it an even longer day. Very long.' He paused to suck up another lungful of smoke.

'You're very tempting.'

Their second 'date', the first time they'd gone to bed, came into her mind in little flashes. It had begun with a cheeky, if slightly hesitant, call on her mobile. 'Jo, hello there, Marcus here... you know, the chef... er... I'm going for a drink after work, I just wondered... if you'd like to come along. To make up for the other night.'

At the sound of his voice, Jo had felt an outrageous tug in her stomach... and lower. 'I'm still at work,' she'd told him. It was 9 p.m. on a Friday night and she'd be at least another hour or so finishing things off.

'Me too. Us late-shift workers.'

'Speak for yourself,' she'd answered. 'I've been here since 9 a.m.'

'You'll really need a drink when you finish, then.'

'Either that or straight to bed,' she'd said, only conscious of the other meaning once she'd said it and it was too late.

'Aha,' he'd said after the kind of pause that meant he was thinking of that other meaning too. They'd met at the cramped and hot bar from their last night out, but this time, Marcus was there on his own. He was drinking a bottle of beer, with his hair dishevelled, tucked behind his ears. In a plain grey T-shirt, he looked grimy but incredibly sexy.

He'd bought her a beer, then they'd squeezed into a corner table together and had one of those conversations she hadn't had for years, where she'd barely taken in anything that was said, barely even listened, she'd just watched him, using his turn to speak as her excuse to stare. She'd liked everything she'd seen, particularly the chunky wrists, the broad, tanned forearms, the expressive mouth drinking from the rim of the bottle, the surprisingly white base of his neck that she glimpsed now and then.

He'd quickly breached the physical barrier between them, putting an arm round her, saying things into her ear, kissing her neck. He was a touchy-feely outrageous flirt. If she'd been much younger, she'd have worried about him, been nervous that he wasn't going to be reliable or particularly trustworthy, but now, he was the serious fun she wanted. Oh. Yes. Please.

'So where are you?' he'd asked. 'Are you moving on from your husband? Are you going to start seeing other people?'

'Other people?' she'd smiled at him. 'I don't think so.'

He'd nodded solemnly as if he understood, was trying to sympathise. 'Not other people,' she'd added, taking a swig from the bottle of beer, putting her hand on his arm, feeling the soft hair beneath her fingers. 'I'm going to start seeing you.'

She didn't need to be subtle, she'd decided, she didn't need to wait to read the signals, she was a grown-up, so she could make the offer. If he wasn't interested, why was he here? If he didn't want to play, then he could say so... no hard feelings.

And then they'd kissed properly: tongues tasting of beer, cigarettes and filthy promise.

There was only one thing to say after a kiss like that.

'Let's go,' she'd told him.

They'd left the bar, Jo savouring the feel of a new hand in hers. Kissing again outside, she realised how close in height they were, whereas Simon had always towered above her.

'I've got my car, you're not far from here, are you?' she'd asked.

The journey was only minutes, but it was still too long. They'd run up the stairs to his flat and when he closed the door and they were together in the tiny hallway, facing each other, she'd felt her heart shake, the blood rush.

In the busy tangle of kissing, he'd tried to slide her jacket off but she'd caught it in her hands as it headed for the floor. 'Sorry, but can I hang this up?' she'd asked.

Not exactly mad, passionate abandon but she was damned if she was going to let lightweight woven wool and silk workwear end up in a heap on this none too clean floor.

When Marcus swung open his bedroom door, she'd seen a clean bed, freshly made as if he'd thought this through, expected to get lucky.

He'd pulled off his shoes, socks, trousers, then his T-shirt, until he stood before her naked. Very erect. An erection pressed so tightly against his stomach it was almost difficult to slide her hand between the two.

For a moment, Jo had felt awkward, too old, too unused to this, too formal, too dressed: a shirt, trousers, tights, not to mention areas of dubious shaving. She hadn't thought this through at all, she'd been caught out.

'Come here,' he'd encouraged her, bare arms folding over her shoulders.

'Get under the covers,' she'd told him. 'And turn out the light.'

'Why?' There was a smile with this.

'Because I say so.'

'Are you shy?'

'I don't think so.'

When the room was dark orange, lit only by a streetlamp outside the window, Marcus had slid his naked body into bed and watched as best he could in the half-light as she'd taken off her clothes.

His hand was on his cock, that much she could tell. 'Come here,' he'd said again with something close to a groan.

And she did. Under the cool covers, with his solid warmth, his bare skin pressed up against hers, she'd felt like she was going to come three times just at the touch of his hand on her thigh.

'Here?' and 'OK?' he'd asked in breathy whispers.

Her skin all over had tingled for him, needed him to rub against her, with his fingers, with his cock, with his lips and tongue.

The fumble of the bedside condom. How could she have forgotten about the excitement, the awkwardness, the pain almost, of wanting someone so badly? The ache from the very centre of her pelvis.

But when he was inside, she'd felt him pulse through her, a different shape, the unexpected chill of the condom, the new rhythm and suddenly she'd been struck by a piercing sense of loneliness that had brought tears to her eyes. She'd heard the long, sustained gasp and felt him shudder and fall back with some disappointment because he hadn't made her come.

He'd wanted to keep trying, but she'd moved his hand away. Didn't want him to. She'd carefully moved off and laid down beside him on the bed, the throb of blood receding. Lying quietly, chests rising and falling almost together, she'd felt a wave of disbelief wash over her. She'd lost her marital virginity and it was just as overwhelming as losing her virginity the first time round.

For over a decade, she'd only been with Simon until tonight. The emotions were all jangled and conflicting. She wanted to be with someone new... it was exciting, adventurous, daring even. It was making her feel alive and excited about the possibility of new relationships. But also, she could feel that she wasn't quite sure. She was holding a big part of herself in reserve. This was still too new.

* * *

'I am very tempting, Jo,' he was saying right now into the receiver against her ear.

'You are. But no,' she replied.

'Are you sure? Sure?' he repeated, warm and intimate.

'What are you doing tomorrow?' she asked.

'I don't know. Might not be interested tomorrow... maybe you should say yes to tonight. Tonight, I'm very interested. Tonight, I'm getting hard just talking to you.'

'Uh oh,' was her response to this.

'Tonight, I'm so interested that you might just want to put your hands inside your pants right now and see what I'm talking about.'

She swallowed involuntarily.

'It's very nice in there,' he added.

'Uh oh,' she repeated, not sure if this was the way she wanted this phone call to go.

'Ohhhh,' he gave a little groan, 'I want you.'

'You are a lovely boy. I'd really like to see you soon. But I have to go now. Is that OK?'

'No! You're not going to leave me like this, are you?' She could hear the giggle in his voice.

'Night-night,' she said, then hung up.

The phone rang back almost immediately. 'Baby, you have to leave me alone now,' she purred into the receiver.

'Jo? Is that you?'

This time it was Declan and no doubt he did want to discuss every item on the 10 p.m. news.

6

WEDNESDAY: 8.15 A.M.

'So, that's the update,' she told Jeff from her car.

'When do you think you'll be back?' Jeff asked.

'Well... all the way to Canterbury, good long interview, I've got Ray coming down to do pictures. It'll be after lunch, I think.'

'We proceed with extreme caution, Jo.'

'Yes, of course,' she told him. 'The family thinking what's happened to their child is linked to the vaccine is a long way from proving things factually. The country is panicking about a whooping cough epidemic and we're telling them the injection that should protect their children might not be safe.'

'We will only run this story if the parents make a good case,' Jeff added, 'And I will want the full medical and government statements to go alongside it... if we run it.'

'Yes, of course.'

'Yeah, so, I'll go through the rest of your list at conference?'

'Unless you want Dominique to go in?'

'I don't think so!' Jeff warned. 'I can't give Dominique a taste of conference power or I'll find you dead at your desk next week with a great big dagger in your back.'

'Fair point.'

'So, the twins is a totally signed-up world exclusive, I take it?'

'Well, it will be by the time I've finished with it,' Jo assured him. 'No, don't worry, the woman who put me in touch with the family is a solid contact.'

'OK then. Drive carefully.'

'Thanks.' Jo clicked the phone off and turned the radio on. More whooping cough, some political stuff, blah, blah, an item about bits of the Greenland ice shelf breaking off and melting into the sea at an 'alarming' rate. They should do something fresh on global warming. She felt readers should be reminded of global warming at least once every two weeks. Three per cent of the world's coastlines were going to go *soon*. 'You're a reporter,' Jeff had reminded her the last time she'd brought a climate crisis story. 'You bring the news, you can't change the world.'

'Maybe I should be trying a bit harder.' She'd said.

'What? To change the world?' He'd smiled at her. 'Come and have a beer,' he'd suggested. 'Your girls are with their dad tonight, aren't they? Beer is very soothing. If all megalomaniacs drank more beer, the world would be a better place.'

'You are very soothing,' she'd told him, closing down the story she was working on. 'I should have married someone as soothing as you,' she'd added, 'I'm sure that would have helped.'

Group therapy in the pub with the other reporters and enough beers to require a taxi home was sometimes the only way of winding down from the hectic Fridays and manic Saturdays of the job.

The talk was always scurrilous, all the outrageously elaborated rumours that could never be printed but that someone had heard from 'an impeccable source' who 'swore it was true'.

* * *

It took Jo a long time to find the address she'd been given. But finally, she was driving up a long, narrow street at the edge of town. It wound gently up a hill; small, detached houses on each side with gardens, cars and motorbikes in front. It wasn't a smart area, but it was neat and tidy. Samantha and Mick Townell were parents of twin boys, one who had suffered a stroke, which the Townells blamed on the Quintet injections given just a month ago.

Jo parked her car and locked up, bringing her bags out with her. The photographer was going to come an hour later. She liked to do interviews that way. Get talking properly without someone with a huge camera and associated equipment scaring the interviewees to death.

Scooters, bikes, plastic tractors, swings and a slide were strewn about the hilly front lawn, but there was no sign of children. The house looked neat from the outside. Paint shiny, small leaded-effect windows, with the white toggle of a blind hanging in the centre of each one. Before she could reach up and press the bell, the door was opened and a woman with short blonde hair wearing a smooth white shirt and cropped beige trousers was standing in front of her, holding out a hand and introducing herself as Samantha.

'Come in... sorry, we're in the kitchen having a snack, we couldn't wait any longer.'

'Sorry I'm late,' Jo apologised, 'it took me a while to find it.'

They had the cursory little chat about directions, driving from London, traffic and so on. Jo was as relaxed and friendly as she could be because handling the warm-up talk well was an important part of the job.

The Townells hadn't signed any sort of contract yet, so they were under no obligation to talk to her. They could pull out at any time, and it had happened often enough in the past: she'd arrived at out-of-the-way addresses after hours of driving only to have the door slammed in her face because people had changed their minds about an interview. Or worse, another newspaper was already there. 'Assume nothing' was the newsroom motto. Take nothing for granted. Check every single fact and waterproof your story, your contacts. Your exclusive.

'Come and say hello to the boys,' Samantha said, so Jo followed her into a small kitchen where the two-year-olds and their father, Mick, were sitting at the table.

Mick, a friendly-looking, casually dressed man, stood up to shake her hand, encouraging his sons with a: 'Say hello, boys.'

The two curly heads moved in her direction and smiles and waves followed, then the faces turned back to their plates. 'They'll be shy to start with but I'm sure they'll get used to you,' Samantha explained. 'Shall we go into the sitting room? And would you like some tea?' Samantha asked.

'Tea would be great. Just milk, please.'

So, finally they settled down in the spotlessly tidy room. Teacups in front of them – boys now out in the back garden with their dad – Jo, ready to record with her notebook and biro on her knee.

'So, d'you want to tell me all about it?'

And Samantha began. A little falteringly at first, but then gathering strength, until the story was flowing. Jo listened. She sometimes slipped in a clarifying question or two, but mainly she listened, thinking occasionally how confessor-like her job was, and the terrible things she'd heard over the years. All spilled out into her recorded files. The voices played over again in her earphones back at the office, their words typed out onto the computer screen in front of her, then appearing in black and white on the pages of the paper on Sunday.

It was a strange job, because she couldn't give her interviewees much in return. She was not there to comfort them, to bring help, to advise, she was there to listen, then to tell others and only occasionally could her articles at least serve as a warning, to try to prevent tragedies from happening again.

* * *

Samantha and Mick had tried to have children for five years. Their boys, Ben and Ellis, were born after a third IVF attempt. There was grief enough in that story. But what Samantha went on to tell was even worse; it made Jo wonder, yet again, why pain was doled out so unfairly in life. Why were some people allowed to lead charmed, virtually unshadowed lives, when others were given the lion's share of grief?

'The boys made it to 36 weeks,' Samantha was telling her. 'That's when I went into labour. I had a Caesarean because the doctors felt it would be safer for us all. And they were a good weight for twins, both just over five pounds. They went into special care for a week, but they were thriving. Doing really well. It was just mad, the first few months. We were on this wonderful, unbelievable high.' The words were tumbling out, Samantha smiling at the memories: 'I mean, two healthy baby boys. It was all we could ever have hoped for. Much more than we'd ever hoped for. We were exhausted, but the magic of it never wore off. In the middle of the night, getting up yet again, I'd think about the women I met through the IVF.

Think about how much they'd love to be woken up by a baby crying in the middle of the night.'

Jo scribbled this down in her notebook and underlined it.

'The boys' development was closely monitored, because they were premature twins,' Samantha went on. 'I'd go for developmental checks every couple of months, hand-eye co-ordination, hearing, sight, that sort of thing. It was all normal, they were coming along fine. I've got their log books. I can show you.'

'That's great, we'll do that afterwards, you just tell me what happened next,' Jo reassured her.

'March the 6th. I will never forget the date,' Samantha began, very serious now, turning from the window to face Jo and look her directly in the eye. 'Mick came with me, because taking them for their baby vaccinations had been an ordeal. I'd had to put one screaming baby down to hold the other one for the injection and I thought it would be better if we were both there, especially as they were toddling about by then, curious, getting into all sorts of mischief. So, we went to the doctor's surgery. They were exactly 24 months old. I was always keen on vaccinations, wanted them to have them as soon as they could. Had them all at the recommended ages, even though the boys were born a month early. No one had suggested to me I should treat them as aged minus one month and delay everything for a month at least. So, we took them in and—' Suddenly Samantha stopped, she looked out of the window and into the garden where Mick was trying to interest one of the boys in a tricycle. Her hand went up to her eyes and wiped away the tears that suddenly spilled out. 'I'm sorry,' she said.

'Don't be sorry, take all the time you need,' Jo soothed her.

'I have dreams about that day,' Samantha said quietly, and Jo noticed that the hand wiping away the tears was trembling. 'I dream that we pull up outside the surgery and Mick gets a phone call on his mobile, or I change my mind, or one of the boys is sick, something makes us drive away again and Ben is still fine.' Her voice was a whisper now.

'I'm so sorry,' Jo said and really did mean it.

'We went in,' Samantha continued. 'Mick stayed in the waiting room and I took them in one at a time so they wouldn't be frightened, because injections always make children cry. And they have to have two at a time – Quintet and then the Meningitis C, which makes it really hard, because after the first one they know what's coming. You feel bad enough, putting them through the pain, let alone—' She broke off to dab at tears again. 'I'll have to go and get some tissues, I'm sorry, I didn't think I'd get so upset.'

'It's OK, I've got plenty of time,' Jo smiled, but once Samantha was out of the room, she grabbed for her phone and messaged the photographer to stay away for another forty minutes at least.

When Samantha returned, she looked composed. She took up her seat on the sofa again and continued. 'The injections had an immediate effect on the boys. They cried and cried. Looking back, I can't believe I didn't say, after Ellis had been done, "Wait a minute, this isn't the way he should be reacting." He was inconsolable. Bright red, screaming. But I just handed him to Mick and snatched Ben up before he got upset and headed back to the nurse.

'Once they'd both been injected, we sat in the waiting room for twenty-five minutes trying to calm them down. The other patients were joining in, trying to help us out. We were cuddling the boys, rocking, bouncing, whatever we could. The nurse came out to look at them, took their temperature and said they were fine, they'd just been upset by it all. So, finally we decided to bundle them into the car.

'They were still screaming by the time we got home and when they did finally quieten down, they fell asleep. We put them to bed and they slept for the whole afternoon. I remember joking about it at the time with Mick. It was so wonderful to have a full afternoon off. We were saying, "must take them for more injections". Terrible to think of that now.'

'So what happened after that?' Jo asked gently.

'I ended up waking them. But they were groggy, tired, just not themselves for the rest of the day. They didn't eat much. Ben had a temperature and I gave him Calpol, because that's what they tell you to do if they're unwell after the injection.

'They both slept through that night and the next morning Ellis seemed better, but Ben was groggy, drowsy, just not himself,' she said. 'I had the vague feeling for several days that he wasn't right. But I didn't contact anyone about it, I didn't phone the doctor, the health visitor or anyone, because I thought I was being over-anxious. I told myself maybe they were coming down with a virus.'

Samantha cleared her throat, then said, as matter-of-factly as she could:

'It was twelve days after the injection that Ben had his stroke. Paediatric stroke they call it in children. All the symptoms you're told to look out for in older people, happened to him. He couldn't move his left arm. The left side of his face dropped. At first, I thought I was imagining things. I was here in the house with them both, on my own. Then I got really frightened and phoned 999. Once I explained what was happening, they sent round an ambulance for us very quickly.'

Jo sympathised: 'How frightening for you.'

'Oh God,' Samantha's fingers went up to squeeze at her eyes again, 'it was terrifying.' She went on to detail the treatment Ben was given and then outlined where he was now. 'Well, you'll see when you meet him. His face is still droopy on that side, he can only half open his eye. A little bit of movement is coming back to his left arm and left leg, but we're looking at months and months of rehab, physio, speech therapy to get everything working again and have him developing as he should. The outlook is quite positive —' Samantha broke off, 'I have to stay positive,' she added, her voice wobbling again, 'But I wish it had never happened.'

She spoke of doctors who asked if Ben had been ill or had been vaccinated recently, who asked about family history of strokes and blood clotting illnesses. 'My Mum died of a stroke in her sixties and I think she did have trouble with clots. I remember her being on blood thinners, but I don't know much about it,' Samantha said. Now Jo was listening extra carefully. Jayne had mentioned that children with a family history of this kind of illness had to be screened out from having Quintet. The government knew this but hadn't done anything about it. If anyone had asked Samantha, she could have told them about her mother.

Samantha blew her nose and added firmly, 'I'm talking to you because I want to find out if that injection was to blame. Because if it was, they need to help Ben get better. And they need to make sure no other child is harmed like this.'

'Of course, I understand... have you spoken to a lawyer? Do you think you would consider going to court?' Jo asked.

Samantha looked anxious, 'Lawyers... courts... it all costs a lot of money. No, we've not gone down that route. But we're talking to you and we're talking to Ben's doctors. We're hoping we can work out what's the best next step.'

'The IVF was expensive,' she added. 'Having twins is expensive. Can we risk a court case? I don't think so. Someone somewhere should be held to account for this. But I don't think we're going to be the ones to do it.'

'How does Mick feel about it?' Jo asked.

There was the sound of voices at the back door and Samantha stood up, telling Jo she could speak to him herself.

* * *

Mick was maybe going to be a little pricklier to interview, Jo reckoned. She watched him sit down and cross his arms as she switched on 'record' and selected a fresh notebook page.

He talked about his children, about the day of the injection and the problems Ben had had ever since.

'To my mind, there's no doubt the injection caused the stroke,' he said. 'The manufacturers know perfectly well that some children can be damaged. The government has a fund set aside for vaccine-damaged kids. But I've no idea how you're supposed to get any compensation when not a single doctor wants to help you or will even admit that there is a connection.

'No doctor at that hospital wants to put themselves on the line for us. Testify in court? Challenge the official line? I don't think so. Far easier if they write it off as "one of those things", "hereditary", whatever. They've no proof it was the vaccine, but they've no proof of any other explanation either, as far as I can see. It's very unusual for a toddler to have a stroke.'

Jo nodded and took notes at speed.

She was hoping this was going to be a clear cut story for once. The vaccine company and the government knew children with a family history of a clotting disorder shouldn't have the injection, but they hadn't done anything about making the public aware – and now here was the conse-quence. Enormous distress and damage to one family and their child. She could hear Samantha talking to the boys as she made lunch for them in the kitchen while Mick gave her his side of the story.

Finally, after what felt like a slightly awkward break in the conversation, he leaned over and said in a low voice: 'Jayne didn't say anything about how much you'd be paying us for this article.'

This was the tricky moment. Of course newspapers paid for stories. But not for all stories. And they only paid big when they had to. Jo knew any payment for this story would come straight out of her own small departmental budget. The one which had to cover freelance photographers, news agency stories, the occasional expensive scoop, expenses and so on.

'I wasn't expecting to pay anything for this interview, to be honest, Mick,' Jo said as nicely as she could. 'I thought you wanted to speak to us to highlight your situation, see if we can get some action on your sons' behalf.' Then the killer line: 'Would you like us to make a donation to Jayne's support group on your behalf?'

'Well, I was thinking of money that would go towards Ben's care more directly.'

Understandable that he wanted money for the family... of course. And her paper had a reputation for paying big for good stories, but those stories usually involved celebrity scandals... health stories, even important ones, didn't usually attract payments. But this was important and maybe she could do something. 'Will you leave it with me? I'll phone you back and we can talk about that,' Jo said. 'We're hoping to go really big on the whole vaccination issue this week,' she went on, 'I'm sure you know about the whooping cough outbreak. Parents are really worried about all the issues surrounding the new injection.'

'It's just,' he countered, 'we've never gone to the papers before. One twin being damaged by a new vaccination, I thought that would be a big story for you. I thought that would be worth something. I'm not sure if I want to go through all this hassle and publicity without getting something for the boys out of it.'

It crossed Jo's mind that maybe he'd been talking to another newspaper or had sounded out someone who claimed to know the papers. Jo tried to put herself in his shoes, if her child was looking at lots of physio, rehab and there was doubt about whether he would be fully OK again, wouldn't she want as much money for a fighting fund as she could possibly get?

'I'm sure we'll be able to do something for you all. Will you leave it with me for a day or so?' she asked him again. 'I'd love to meet your boys properly,' Jo said, wanting to move on quickly. As she stood up, she was relieved to see the photographer's car pulling up outside the house.

7

WEDNESDAY: 4.15 P.M.

The screen was blurring in front of Jo's eyes. No escaping the fact that her tired eyes needed her to put on her reading glasses. Reading glasses! Reading glasses? Just not what you were supposed to have at thirty-five. She'd never told Marcus about the reading glasses, had she? There had been a rash of emails to come back to. Press releases, and more press releases, she had scanned and deleted many:

New Rural Recycling initiative launched
Small cars not as safe for pedestrians
Hospital waiting lists up

Then Green Tony with a few lines about how he'd put their idea to Savannah and she was *thinking about it.*

Oh hell... Jo really didn't want to doorstep Savannah. It wasn't just that her taste for badgering people on their doorsteps seemed to have diminished over the years. It was also because she admired Savannah too much. Jo was somehow hoping to make Savannah into a top contact one day. Turning up on her doorstep wasn't exactly going to be the start of a beautiful relationship, was it?

What else was in this list? Her contact, Jayne, asking how the interview with the Townells had gone. A few lines from parents she'd interviewed in the past asking if she would like them to comment on the current outbreak. New research from a meticulous, reliable scientist she'd used before about pollution causing a huge rise in brain diseases. She transferred that to the holding file and sent a return message to ask if the story had gone out to everyone yet or could they hold it for her exclusive until Sunday.

There was an email in her basket from:

noreply@yahoousergroups.com

an email address she didn't recognise. She double-clicked to open: It was an early news report about the whooping cough outbreak that looked as if it had come from the BBC's website. It named the first official whooping cough case, a girl from Bedfordshire who'd been so severely affected, she'd been hospitalised.

A quote from the child's father, Morris Theroux, was included:

'We can't understand how this has happened because Katie had been vaccinated.'

Underneath in a different typeface were the words:

Not all cases of whooping cough are the *same*.

And that was it, nothing else. Jo typed out a reply:

Hello, who are you? Would you like to tell me more?

and sent it, but as she'd suspected, it just came back with a 'Delivery Failed' notice.

No time to worry about that. Her desk phone and her mobile began to ring at the same moment. She asked Dominique to deal with the desk call and answered her mobile.

The receptionist from the clinic where she was planning to have the girls injected against whooping cough was on the phone, offering an appointment in two weeks' time.

'You really haven't got anything before that?' Jo pleaded.

'If you can come at fairly short notice, we can put you on standby for a cancellation.'

'Well, OK, if that's the best you can do,' she answered, knowing Simon was going to freak out at this. Two weeks!

Dominique was looking quite animated at the call she was taking, scribbling down lots of notes.

'I'm meeting my Oxford Green pal tonight—' Aidan was up at the side of her desk. 'I think he's going to be quite useful. He's in with them all without being too tied up in party politics. There are maybe some things he could find out for us, maybe some things he'd like to leak, that's what I'm hoping.'

'Oh, right.' Jo wasn't really very comfortable with this. She had her own relationship with the Green Party to maintain, she didn't want Aidan stumbling in and upsetting things – or nicking any exclusive stories. But then, she pulled herself up, this was a free country. There must be plenty of other reporters Green Tony cosied up to as well.

Aidan was leaning over Jo's desk in a way that made her push her chair back slightly from him. He was dressed in one of his soft, tactile corduroy suits that matched his soft, chocolatey hair which flopped constantly to one side, so he was always pushing it back. His face was creamy pale, punctuated by a large mole in the middle of one cheek, and he had high cheekbones and naturally arched eyebrows. He was clever, very well read, idealistic in the way almost everyone who becomes a journalist is, to start with. And Jo knew perfectly well that she was just a little bit too taken with him.

Sometimes she wondered if Jeff had assigned Aidan to her department as a sort of morality test; if there was a bet on somewhere in the executive upper echelons, odds on as to whether or not she was going to do what certain male department heads had been doing for decades: seduce the fresh-faced new talent on the news floor.

Of course, if she didn't have any shame, or morals, or sense of decency, she could take Aidan under her wing, devote some special attention to him... She looked up from his expressive hands to the smooth face.

'Aidan,' she began. He was looking at her just a little too intently, probably about to take notes on what she was going to say to him. 'Journalism isn't just about stitching people up. You can make friends, you can do stories on people you admire and with people you admire, just as much as you can do stories on people you're trying to expose.' She gave him a smile. 'I just wanted to make sure you were aware of that. Don't go looking for trouble that isn't there. You can get pretty far as a journalist who people like and trust. It's not all Watergate, you know, conspiracies, secrets and cover-ups.'

He smiled back, a charming dimply, arched-eyebrow thing. So, she quickly picked up the phone and dialled the first number to come into her head, to make sure he went away, stopped leaning over her like that.

There was a whole list of contacts she phoned at least once a fortnight to check on, to make sure nothing had happened or was about to break that she didn't know about. She was already behind on this week's calls.

'Hi, Dr Wilson's office, please.'

'Putting you through.'

'Is Dr Wilson about?'

'Who's calling please?' She recognised the voice of Ted's secretary.

'It's Joanne Dundas.' Her married name and alias.

'I'll see if he's available.'

After a moment or two she heard Ted's warm hello.

'I've nothing for you yet,' he added. 'God, woman, leave me alone for a week or two and maybe I'll get some work done.'

'Nothing! Are you sure, not even the slightest preliminary indication?'

'No!'

'But how am I going to make sure you come to me first if I don't phone you up regularly and flirt?'

'I will come to you with a lovely big leak, you have my word, you know you do. But you can flirt away anyway.'

'Oh, Ted. But how can I be sure your partners won't be giving some lovely big leaks to someone else?'

'Leave them to me.'

'So when can I pencil in a date?'

'For dinner?' he asked, almost certain that wasn't what she meant.

'No, for leaks. Dinner! Pah. I'm far too busy to have dinner even in my own home.'

'No time for dinners. Single life can't be much fun for you then, can it?'

'No, no, it's fine. Honestly. We will do drinks very soon, OK? Meanwhile should I keep my phone in my handbag? Should I hold it twelve inches from my head when I'm talking to you? Or what's your entirely off-the-record, unofficial advice?'

Jeff was at her desk now, a big notepad in hand, ready to get an update on how the day's stories were progressing.

'You are absolutely outrageous and shameless. I'm not giving you anything yet. Not one word.'

'Do your children have mobiles?' she asked.

'I'm not telling,' was his answer to this.

So, still no word on the three-year-long, government-funded study into the long-term damage caused by mobile phones yet... But one day very soon. She was looking forward to that story. One night, after a very nice dinner and two bottles of decent wine, Ted had told her that he was expecting to break very bad news. Manufacturers might face radically altering the designs of their phones, having to put health, exposure and age restrictions on them and site all mobile phone masts well away from built-up areas.

Out of the corner of her eye, Jo saw something flick past. Then again. What was that?

She bent down, phone still against her ear. Flick. It was a wire poking out of her top drawer.

What the hell was that attached to?

'OK. Speak to you soon, Ted, take care.'

She put out her hand to catch hold of it when it moved again, and she realised it was a long, straight tail.

Her scream was tempered by the fact that she was on the phone and in the middle of a busy office.

She tried to strangle the last of it.

'What's the matter?' Ted asked. Jeff's face, as he stood on the other side of her desk, was the picture of concern. Aidan and Dominique had both turned to stare in her direction.

'Nothing, nothing,' Jo managed. 'It's a— it's a— thing— in my drawer. I have to go.'

'Are you sure? Are you really OK?' Ted asked.

'Yup, yup, fine. Speak soon,' she said, pointing frantically at the drawer, hoping Jeff would go and investigate, while she tried to move as quickly as she could round to the other side of her desk, stretching the receiver wire as tight as it would go.

'Bye.' She put the phone down.

'Jeff, there's a frigging rat in my drawer!' she burst out.

Jeff didn't waste any time, he pulled open the drawer and they both caught sight of the tail and the brownish-grey back legs of the rodent. Inside the drawer, a packet of nuts Jo had no recollection of bringing in, had been shredded to pieces.

'Jeez,' Jeff shut the drawer abruptly. 'It's a mouse,' he said in an effort at consolation.

'Don't lie, it's a freaking rat!' Jo realised her hands were shaking. A rat. A rat's tail and she'd tried to grab it. *Aargh*.

Dominique was on her feet, Aidan was coming over to see and so were a few more interested parties.

'It's a young one, though,' Jeff said, still looking at the drawer. He moved slowly round her desk, assessing the rat's chances of escape. 'Anyone got a big, padded envelope?' he asked.

'No, no way, you are not rat-catching in my desk.'

'Got any better suggestions?' he asked. 'Do you want to wait the month it'll take janitoring or pest control to make it up here?'

'No! Get the rat out! But I can't look. I really can't.' This was horrible.

Aidan, with a slightly incredulous look, handed Jeff a big brown envelope: 'I don't think it's going to just hop into this, is it?' he asked.

'No,' said Jeff, eyes fixed on the drawer. 'I'll have to stun it with something first.'

A little crowd had gathered round, while Jo tried to back away from her desk as far as possible. She really did not want to see an agitated rat scampering out of her drawer and across the floor. Jeff armed himself with the nearly full 1.5-litre bottle of Evian water on Jo's desk and carefully opened the top drawer. About fifteen people had gathered around the desk now. There was the hush of amused suspense.

'He's not here any more,' Jeff said in a low voice, slightly conscious that his authority over the newsroom was possibly at stake here. He slid the top drawer shut, opened the one beneath it then put his head down low to peer into the stacks of papers and files Jo had stashed in there.

'Nope. OK, third and final attempt.' He opened the last drawer with something of a flourish, paused for a split second, spied the rat and banged the water bottle down on it. A cheer erupted from the onlookers. Jeff put his hand into the drawer and pulled the animal out. He quickly stuffed it into the envelope Aidan was holding out for him.

'Is it dead?' Jo wanted to know, feeling both horrified and impressed with Jeff's hitherto unknown talent for rodent-catching. She knew he was always calm under pressure, but this was a whole new level of grace under fire.

'I don't think so,' Jeff replied.

'What are you going to do with it?'

'I'll go down to the back courtyard and let it go there. Either that or find it a new home in Spikey's office.'

'Why are there rats in our desks?'

'Because we leave food all over the place,' Jeff replied. 'Or maybe it's because the accountants on floor five have still not pulled the plug on the cleaning contractors even though they were investigated by our reporters and found to be not only useless, but employing illegal immigrants at half the minimum wage. Funny old world,' he added.

8

WEDNESDAY: 9.45 P.M.

Once her girls were in bed, Jo made herself a cup of tea and used her trusty, bashed-at-the-edges laptop to go online.

Yes, yes, yes... obviously she could be chucking some soup together to see her through the busy end of the week ahead, or making small inroads into the laundry landslide, or even unpacking some of the last removals boxes cunningly disguised with a tablecloth in her bedroom. But she was too tired, she couldn't face it. Whereas the lure of just a little preliminary research into Quintet, a teensy scout-about of the top ten hits from a Google search... well, she couldn't resist that.

She typed in 'Quintet', then the manufacturer's name 'Wolff-Meyer' and began her search.

Financial reports, NHS sites, doctor comments all came up, so she began a methodical trawl through everything that sounded interesting, in the hope of finding some clues.

When her home phone on the desk began to ring, she didn't take her eyes from the screen as she picked up: 'Jo Randall,' she said automatically.

'No, it's not your news desk, work slave. It's me.'

'Hey, you, I was just thinking about you.' Jo was pleased to hear Bella's voice on the other end of the line, 'I'm on the internet...'

'Aha,' Bella interrupted. 'Working or doing Mummy porn?'

'Mummy porn?'

'You know, on the Mini Boden website planning fantasy child outfits?'

'Oh, ha ha,' Jo replied. 'No, I'm working. I'm deep in Reuters finance trying to make sense of rows and rows of figures.'

'Looking into anything interesting?' Bella asked.

'Oh, you know me, just the little cottage industry that is global pharmaceuticals.'

'Hope you've got a good lawyer then,' Bella warned. 'They are very, very litigious. Who are you investigating?'

'Wolff-Meyer, the Quintet manufacturers.'

'Well, well...'

'Know much about them?'

'Might do.'

'Come on then, tell me something interesting,' Jo wheedled.

'Would you like to know how much money they made last year on vaccinations alone?'

'Yes.'

'A cool £900 million.'

Jo whistled.

'They have big money, big, big money. And they have big investors: banks, the major pensions companies, probably the government too. No one wants these guys to fail.'

'No one wants any vaccination scare stories to send share prices tumbling then?'

'No, definitely not.'

'Not even the government.'

'Especially not the government.'

'Oh, good, nothing I like better than a challenge.' Jo was scribbling notes. 'Medicine has been great business ever since the days of the witch doctor,' she added.

'I suppose so – Jo?' Bella ventured.

'Yes?'

'There's more marble in their London headquarters than in the Vatican.'

'And how would you happen to know that, Bella?'

'Well... there's something I didn't tell you the last time we spoke about Quintet.'

'Yes?'

'It will probably interest you just a little bit too much to know that I updated all the virus software in their London office four months ago and I now hold a regular maintenance contract with them.'

'No!' was Jo's response, her heart beat revving up as she felt an internal *'yeeees!'*. There had to be some way this amazing stroke of luck could be put to good use.

'So you're in cahoots with them. I might have guessed,' Jo teased.

'I hardly think a computer contract—' Bella began.

'I'm going to have to take you out for a series of stiff cocktails, my friend,' Jo said. 'And talk to you about Messrs Wolff and Meyer. See if three margaritas later, you can come up with something interesting for me that you didn't even *know you knew*.'

'I don't think so, Jo, just put me down as one of the company's techies. I'm sure there's not that much I can help you with.'

'We'll see. I'm deep in research. I will let you know if there are areas requiring further investigation.'

'The weather forecast for Sunday is great,' Bella informed her, 'which is why I'm phoning. I thought you and the girls – and maybe, you know, your *boyfriend...*' big tease at the word, 'could join us for a barbecue at the allotment?'

'The allotment,' Jo snorted, ducking the boyfriend dig. 'Who even are you?!'

Bella with an allotment. It still made her snigger. Bella had somehow imagined herself spending the weekends digging, weeding, growing lovely organic deli food and picnicking with her boys in the fresh air. Yeah, right, maybe if Bella had had a personality transplant that might have been possible.

Instead, her allotment was riddled with weeds, overgrown lawn and catastrophic under-production of fruit and vegetables. When the tuts and complaints from her allotment neighbours grew too strong, she'd *hired a gardener* for a slash and burn repair session. Bella had high-heeled wellies, a designer trug and cute little gardening implements from the Conran shop, but Jo had absolutely no recollection of ever having seen Bella on her hands and knees attempting one tiny little bit of work in said allotment.

Mainly Bella held noisy barbecues there and Jo suspected this was because she didn't want her immaculate home garden to get too messed up. Don pottered about the allotment a little, admittedly, with a hoe and a pair of clippers. But mainly he sat in his deckchair with a bedraggled fisherman's hat on his head and read the foot-high stack of newspapers at his side. Occasionally, his sons, Markie and Murdo, poked him so vigorously that he had to get up and join in a game of kickabout, badminton, swing ball, or whatever wild and vigorous activity they were pursuing that day.

'Allotment 12.30-ish?' Jo suggested. 'Me and my daughters only,' she made it clear. 'We'll bring potato salad and pudding as long as you get the posh burgers sorted out.'

'OK. Deal.'

'How's your week going anyway?' Jo asked.

'Same old, same old. People I'm working with have turned into total pains in the arse, so I'm stressed and in a bad mood all the time, Don's going away for a few days on some sort of ideas-creating, brainstorming jolly in Dublin. More like a brain-damaging session in Dublin. Even if they come up with any good ideas, they'll all get too pissed to remember them. Murdo has started to wet his bed again, which means I'm blaming myself for... well, everything... You know, life. All lovely.'

'Finished ranting now?'

'Yes, feel much better. You?'

'I'm fine.' Jo left it at the short answer.

'Oh, good. I'll look forward to hearing all about it on Sunday.'

'Or maybe speaking about it before then?'

'Yeah, well... we'll see.'

* * *

Not long after she'd hung up the phone, her mobile bleeped with a text.

Fancy a fck?

it asked. Followed by a smiley face.

Oh *please*.

Too busy but call me.

Jo typed back. Just seconds later the phone rang and his sexy voice was in her ear.

'Are you sure?' he was saying, 'I'm getting out early tonight, it's quiet.'

'I'm sorry,' Jo told him, 'I'm still working... Tell me about your day anyway.'

'Hot and sweaty, but delicious. That's all you need to know about my day and about me.'

'Mmmm.'

'And you?' he asked.

'Me? The usual, trying to save the free world from the evil clutches of – insert villain of the week into this space,' she joked.

'And why can't I come round?'

'I've got to do the washing, unpack things... it's Mel's birthday tomorrow, I have to wrap her presents and bake a cake...' She had a feeling she'd let something out of the bag now.

'Can you wrap a kitten?' he asked.

'Please shut up about the kitten. I haven't got her a kitten. I'm the worst parent in the world.'

'You are, but not because of the kitten,' he answered. 'You're the worst parent in the world if you don't let the professional chef you know come over and bake her birthday cake.'

'Oh.' Yeah, he was going to be hard to resist now.

'I'm very good at cakes,' he wheedled. 'I've probably spent more time baking than you've—'

'Spent shagging?' she answered for him. 'Although not counting the past few weeks.'

'Yes...' he lingered over the word, managing to load it with meaning.

'OK, OK,' her resistance was over. 'Come and bake the cake. Please.'

'OK, I will come over for some late-night baking, but I'm not promising anything else...'

'No?'

'No... right, you have to go and check your cupboards for the following ingredients—'

* * *

Marcus arrived not long after 10.30 and as soon as he was in the house, she was kissing him, licking his soft salty skin and telling him that they should go to bed immediately and never mind the cake.

But he'd come with a rucksack full of the things he needed and he wasn't going to be distracted.

'Will you just get off?' he insisted. 'Jo, leave me alone!' He took her hands off his shoulders, then out of his pockets. 'Baking,' he reminded her. 'Focus. Baking is a serious science,' he added, 'I hope you've got scales that work in your crap kitchen.'

'Crap kitchen?' She felt mildly insulted by this, even though the cramped dark-pine, grey-granite arrangement fitted at expense by the previous owner didn't really appeal to her much either.

He washed his hands at the kitchen sink, while she watched with her arms tight around his waist and her head hooked over his shoulder. She let him lead her round the room like this as he went into cupboards and the fridge to round up the ingredients he hadn't brought with him. 'So, we're doing sponge,' he said. 'Let me see the size of your baking tins.'

'Why does that sound so rude?' she said and kissed his neck.

'Because you're a filthy old lady.'

'Am not!'

'Are so!'

She showed him her tin collection and he almost seemed impressed. But then cake baking was a favourite rainy Sunday activity she liked to practise with her daughters. 'But it's to be a dress, you know, sponge layers stacked up,' she explained, 'so Barbie can be plunged in all the way up to her monstrous chest.'

'Got you, got you.' He was looking at the tins, tucking his hair behind his ears, frowning a little, working out how much cake batter would be needed, and she couldn't resist curling into him again and licking his neck. 'Get off!' he told her again. 'We aren't going to get anywhere like this.'

'Couldn't you bake naked?' she asked him. 'No, naked apart from an apron, maybe? I have this butcher's one. Very macho.'

'You are a filthy old woman,' he repeated, but then got hold of the hem of his T-shirt and pulled the top off over his head and threw it onto a kitchen chair. 'How about topless baking, will that keep you happy? Obviously if a health inspector turns up at the door, I'm in big trouble.'

He picked up a bag of flour and began to shake it carefully into the scales.

Much as Jo wanted to run her hands all over his bare skin and pull him down to the floor on top of her, she restrained herself. 'I'm going to sit down over here and just watch you, OK?' she told him. 'The topless chef.'

'OK.' Without taking his eyes from the scales he added: 'Obviously, if you want to touch yourself, I'm fine with that.'

She bunched his T-shirt up into a ball and threw it at him.

'What do you like about me so much anyway?' he asked, heaping sugar on top of the flour.

'You mean apart from your fabulous body and what you do with it?' Jo smiled.

'I know it's hard to look beyond that,' Marcus joked back, clearly flattered.

Jo put her elbow up on the kitchen table, leaned her head on her hand and considered her reply.

'You're like a début album by a band I've never heard of,' she said finally. 'That's what I like about you.'

'Huh?'

'Well, Simon was a greatest hits compilation I'd heard thousands of times before... and you are not. That's what I like so much about you.'

'I see,' Marcus said.

'I never cheated on Simon,' she felt the need to add. 'Last year, I thought about cheating on him *a lot*. In fact, I thought about it constantly,' she confessed. 'The postman, the Frenchman behind the counter at the deli always going on about his amazing saucisson, just about everyone in my office, including the Fashion girls, Mel's very handsome teacher, you name them, I had a bedroom fantasy about them,' she laughed at her confession. 'Simon and I were so fed up and so pissed off with each other, one of us was bound to go off and have an affair,' she added. 'I thought it would be more grown-up to split before that happened, rather than after.'

'And his new bird?' Marcus asked.

Jo shook her head. 'I don't think that happened before we split. She was his shoulder to cry on and things developed from there. I've no reason not to believe him... and anyway if they were seeing each other before, do I need to know that? Probably not.'

Marcus broke eggs. She liked the way he did it: with a deft flourish, a twirl of forefinger and thumb before tossing the shells into the sink.

'I'm much more interested in you, Marcus,' she said. 'Why are you here? In a crap kitchen, baking a cake for a little girl you haven't even met?'

'I dunno,' he answered. 'Maybe you're like the first new release in a decade by one of those great bands from the Eighties.'

'Oh *God*!' she burst into laughter, 'I was a child in the Eighties. A mere child!'

Marcus cubed butter with a small knife and slid the pieces into the mix.

'I hardly know anything about you,' she went on. 'Have you got brothers or sisters? I don't even know that and I'm *sleeping* with you.'

He turned to give her a little grin. 'Début album, remember, band you've never heard of...' but then he answered, 'I've got a younger brother.'

'Me too,' she said.

'Yours first,' Marcus said, turning on the mixer.

'He's called Matt,' she said over the whirring, 'he's thirty-one, he works in the oil business, married, one son, currently living in the States.'

'But do you like him? Is he a nice guy?' Marcus asked.

Jo sighed. It was a tricky question, tricky subject: 'Not much, I suppose. I liked him when he was small, but he got more and more annoying with each passing year.'

Marcus switched the blender off and checked the mix: 'My brother's cool,' he threw in. 'He's a chef too. Works in a luxury resort in Africa.'

'Nice one,' she said.

'I'm thinking about going out there for the summer,' he said, and licked the back of the teaspoon he had dipped into the mix to assess it.

'Sounds good,' she said.

'He says it's busy, but good pay and you can drink under the stars every night, swim in the lake every morning. We'll maybe do a bit of travelling together once the season's over.'

'When does the season start?' she couldn't help asking. It was mid-May now.

'Middle of June,' was Marcus's reply.

Middle of June. She smiled at him. So, the Marcus question – the Marcus situation – looked as if it was going to resolve itself. Nicely, casually, just as easily as it had begun. Except... she didn't think that it would be just nothing to wave him goodbye. Yesterday, she'd thought this was just casual, a fling, as easy to end as it had been to begin. But today, she knew that if he went away, it would hurt. 'Why don't you come?' he offered, pouring cake mix from the bowl into the tins.

But this just made her laugh.

'Me? Ha. No,' she ran a hand through her hair, 'Nice of you to ask, but, you may not have noticed' – she waved her hand about – 'I have children, this big job thing... career, I think it's called, my house, my mortgage, my divorce to sort out. So, no, I can't just pack my beach bag and—'

'Fuck it,' Marcus said. He was shaking each cake tin in turn, gently, settling the mixture to an even level: 'Once the summer holidays start, just come over, you and the girls, swim, get tanned, live in my beach hut with me.'

'Aha.' For one long, lovely moment, as he pushed the cake tins into the oven, she allowed herself to think about it: *Mel and Nettie on the beach all summer long, Marcus, wood-brown and naked, rolling over in bed towards her, hair curly and tangled, bleached in the sun.* And then: *cut.*

'No,' she smiled, 'I don't think we can come... But you probably have to go.'

'Why?' He crouched down beside her and slid a hand up her leg.

'Because you can,' she replied, hands on his shoulders squeezing the muscle there. 'Because you're twenty-six and footloose and have all these adventures ahead of you. God, when I was twenty-six, I was so boring. I'm boring myself just thinking about it. I wish I'd done so many more crazy things.'

'Not so boring now,' he said, brushing his lips against hers, undoing buttons so he could touch her bare skin, 'I've set the timer for forty-five minutes. Although I'll skewer after thirty-five. What can we do in thirty-five minutes?'

His fingers were already inside her bra. He was kissing her stomach and moving downwards.

'Make icing?' she replied.

'Oh, yeah. I want to make icing with you.'

Could she go? She wondered. *For a summer holiday? To Africa... just to see what might come next?*

9

THURSDAY: 10.25 A.M.

'I've got IVF twins who are Quintet victims, according to their parents, and I'm aiming to find other children who have suffered to make the story stronger,' Jo told the morning news conference, treading the fine line between trying to make it sound as good as she could without exaggerating. Because this story meant a lot to her. She wanted it in the paper, but she didn't want to oversell it and potentially blow it.

'OK, let's see what you come up with,' was Spikey's verdict.

'The wind farms story is going well,' she updated them on Aidan and Dominique's research. 'We all seem to be coming down on the side of building them in the North Sea. Although that's the most expensive option.'

'Hmm... Can Pictures mock that up for us? Massive windmills in stormy seas?'

'The picture desk editor nodded.

'Nice,' was Spikey's verdict.

Jo registered the predictable little prick of jealousy that he seemed to like the other story better than hers – the one she was far more invested in.

'What else is on your list then?' he asked.

'Britain's asthma league table and how it relates to the air pollution stats – quite nicely, in fact. We're shelving *How Green are the Royals* for now, as agreed... the latest research into the causes of senile dementia... a few other bits and pieces, eco-tourism, and that's us for the week so far.' Jo smiled around the table.

'Nothing splashy then,' Spikey concluded. 'And no Savannah Tyler. Which is a bit disappointing.' She caught the glance shot in her direction and felt stung.

'The whooping cough vaccination story is really important, I think,' she heard herself reply, feeling her stomach churn and cheeks flush as she stood up to him. Aaaargh, she hated to do it, but it had to be done, or else she'd let him ride right over her, making her feel as if all the years spent working to get this job weren't worthwhile.

'The disease is proliferating,' she added, trying to sound incredibly authoritative. 'Another seven cases have been reported this morning. And all those children have already been vaccinated, so something strange is going on.'

'But we're not really getting to the bottom of that, are we?' Spikey was clearly in the mood for a fight today.

He slid a weighty silver pen through his fingertips and rapped its end on the table a couple of times.

'What's the government saying? What about the manufacturers? Can no one shed any light on what has started all this?'

Jo, noticing that Vince was taking a deep breath and about to wade in, answered quickly: 'We're looking into all these aspects. We're asking the right questions. Obviously, when we write about vaccination side effects, we're writing about something the Chief Medical Officer doesn't want made public. We're not going to get a lot of support from the authorities or the drug companies on that.'

'Time for a couple of bodies from News to be helping, Jo, I think,' came Vince's suggestion.

'Thanks for the offer, we'll certainly come to you, if we need you,' she said, as sweetly as she could, while thinking completely poisonous, how-Vince-must-die thoughts.

'Well, it's not the splash,' the editor said in a way that signalled this was his final word on the subject. 'Page three at best, probably five,' he wrote in his notebook.

'And Savannah?' he added. 'Didn't we say she'll be doorstepped if there still isn't any word of her doing an interview?'

Jo could feel her heart sinking further.

'I'm very close with this,' she said, much more confidently than she felt. 'If we barge in now that will be the end of it. She won't talk, they won't deal with us. Just give me a bit longer. I'm optimistic and it will be worth the wait. And if we don't get her on her own, we can interview her with another Green candidate. Sort of a 'Green Dream Team' angle.'

Spikey let out a theatrically deep sigh.

'You know no one wants to read that,' he said.

Brutal, but fair, she couldn't help thinking.

'We want the scoop on Savannah,' he added. 'OK, you've got the rest of this week. But the by-election's on Thursday next week, so this Saturday morning, News will doorstep her if you want to stay out of it,' was his verdict.

'Right. Leave it to me,' was the coolest reply she could manage. She saw the smug expression on Vince's face but then caught an encouraging smile Jeff fired in her direction and felt a little bit soothed.

Now it was Jason Caruth from Politics. Jo could barely stand him either. He always whipped every little story up and tried to make it sound like the scoop of the year. But his stories had a horrible habit of sinking like soufflés after a few checks on a Saturday afternoon, leaving everyone frantically searching about for things to put in the paper in their place.

'Hold the front page,' Jason opened with a smile. Jo hoped he was being funny: 'Love across the party lines.' He paused for effect, but the response was muted as nobody expected it to be true.

'One Labour MP's son is dating the daughter of a Tory lord,' Jason explained.

There were chuckles at this. It was cute.

'Nice,' Spikey said and wrote a note on his list. 'Nice headline, but not a splash. So, it's Thursday morning and we await the front page. You know I don't like that. What's Showbiz got for us?'

Or, as Jo rephrased the question in her head: 'Which celebrity Hollywood millionaire is *opening their heart* about the trauma of their recent *illness* – really just the time they spent in hospital recovering from cosmetic surgery – to plug their latest film?'

'Victoria Beckham,' the Showbiz deputy editor replied and everyone round the table groaned.

The Showbiz deputy, Elaine, a stick-thin, long-haired young lovely, drafted in from *Elle* magazine and doing her first conference because her boss was away for the day, looked mortally offended. But it probably hadn't been like this on *Elle*. No, here she was dealing with the testosterone-fuelled shark tank of the newsroom.

Spikey wasn't in the mood to discuss the showbiz agenda in depth so he merely nodded, scribbled on his pad and wound up the meeting with the words: 'Go away everyone and get me a splash by the close of play, will you? Keep me off the pills,' which may have been his idea of a flippant joke, but it prompted a slight mass panic as the conference attendees struggled to avoid each other's eyes and choked back snorts of frantic laughter.

Jo got back to her desk to find a Post-It from Dominique stuck to her computer screen.

Phone Mick Townell

it ordered.

The father of the twins. She would phone him just as soon as she could. Right now, there was an entire list of calls to be made.

Vaccine manufacturers, for a start. Then the Canadian Department of Health – no, time difference, couldn't do that till the afternoon. Green Tony. He had to get her something!

She scanned her email to see what was new. Press releases, press releases, nothing looked interesting. But then at the bottom of the list:

noreply@yahoousergroups.com

That strange anonymous address again. She opened the message. This time it was a fragment of newspaper cutting that had been scanned in. She enlarged the screen so she could read the print.

Doctor who offered single injections hounded by smear attempt

was the headline. There followed a news story she remembered vaguely about a GP who allowed patients to pay for single vaccinations until he was called up before the General Medical Council on misconduct charges. This cutting was from the end of the two-day hearing when the doctor had been exonerated, cleared of all charges.

'I vowed I would clear my name and I have,'

Dr Paul Taylor had told reporters afterwards.

'The medical establishment wanted rid of me by fair means or foul. They threw the book at me, but they've failed.'

The piece went on with background information to the case, also more about the doctor, where he lived, where he practised, how he became interested in single vaccinations.

Underneath the newspaper cutting was the simple typed line:

You should speak to him.

Plus a telephone number for his surgery.

Jo made another attempt to reply to the email but her message was sent straight back to her.

Anonymous tips – always a very suspect thing to act on. This could all be a red herring... a set-up.

She did a quick search of news stories about Dr Paul Taylor.

After a quick scan, she dialled Dr Taylor's number.

But Dominique was waving at her. 'Mick Townell, line three, says he really needs to talk to you,' she explained. 'Urgent.'

'OK.' Jo didn't like the sound of this. She hung up the call she was making and picked up the other line.

'Mick, hello it's Jo Randall, sorry I didn't get back to you earlier. I was in a meeting. How's it going?'

'Er, fine... we're all fine...' Then there was a loaded pause that made her feel uneasy before he added: 'You've never come back to me to say how much you'd pay us for this story.'

Oh, right. It was going to be one of those conversations, where she tried to talk the interviewee out of the ludicrous amount of money they'd thought they could earn from her newspaper.

'Mick...' She decided not to bother with the publicising your case/donation to the charity of your choice line again. Instead, she told him: 'We can give you £500 for your time. How does that sound?'

'To be honest,' he began, 'it's a bit low. The *Daily Mail* have phoned us—'

Oh, crappola was the only coherent thought forming in Jo's mind. This story was about it be taken away from her by a rival. And that was not what she wanted. 'And they've said £3,000 at least. Maybe more for a full interview and photographs.'

'OK. Well, I can tell you that they've been known to exaggerate. What you're offered before and what you get afterwards can be two different things. But anyway, have you agreed to do the story with them?'

'Well... not exactly.'

This didn't sound like the truth.

'I said I'd speak to you first.'

But Jo knew that someone from the *Daily Mail* news team would already be in their car gunning it down to the Townells' home.

'Mick?' she asked, 'Have you got email access at home?'

When he said he did, she told him: 'I'm going to go and speak to my news editor right now. Then I'll send you a contract through. We'll pay you £5,000 if we use your story on the front page.' She was on safe ground here: judging by Spikey's reaction, there was no chance of that happening: '£2,500 if it's used anywhere else in the paper. But you have to sign up and speak to us only. How does that sound?'

'That sounds fine.' There was relief in his voice. He obviously hadn't enjoyed this conversation much, which was a good thing because it meant he might stay away from the *Mail* when they arrived at his front door.

'Phone me as soon as the email comes through,' Jo instructed him. 'I'll speak to you in a few minutes,' she said in a friendly tone. But at the end of the call, she slammed the phone down hard.

'Shit,' she announced loudly. 'We've got a major problem. Aidan, I need you to go to Canterbury. Very sorry. But I need you to go right now, do not pass Go, do not collect £200. Here's the address.' She handed Aidan – already on his feet scrambling things into his briefcase – a Post-It note. 'Don't even stop to blow your nose. I'll brief you *en route*, but in a nutshell, you're keeping the vaccine-damage family I've interviewed away from the *Mail*.'

Aidan had the decency to nod and not look too ticked off. She knew she was taking advantage; if she'd asked Dominique to do this job, she'd probably have been dealing with a temper tantrum. Dominique liked to work on her own thing, did not like to do anything which could be interpreted as an errand for Jo.

'Thanks very much,' Jo added, 'I really appreciate it. Really sorry to land you with the babysitting job.'

Now she had to tackle Jeff and get money out of him.

She walked over to the news desk and stood by the side of Jeff's chair, waiting for him to finish a phone call. Jeff, her mid-40s, completely dependable news editor, always in a somehow fresh-pressed shirt giving off a whiff of limes, even though he was in that chair round about ten hours a day. Though he did frequent the office gym. Allegedly. 'Otherwise, I'm a heart attack waiting to happen,' he'd tell her.

'Good, good. That sounds very good,' he was telling the person on the other end. 'The editor will love that.'

She hoped this meant she'd caught him at the right moment.

'Jo?' He put the receiver down and swivelled his chair to face her, although she could see the flashing lights of two other calls holding on his line.

'Got any money?' she asked him.

'For a coffee?' he replied.

'No. For an exclusive.'

'Uh oh. I don't like the sound of this.'

'The Townells want £2,500 for their story. I can only stump up £500 and that's if I put off the freelancer who was going to file on eco-tourism for us.'

'Two and a half grand?' Jeff wanted to check, 'for the whooping cough vaccine twin?' He rubbed the palms of his hands over his face. 'Or else...?' he asked.

'They go to the *Mail*. And they've already spoken to the *Mail*, so Aidan's on his way down there to guard the door.'

'Oh, damn,' he exclaimed, 'I thought we were going to get this one, at least, for free.'

'Me too,' she added.

'Two thousand five hundred quid... won't take any less?'

She shook her head: 'Don't think so.'

Jeff's pen was being squeezed mercilessly between his chunky fingers.

'OK, OK, well, we can juggle some things about. Defer a few payments... and sort this out somehow. You say OK.'

'Thanks,' she fired him a smile.

'I better get some decent stuff to go with it. Make it worth a page three with a sidebar on the front, huh?'

'Yes, please, Jo.'

✳ ✳ ✳

Mick phoned back once he'd received the contract by email and made something of an embarrassed apology.

'This is fine,' he told Jo. 'I've phoned the *Daily Mail* to say forget it, but they say someone's already on the way down.'

'You can't even speak to this person,' she warned him, 'or you're in breach of our contract. OK? My deputy, Aidan' – that would annoy Dominique – 'is on his way to help you. The *Mail* will be very persistent. But just keep away from them, please.'

There was a pause while Mick registered what he'd done – made himself the subject of a little Fleet Street dogfight.

'Aidan Brodie is my reporter, he'll phone you before he rings at your door, so you'll know it's him. If I were you, I would get out of the house for the day, because the other reporter will be very persistent. I'm sure you'll be promised all sorts of things. But to be honest, Mick, £2,500 is a lot for the story.'

And that wasn't a lie. Although vast sums were occasionally paid out by papers for big celeb stories or news of international profile and saleability, ordinary people rarely made four figures. Especially at her paper, which was always operating on freshly squeezed budgets. The *Mail* had more money and, in her heart of hearts, Jo had already resigned herself to the fact that this story might be snatched from under her nose. And it was an important story – a clear cut example surely of the government and the vaccine companies knowing about the possibility of harm and not acting. Important to the world at large and important to her. Damn, damn, damn.

She might have to go to Canterbury, too, she decided. But first, she would phone the doctor, as her anonymous friend had recommended. Ringing the surgery number got her through surprisingly easily to Dr Paul Taylor directly.

Jo explained who she was, said she was planning a story on the new Quintet injection and would he like to talk to her.

'Jo Randall,' he said pleasantly, recognising her name, 'I've read lots of stories by you.' And then he hung up, which was the kind of thing you got used to in her line of work. But still, it came as something of a surprise.

She gave a long sigh and began to punch his surgery number back into the phone. But a call flashed up on line two, so she decided to take that instead.

'Jo Randall.'

'Hello, hello there, Ms Randall... sorry about that. It's Dr Paul Taylor here, I'm calling you back on the mobile. It's just... well... easier this way.'

'Oh. OK. Hello.'

'Quintet,' he said quickly. 'You're doing something on Quintet, are you? About time too. I don't know much about this injection. But it comes with risks, especially to certain groups of children.'

'Have you got any evidence... anything in the way of facts?' she asked.

'Would you like to meet up? That would be best, then I can tell you more.'

'Yes, good idea—' but before she could get out the wheres and whens, the doctor added: 'I take a break between twelve and one today. I know you journalists are always in a hurry. So, I'll meet you at ten past twelve on Primrose Hill, the first bench you come to if you take the Fitzroy Road entrance. Does that sound OK?'

'Ermm, well... yes. Unless you'd prefer a café round there or something a bit more comfortable?' She knew she would.

'No, no, the park is fine. You'd better take my mobile number, just in case you need to change the plan.' He gave her his number, then hung up again without any further warning.

'Oh for goodness' sake!' Jo said out loud, irritated. She suspected he was totally cranky and she didn't have time for this. She dialled Green Tony's number. He picked up on the first ring for a change.

'Green Party HQ.'

'Tony, it's Jo Randall, your most persistent caller. Your telephone stalker, your serial dialler.' She tried to sound friendly, although by now she was irritated with him too.

'Ah, Jo.'

'Don't "ah, Jo" me. This better not be another one of your long-winded excuses.'

'Savannah just isn't ready for this yet,' he said. To her ears, this sounded pompous.

'Well, she better bloody well get ready, cos the news team are going to be staking her out all day, every day starting Saturday, unless I get this interview.'

'Oh, rubbish,' was Tony's response.

'They are. The editor has spoken. He's desperate – in love with her or something – she has to talk, one way or another.'

'How very sinister,' Tony said. 'Well, they'll be wasting their time. Jo, please don't do this to her or you're going to be way out of favour. You'll go into the Siberia section of my contacts book.'

'And just where do you think you are in mine?' she shot back. 'You're in the freaking Arctic, about to go into bloody global-warming meltdown.'

At least he laughed at that.

'She's thinking about it,' he said, wanting this conversation to be over.

'She is never off the telly, Tone,' Jo commented. 'Why won't she do a newspaper chat?'

'She's nervous. It's so much more personal. More open to interpretation by the journalist. She finds TV quite easy. She can say what she wants, the way she wants to say it. Newspapers give her the jitters. Her campaign has been flawless,' he gushed. 'She couldn't have done better if she'd been running for the White House. She doesn't want to muck it up now.'

'This isn't about mucking it up. This is the icing on the campaign cake. This is *me*.' Jo didn't like the pleading tone in her voice now. 'I'm a huge fan of hers.'

'I know. Just leave it with me a bit longer. Please.'

'Why don't you let me ask her?' Jo tried. 'I can tell her what I'd like to talk about, reassure her.'

'Very persuasive, Jo, but I don't think so.'

'Just ask. Please.' *Jesus.* This was getting tiresome. The wannabe politician, for God's sake, making like a Hollywood diva. It was almost strange. For a moment, it fleetingly crossed Jo's mind to wonder what Savannah was so anxious not to reveal.

Once she and Tony had said their goodbyes, she hung up and looked at the latest text on her mobile:

Need to talk, see you at bday party. Simon.

A lovely family birthday party at Simon's flat with her parents and Gwen in attendance. That would cap her day just perfectly.

'I have to go out,' she told Dominique and began packing her handbag.

* * *

Half an hour later Jo was sitting on the designated park bench in the sunshine watching the good mummies of north London pushing their organic babies about in designer buggies.

She was just finishing off the sandwich she'd bought round the corner and thinking how nice this was – *Woman escapes from office to enjoy sun and sandwich* – when she felt a tap on her shoulder.

'Can I ask your name?' said the short man behind her. He was wearing a raincoat with the collar up, a hat and dark glasses.

'Can I ask yours?' was her frosty reply. 'I'm meeting someone on this bench at ten past twelve,' the man said.

'So am I. Look, it's bound to be me you're meeting, I'm Jo Randall,' she said.

'I'm Dr Taylor.' He held his hand out to her and they shook.

'Bit warm for a raincoat and hat, isn't it?' she couldn't help asking.

'Er, yes... probably. But I have to be careful.'

When her eyebrows shot up, he added: 'Maybe if you'd been hauled before the General Medical Council on entirely trumped-up charges, which proved that your confidential files had been closely examined, and maybe if you'd had notification from Scotland Yard that your surgery phone was being tapped, you might see it slightly differently.'

'Well, yes,' she agreed, 'I probably would.'

Dr Taylor sat down at the other end of the bench. Perhaps in response to her comments, he took his hat off, revealing sparse hair the same sandy colour as his beard, and undid the belt of his trench coat. Underneath the coat, his thin frame was clothed in a dapper suit, shirt and tie.

'Do you think you're being followed?' she asked him.

'No. But I was worried that you were.'

'Being followed?!' she asked, incredulous. 'I don't think Wolff-Meyer is tailing every reporter in London, are they?'

'You're not just any old reporter. If anyone's going to investigate Quintet properly, it's going to be you, isn't it? Because you do your health investigations very thoroughly. You have respect, even in the medical community.'

'Well...' She felt a slight flush at the compliment. 'Here's hoping.'

'You have to realise,' Dr Taylor went on, 'if you're going to take on a corporation like Wolff-Meyer, they will be *very* interested in you. Very interested.'

She couldn't help smiling at this. 'They know where the office is, they can come and find me any time they like,' she said and tried to make light of it. But really, it gave her a shiver of nervousness. You couldn't blunder into stories like this, you did have to be careful. Jo reached into her handbag for her smallest notebook and a pen, then set her tape recorder out between them. To reassure him, she placed another notebook on top to disguise it.

'That's not going to bother you, is it?' she asked. 'I record all my interviews.'

'No, no, fire away.'

'Have you always been a private doctor, or did you originally work in the NHS?' she began as a warm-up.

'I was NHS for years,' Dr Taylor told her. 'Here in London and also in my hometown. I must have done almost twenty years in the NHS. I'm committed to the idea of an NHS even though it's like working in Communist Russia. I only began to go private when the NHS decided they weren't going to allow single vaccinations any more. Even though single injections were and are, as far as I can see, safer and much more widely trialled and trusted than combinations.'

'Do you think combination injections cause problems?'

'I don't think, I know,' he said. 'The possible side effects come listed on the side of the box.'

'So, Quintet?' she asked. 'I take it you'll be anti-Quintet just because it's a combination vaccine?'

He gave a small laugh and began to brush at something on his trouser leg: 'There are a lot more reasons to be anti-Quintet than that. This is the injection that will give all the other combinations a bad name.'

'How so?' she encouraged him.

'Well, Quintet: how long have we had it in Britain now?'

'Three and a half months,' she prompted him. 'But it's been in use in Canada for several years.'

'Oh yes, Canada,' he said, smiling. 'We all think Canada must be a very safe and progressive place to test out a new vaccine. But I can give you some contacts over there who'll fill you in about vaccine data procedures over there.'

Dr Taylor suddenly seemed to take an intense interest in a woman about three hundred metres away.

'Has she got a camera?' he asked.

'Who? The woman in the red top?'

He nodded. His hand was reaching for his hat.

'Calm down, will you?' Jo tried to soothe him. 'She's probably taking pictures of her dog. Look, over there, it's one of those beige poodles. Do you think industrial spies come with poodles?'

The doctor put his hat on anyway.

'It may interest you to know, Ms Randall, that there have been two changes to Quintet since it was licensed, but no authority made Wolff-Meyer apply for a fresh licence. One of the injection's preservatives has been changed from a mercury-based ingredient to an antifreeze-based ingredient. The whooping cough element has also been altered. What you need to know is that this alteration has been blamed for a spate of whooping cough outbreaks.'

Jo was scribbling and underlining at speed. If this was true, it was all much better info than she'd expected. He went on to tell her of a Canadian parent-run website where she would be able to make contact with families who believed their children had been damaged by Quintet.

Just as she was noting down these details, she heard the tiny click that meant the first side of her tape had come to an end. She stopped him for a moment, popped the tape up and turned it over.

'Quite an old-fashioned way to store information these days, isn't it?' Dr Taylor asked.

'Kind of reliable though,' Jo replied. 'Digital recorders scare me. I think I'd find it hard to track down small conversations in the middle of huge digital megabytes.'

'And where do you keep your tapes?' the doctor asked.

This wasn't a question she was keen to answer.

'At work,' she replied, although this was only partly true. Many important tapes were also stored in a jumbled disarray in a suitcase on top of her wardrobe at home.

'I shouldn't need to tell you that if you're going to investigate vaccinations, make copies, store them in different places and take care. If you poke about in the right corners and start asking the right questions, they will come looking for you. Just think about what happened to me,' he warned, making eye contact again, so she wasn't in any doubt about how seriously he meant this.

'But you got off, you're still practising,' she reminded him.

'Yes, but my peace of mind, not to mention my faith in human nature, has been rather dented.'

He took another long look at the woman in the red top and scanned the open green parkland in front of them: 'Why is Quintet so particularly interesting this week?' he asked. 'Because of the whooping cough outbreak?'

'Yes. But we've also had a family approach us who say it has caused one of their twins to have a stroke.'

The doctor nodded, 'Yes... that wouldn't surprise me. Some children will be much more susceptible than others.'

'But a case of measles or whooping cough can be very nasty too,' she reminded him.

'In medicine we are often stuck between two evils: the illness and what it can do to you, or the medicine and what it can do to you. But we certainly don't want to be creating new evils,' Dr Taylor said.

'Hmm...' as Jo paused to consider this, her mobile began to buzz at her from inside her handbag. 'I'm so sorry, but I just need to check who that's from.'

Jo pressed the message button and the text slipped across her screen:

Phone ASAP Mail here, Aidan

'I'm so sorry, slight crisis at work, I'm going to have to call this person back.'

'No problem, I'll go for a little stroll, shall I?' the doctor asked.

'Thanks,' she replied, dialling Aidan's number, wondering if the worst had already happened: Aidan outside on the pavement, the *Mail* cosied up inside with the Townells, stealing her nice little exclusive from right under his nose.

'Aidan, Jo. What's happening?' she asked as soon as he picked up.

'I'm really sorry—' Uh oh. She could hear the anxiety in his voice. 'The reporters from the *Mail* are outside and Mick wants to let them in to hear what they have to say.'

'No, no, no,' she warned him. 'That can't happen. Is Mick around? Why don't I talk to him?'

After just a few moments of talking to Mick, Jo realised she wouldn't be able to manage this situation from London, she would have to go and join Aidan at the Townells' home. Mick only wanted to talk about money: he was desperate to pit one paper against another and drive the price of the story up. This was going to be very messy, if she was going to hang onto the story now, she'd have to negotiate a higher payment, maybe in instalments, appeal to Spikey for more cash...

Once she'd hung up, Dr Taylor made his way back to the bench and sat down with the words: 'There's something else you should be asking me about.'

'Oh.' She was surprised. 'And what's that?'

'Do you have a good understanding of the way vaccinations are made?'

'Um, not really. I'm sure you know much more,' Jo replied.

'I didn't know much about it either,' the doctor admitted, 'but I've since found out that laboratories grow varieties of a disease: mutations, even genetic modifications. There's a lot of playing about with viruses and microbes going on. I don't need to tell you that there is scope for harm to be done.'

'Right.' She wasn't sure where this was going. What could she find out about it anyway? How microbes were manipulated... sounded like the kind of thing that required a chemistry degree to even begin to understand.

'I went to a talk in Oxford recently,' Dr Taylor went on. 'Various doctors and experts who came from both sides of the vaccination fence. It was a lively evening. And that's when the manipulating and mutating of diseases came up. One of the speakers warned that in trying to fight old diseases, we might accidentally create new ones.'

'Do you have a note of who was talking there that evening?' Jo asked, hoping that a whole new trail might be opening up before her.

'When I get back to the surgery, I'll have a look through my papers and find that information for you.'

'Thanks for your help... and for putting your trust in me.'

'Strictly anonymous, of course,' he added. 'And please, be careful.'

* * *

By the time Jo arrived at the Townells' home in Canterbury, the crisis point was close.

As she pulled her car up in the road, she saw two cars parked ahead of her and Mick Townell at his garden gate, talking to a couple of reporters she recognised, while Aidan looked on helplessly from further up the garden path.

Jo got out of the car as quickly as she could and headed for the house. 'Hello, Mick, sorry about all this!' she called out to him, with a big, and she hoped reassuring, smile on her face.

She gave a little smile and a curt nod to the rival reporters. One of them was health editor, Meryl Payne – Jo already had experience of this woman's persistence. Damn, damn, this would be a fight.

She opened the garden gate and didn't allow Mick to think about whether or not he was going to let her in: 'Let's talk about this in private, inside, please,' she said firmly and carried on towards the front door.

'There's no need to let her back in, Mr Townell,' Meryl said immediately. 'We're more than happy to sign you up straight away. I can make the payment immediately.'

Jeeeeez.

'Mick, please, can I just talk to you for five minutes in private?' Jo urged him.

He followed her up the path, and with relief she saw that Meryl and her colleague were staying put at the gate – for the moment.

Mick showed her and Aidan into the sitting room. It wasn't looking so tidy today. Samantha was there with the twins, who had emptied every single toy box and scattered Lego, bricks and other small plastic objects right across the floor.

'Hello,' Samantha greeted her. 'I'm really sorry about this,' she added, looking properly sorry as well. Jo guessed that if it had been up to Samantha, the *Mail* would never have been involved.

'OK, well, here I am, let's not beat about the bush.' Jo tried to keep smiling and sounding friendly. 'What would convince you to do the story with us and not the *Mail*?'

'A proper amount of money,' was Mick's immediate reply.

'Right. Well, have you got a figure in mind?' She dared to take a seat on the sofa beside Samantha in the hope that this would get Mick and Aidan to sit down as well and make them all feel a bit calmer.

'The girl out there is talking about five figures,' Mick said.

Ouch, ouch. Yes, there was no denying newspapers did pay for big stories and this was a good story, but... but... she doubted very much that it was worth that much to Jeff or Spikey.

On the phone, on the way down, she had been carefully briefed by Jeff as to exactly how high she could go. And how low they were hoping her to stay.

'We're very committed to this story,' she began. 'We've done the interviews, the photos, you won't have to do anything else. I've been interviewing doctors, I'm planning a big report on this. I'm going to do a proper job and take it very seriously. I hope you'll agree it's not just about the money.'

Samantha was nodding at her, holding Ben on her lap.

Mick puffed air into his cheeks and let it out slowly.

'I am not going to be undersold here,' he said finally. 'We need the money... for the boys,' he tacked on.

'We can pay you £5,000.' Jo decided to name a figure which wasn't quite at her limit, giving herself a little to play with.

She looked over at Aidan; the expression of surprise on his face that had been there since she'd arrived widened. 'That's not enough,' was Mick's reply. 'They've already told me at least £10,000.'

'You won't get that, Mick. They will promise one thing and deliver quite another.'

'Same with you,' he said.

'I have a new contract in my bag.' Jo took the file out. 'We can sign it here and now.'

There was a loud rapping on the front door.

Before Mick was even up from his seat, Jo was at the door, which she held open for just the time it took to say, 'Could you please let us finish?' to Meryl and her colleague.

There was an uneasy silence in the sitting room when she got back.

'I think Samantha and I need to talk about this,' Mick said. 'Could you wait in the hall?'

This wasn't good, wasn't good at all. But she backed out of the room and once Aidan was out as well, she shut the door on the Townells.

'We'll give them a couple of minutes,' Jo told him. 'Are you OK?'

'Bit rattled,' he admitted. She smiled at him: 'At times like this, you can see why journalism and heavy drinking tend to go hand in hand. I really want this story, but the *Mail* probably has more money. And we all know money talks,' she whispered.

He nodded at her and let out a nervous sigh.

They heard the letterbox lifting and a folded piece of white A4 paper slid onto the doormat.

'I think we better take a look at that,' Jo said, crouching down to pick the page up.

She gave a whistle at the contents: '£10,000 is on the table from the *Mail*, and my top limit is £7,000.'

'Oh dear,' Aidan said.

'Let's just fold this up for now.' She took the paper, folded it in half and put it back onto the floor.

'This story appears to be very clear cut – so rare in medical stories,' she added, more loudly now, hoping Mick and Samantha could hear as well as Aidan. 'The vaccine company knew, the government knew children like Ben are at risk. And they didn't act. So I really want to do this one.' The door to the sitting room opened.

Jo was in the middle of what she thought was a very persuasive speech about 'the best paper for the story' when she noticed that Mick and Samantha's eyes had left her and moved to the window.

Jo turned to see Meryl holding up a large sheet of paper with the words:

£14,000 – Let us in

written on it with marker pen. 'Well, as you can see, they're being ridiculous now,' Jo said. She went over to the window and snapped down the blind. Meryl's response to this was to move to the next window.

Jo went over and pulled that blind down, too, but this wasn't good. It was already getting very undignified. She wondered what Meryl would do next, bring out a megaphone?

'They're just being childish. You can't take your story to people like this,' Jo told the Townells, with a lot more confidence than she felt.

'You're right,' Mick said. 'I need to put a stop to this.' He stood up, obviously intending to head for the door.

'No, no.' Jo stood in front of him. 'I don't think you should go and speak to them. That will just make it worse,' she said.

'I'm not going to be made to feel like a prisoner in my own home,' he said and squared up to her.

'No— no one's suggesting— of course not—' she had a horrible feeling that Mick had never been on-side from the start and this was her last chance.

'I can do £7,000,' she told him 'and guarantee you get every penny of it.'

Mick gave her a nod but then brushed past and went to the front door.

A conversation then went on there, which she couldn't quite make out. She gave Aidan something of a resigned look.

Casting her eyes over the sitting room, Jo saw that Ellis had found her handbag. While the adults had been distracted by the tense negotiations and signs at the window, Ellis had been busy round the side of the armchair investigating the contents of her bag. Now pens, notepaper, tapes, tampons, lipstick and God knows what else were scattered in an arc around him.

'Samantha!' Jo warned, pointing to Ellis and his little trail of destruction.

'Oh no!' Samantha rushed over to the toddler and lifted him out of the mess. 'Sorry,' she said but it was drowned out by the screams now bursting from Ellis.

Just as Jo began to scramble her belongings back into her bag, Mick came into the room.

'I think it's time for you to leave now,' he said briskly.

Behind Mick was Meryl, another reporter and a photographer.

'Right, well.' Jo took a final cast about the carpet; she seemed to have everything. She wouldn't bother upsetting Ellis any more by wrestling the unwrapped super tampon from his hand.

'Goodbye, Samantha,' she managed, determined to leave with some shred of dignity intact. 'Nice to meet you all. I am sorry it won't be me helping you to get your boys the justice they deserve.'

The smug look on Meryl's face wasn't helping. 'Right, Aidan, we'd better be off then.'

The walk across the living room, along the corridor and to the front door felt burningly long and painful. Jo stumbled over the raised threshold and almost fell down the steps into the garden, prompting a pithy 'Bugger!' to escape her lips.

Only when she was back at her car did she face Aidan, who looked flushed and slightly traumatised. 'I'm so sorry,' she reassured him, realising she had to be the grown-up here and make him realise that although this wasn't great, it wasn't the end of the world. 'It happens once in a while. The desk call it snatching defeat from the jaws of victory. OK, what we have to do now is work as hard as we can on all the other elements of this story, so we can do a brilliant follow-up once the *Mail* has broken it.'

But really, Jo suspected, that wasn't going to be the same. Did they know everything she knew? Or could she bring anything new to the party?

'Bloody hell,' Aidan said, 'they were so persistent. I think Meryl would have written the figure on her bum and mooned it in the window if she'd thought it would help.'

Jo began to giggle, then found she couldn't stop herself. It was stress relief. Aidan began to laugh too. 'I'm going to have to phone Jeff,' Jo said when the laughter had finally passed. 'Better light an emergency cigarette first. D'you want one?' she offered.

Aidan shook his head.

'Jeff? Jo here.' She'd got through to him on the first attempt. 'Total cock-up central. We're out, the *Mail* is in. What more can I say? Can't argue with £14,000. Yup... Aha... OK.'

And she hung up, which puzzled Aidan. He'd obviously expected them both to have to go through a long-distance telling off.

'Don't we have to try again?' he asked.

Jo just shook her head: 'If you were on your own, you'd have to. But I've been working here for five years, I've earned the right to say when it's over.'

* * *

Back at the office, the approaching end-of-the-week chaos was beginning to build.

As soon as Jo walked through the heavy swing doors Jeff beckoned her over although the phone was clamped firmly between his head and shoulder.

Once he'd hung up, he swivelled on his chair to face her. Not for the first time in her working life, Jo was extremely glad that Jeff never got very angry. He certainly never shouted, well not in his newsroom anyway. Thank God. There were quite enough stories about violent and insane editors and news editors who would chew you up and spit you out for spelling mistakes, let alone losing scoops to rival newspapers.

'So, we're completely out on our arse over the twins, then?' was his appraisal of the Townell situation. She could see Mike, his number two, as well as Rod and even news desk secretary, Binah, all suddenly attempting the 'we're extremely busy and not at all interested' look as they stared at screens, flicked through notes, played with pencils but strained to listen to every word of this conversation.

'Is this Aidan's fault or yours?'

'Mine. But I'm trying to see it as a blessing,' Jo said, instigating damage limitation.

Jeff's eyebrows went up. 'Look at it this way, if the *Mail* runs the Townell twins tomorrow or Saturday, they'll just be whetting the appetite for more cases and further information, which I'm planning to give our readers on Sunday.'

'Have you got more cases?'

She mentally crossed her fingers behind her back as she replied: 'I'm waiting for a contact to call back. I'm also hopeful of getting some Canadian cases – the injection's been over there longer, so more cases have cropped up.'

'Hmm,' Jeff didn't exactly sound ecstatic. 'It's not really setting the world on fire, is it? And Savannah? I'm only asking because it's Thursday 3.20 p.m. and there's nothing in any of my news queues that says "front page".'

'Savannah. I have no freaking idea,' she admitted. 'Short of going round to Green Party headquarters and offering them my body, I'm not sure what else I can do on this.'

'Right, well,' Jeff smiled. 'As you know, it's not usually news desk policy to ask reporters to exchange sex for stories... huh, Rod?'

'No.' And Rod, who had once brought in a cracking exclusive that had unfortunately involved betraying the confidence of the girl he was sleeping with at the time, had the decency to blush. But he was saved further humiliation when his phone burst into life.

* * *

Back in her corner of the office, Jo found Dominique and Aidan working industriously, Dominique on the phone, Aidan bashing at his computer in a concentrated way.

'Are you OK?' she asked him.

'Not too bad.' He looked up and attempted a smile that came off looking a little sorrowful.

She nodded. 'Well, learn what you can from it, but sometimes you have to accept the fact that someone else is going to win – at least for today. We'll get them back tomorrow.'

10

THURSDAY: 4.50 P.M.

'So, I have found a Canadian family,' Jo told Jeff several hours later. 'Full chat, and they're going to email us over a happy family pic and, you know what? The Canadian child, Casey, his dad is a nurse. So, a bit of medical establishment credibility for you.'

'That's good, Jo,' Jeff said and she paused for just a moment to enjoy the compliment. Much deserved after the frantically busy two hours she'd spent phoning, chasing and interviewing. 'And now for the bad news,' she carried on quickly. 'I can't stay and write this stuff up now. I've got to get to my daughter's birthday party, or else,' she appealed to Jeff especially. He had teenage boys and as he was always in the office, he had probably missed birthdays, Christmases, school plays, almost all the important milestones in their lives, and Jo was determined not to do the same. Anyway, it was different: if Daddy couldn't be there, that was one thing, but if Mummy couldn't, that was childhood trauma. Punishable with months of guilt, angry recriminations and the constant worry that you were screwing up your children.

'By the way, I've asked the techies to come and take a look at my office computer, it's on a permanent go-slow these days, so just get them to give me a call if they need to access any password areas,' Jo remembered to tell him. Bloody office computer must be about fifteen years old. What it really needed was to be launched out of the window and urgently replaced.

'When are you going to file your copy? Tonight?' Jeff asked, hand hovering over a ringing phone, wanting to catch her answer before he picked up.

'I'll try. Otherwise, I'll be in early tomorrow morning.'

'Simon coming to the birthday party?' he asked.

'Yeah.' Slight grimace at the thought of the evening ahead of her.

'Have fun.' Jeff answered the phone now, telling the voice at the other end: 'News desk, one second,' then turning back to Jo with the words: 'Stay off the sauce. It just makes things worse. And anyway, I want you in fresh as a daisy tomorrow. You've got a lot on.'

She smiled sweetly at his concern, then went to gather her belongings and have one final supervisory chat with her team.

* * *

When Jo got into her car it was with the customary glance of annoyance and resignation at the state of chaos in here. Child debris, newspaper debris, every single one of the side door pockets stuffed with six different types of snack remnants. The ashtray had been hastily emptied after a particularly stressful day on the road several weeks ago, so her girls wouldn't spot butts, but it was still grotty with ash.

The car needed all sorts of basic maintenance: the window washing stuff had to be topped up, the oil light was flashing intermittently at her, which couldn't be good. She never checked the tyres. The thing was running on fumes alone because she still hadn't been to the petrol station and yet again had no time to go this evening because already it was 5.15 p.m.

Simon used to deal with the car stuff, and Jo hadn't got into the habit of doing it herself yet. Oh, bollocks to that, she could just find a helpful car valeting service, couldn't she? But she hadn't found time to do that either. She threw her stuff onto the passenger seat and got in behind the wheel, then took a deep breath, mentally tried to leave the office behind and psych herself up for Simon. And Gwen.

Her eye fixed on the car's badge in the centre of the steering wheel. Funny to think it was right here, in this driving seat, five months ago now, that she had made the decision to tell him their marriage was over.

They'd been coming home from Christmas at his parents' house and she'd insisted on driving because she'd needed the distraction. If she hadn't driven, she was certain she'd have spent the entire journey screaming at him to relieve the tension that had built up in his family home over their four-day visit.

Yes, it had probably been a mistake to raise her alternative-ish health views at the Christmas dinner table in the presence of two GPs, a consultant and a psychiatrist. But on the other hand, the conversation had needed a bit of a jog along – or maybe that had been her seventh glass of champagne talking. Added to the powder keg of the day was the fact that her children hadn't liked any gift their grandparents had given them, sending grandmother, Margie, into a huff – but really, bath salts and tea towels for a three and a six-year-old? Because of this, Jo had ignored all blatant hints from Margie to come and help in the kitchen with the preparation of the Christmas dinner. Instead, she'd hung out with the men in the front room, getting lashed.

It was entirely Margie's fault that her husband and two sons were such unhelpful chauvinist pigs, Jo had reasoned, she was damned if she was going to suffer the consequences.

So, she'd almost quite enjoyed the first part of the day: tipsy on the fizz, she'd briefly managed to forget the insult of her Christmas gifts from Simon.

She'd given him a black cashmere coat. His favourite label, his size, a thoughtful replacement for the one he'd worn for years. Just to be generous, she'd bought him a luxurious scarf to go with it. And what had she unwrapped from him? Oh, and in department store wrapping paper, by the way, he'd not done any of that himself: a stainless-steel vegetable steamer. 'You kept saying you wanted something for the kitchen.' He'd shrugged, when she'd found it hard to feign delight.

Indeed, she had been heavily hinting: state-of-the-art cappuccino machine, retro-chic coffee grinder, a Kitchen Aid mixer in a witty pastel colour. A vegetable steamer was *not* the same. And the second parcel was worse: a black and pink babydoll negligee thing about three sizes *too big* and, frankly, just a disastrous cut for someone with hips and no tits.

Words had failed her. She had gawped. Not least because they hadn't had sex for almost three months now and if he thought this was going to solve the problem...

'Do you like it?' he'd asked. Always slow with the signals, Simon.

'No,' she'd said, 'I bloody hate it,' and then, 'Right now, I bloody hate you too.'

'Merry bloody Christmas then,' he'd said, slumping back onto the sagging, insomnia-inducing, pocket-sized double bed in his old childhood bedroom. They'd retreated there to unwrap their gifts to each other in peace after the mayhem of the early morning Santa-fest.

But by the time the Christmas meal was on the table, Jo had been in a booze-induced good mood again, until the alternative health debate had cracked out over the plum pudding.

Then, closely following that row, came the killer Margie remarks.

Maybe Margie had been at the sherry, maybe she wanted to get back at Jo for not helping, or for bringing up such ungrateful children. For whatever reason, committed doctor's wife, housewife and mother Margie had launched into a full-on rant about the children of today: all they ever watched was telly, all they cared about was computer games and pop music, all they ate was junk, their dreadful parents neglected them and left them stuck in nurseries all day long.

This clearly wasn't aimed at Simon's new sister-in-law, who was heavily pregnant and had just finished telling the table that she planned to take two years' leave 'because it's so crucial for their development, the first two years'. No, the tirade was obviously aimed at Jo. At the start, she let it ride, sank her glass of wine, nudged Simon's dad for a refill and exchanged looks with him, seeing some sympathy in his glance. But as the words flowed on, she locked eyes with her husband, urging him to tell his mother to stop, interrupt the flow... at least put up some sort of defence against this.

Simon had held the look but had then calmly picked up his own wine glass and drained it. How had this man, so outwardly handsome, so superficially charming, who had once meant so much to her, become so hardened and cold? In that moment it had occurred to Jo that maybe whatever they'd had before wasn't coming back. Maybe this wasn't a phase. Maybe their marriage was over.

'Margie—' she'd decided to interrupt the diatribe, feeling angry heat rise in her cheeks. 'Could you please stop now, because you're really upsetting me?' She could have left it there, then she would have remained in the right at the dinner table, could maybe still have elicited a little sympathy from her husband and others, but no, she had to continue, go in for the kill and add totally gratuitously: 'What you're saying is complete rubbish. Maybe if you just put down the *Daily Mail* and looked around you once in a while you'd work that out, you silly woman.'

'Jo, that's enough,' Simon had snapped and her disappointment with him had crystallised.

He'd waited until night-time, back in the saggy spare bed, to argue with her in fierce whispers. She'd argued just as fiercely back.

'How dare you tell me off?' she'd whispered in fury. 'Why didn't you say one word to defend me? Your mother can be a complete cow. I don't think she's ever liked me, she's always disapproved of me, and you know what? I'm beginning to think you're on her bloody side.'

'Have some respect, Jo. She's my mother.'

'Have some respect yourself. I'm your wife. I'm the mother of our children. How dare you let her belittle us like that.'

'She's having a hard time at the moment. Her sister isn't well, she's worn out, she can't look after this big house by herself—' Simon had begun in her defence.

'What about me?' Jo had broken in. 'Why do I never deserve any of your sympathy? I'm working all bloody hours, I do the majority of the housework, the cooking, the girls come to me first for everything, not you, I need your sympathy too. I need your support or— I just don't think I'm going to be able to carry on like this. I'm completely exhausted and I'm spending my precious, frigging holiday time driving up and down the country to sleep badly in a crap bed and be insulted.'

'Your life is your choice,' were the only words that Simon gave in reply.

'What the hell is that supposed to mean?'

'Keep your voice down,' he'd hissed. 'Maybe you're trying to fit a single person's job into a married mother's life. Maybe it just won't work.'

'And what about you? You work even more hours than I do,' she'd snapped.

'So, maybe you should rethink what you're doing.'

'Maybe you bloody should.'

'Jo...' and out it had come, the justification that he so steadfastly believed gave him the upper hand: 'I'm a doctor.'

'Simon,' she'd spat back. 'You're a wanker.'

That had been the end of the conversation and they'd both carried on lying there, fuming in silence, back to back, wide awake in the uncomfortably small bed. Another day ended with another unresolved row. Jo had found herself unable to block thoughts of how once, so long ago now, they'd made love so enthusiastically they'd managed to snap the leg off this very bed. It was only on the long drive back to London that it had occurred to her with clarity that her life was too busy, too stressed, too unhappy and that it didn't have to be like this.

She could decide what she wanted to keep and to focus on, and she could get rid of the rest. It wasn't her job she needed to ditch – the job that gave her purpose, fulfilment, a very important reason to get up every morning – it was her husband: the man who brought her down, upset her, depressed her, didn't support her... quite obviously didn't love her any more. Or didn't love her as much, or enough.

* * *

A winking petrol gauge light on the dashboard interrupted Jo's thoughts now. She'd risked driving around like this for two days, but now she would have to stop and refuel and be undeniably late for Mel's birthday party.

She pulled out of the parking space unable to stem the flow of thoughts about her ex-husband. Hard to imagine they'd once worked side by side in a hospital ward, known true team spirit and been united by a cause.

Simon and Jo had met at work, when as a junior doctor he joined Bolton Royal Infirmary, where she was working as a theatre nurse.

Oh yes.

Secret nursing past of newspaper reporter, Randall

She'd spent several years studying intensively, followed by four years in the hospital, working the grinding NHS treadmill, watching Simon whizz from promotion to promotion while she did the same stuff day in, day out for the same low pay. His salary went up as his hours went down, yet nothing changed for her. She was still working shifts, days, nights and weekends, for an hourly rate not much better than when she'd started.

The injustice of it began to jar. She and her nursing colleagues were well trained, experienced, available round the clock for operations, patient care, drug monitoring. But where was there to progress to? Meanwhile Simon was at training courses, conferences, lecture rounds, getting better and better at his job while she felt as if she was stagnating.

When she had Mel at the age of twenty-eight, she'd felt better about herself. But it was the brush with the press that happened when she went back to work after maternity leave that caused her career change. She'd known that the hospital was badly run, but when it was obvious that large chunks of funding were disappearing into a services company run by the hospital Chief Executive's wife, well, then it was time for an investigation.

A friend of hers worked in admin, so Jo had 'borrowed' a key and sneaked into the offices one evening for a rifle through the filing cabinets. Whenever she thought about this, she still couldn't believe she'd done it. If anyone had found her, she'd have been sacked on the spot with attempted theft on her record. But she had burned with the injustice of it. Probably something to do with her new, post-natal state of mind. Now that she had a baby at home, life had finally come into focus. Everything mattered. If she was to be away from her baby, she wanted those hours to matter; she wanted to be doing something that inspired her.

And working tirelessly in a run-down hospital while the Chief Executive and his wife took the piss with public money had begun to really annoy her.

She'd used the office photocopier to make duplicates of the relevant documents, carefully replacing everything in the files. Here was contract after contract for jobs that had never been done: waste recycling, window cleaning, building repairs. None of it had ever happened. One quick tour of the hospital and anyone could see this was a money-making scam.

Just one quick tour. That's when it had occurred to her how to get this situation resolved. She hadn't had much of an idea what to do before – a tribunal? An internal complaints committee? – but now she knew. She would phone the *Evening Echo*, meet one of their reporters, give them the documents, then take them on the tour.

That's how Jo met Gayle Adams, the woman who changed her life. Well, that's how it might have looked, but probably her life had changed the moment she had pushed Mel out into the world and noticed, through the haze of exhaustion and ecstasy, that Simon was giving career advice to the junior house doctor at her pushing end far more enthusiastically than he'd been helping her through this.

One of those moments in a marriage that you notice and file away under 'T' for Troubling. To be brought out and re-examined when another one crops up. She never said anything to Simon about it. What was there to say? He would just have denied it, would have laughed off the suggestion and soothed her in his slightly smug 'I'm a doctor' way. Journalist Gayle Adams arrived in a pocket-sized convertible red sports car, wore a headscarf to keep her unruly copper hair out of her face, and was surely the closest thing to Susan Sarandon that Lancashire was ever going to produce.

She was fiftyish with a smoker's husky voice, a firm handshake, ready smile and enormous handbag.

'So where do we start, my love?' she'd asked and Jo had felt the grip of dread – holding her ever since she'd called the *Echo* – loosen.

Gayle was all right. Instinctively, Jo felt that Gayle would do this the right way.

'I've just come off shift, so I'll tour you round,' Jo had explained. 'If anyone stops us at any point, asks what we're up to, you are lost and I'm showing you to... depends where we are, wherever makes sense.'

'What about the people who know you're off shift?'

'Oh, I've told them you're a friend applying for a job here.'

'At my age!' Gayle had fired back. 'Well, don't worry, I'll be quick, I won't ask any awkward questions until we're back outside again.'

'Does anyone here know you?' Jo had asked.

'We'll have to wait and see. I've met some of the management staff but I could still be lost while visiting someone. Let's not worry about it too much. If it happens, it happens. It's after six, the chances of office staff being around are quite slim.'

Backhanders scandal at the Royal.
Chief Exec Pays Wife's Firm to do Nothing!
Exclusive!

That was how they ran it exactly four days later. Gayle had needed extra time to check the story out fully, to have a photographer wait outside the chief's home to surprise him and his wife with an early morning photo call.

She'd also had to put the accusations to the couple to see what they had to say.

'Outrageous suggestions... I'll be conducting a thorough investigation... no truth in these allegations whatsoever...' had been the chief's line. 'Some operational difficulties... technical problems... may be behind schedule in some areas,' the wife had said. It was fudged enough for there to be no criminal investigation, no criminal charges. There was some sort of botched NHS-style internal inquiry, as a result of which 'procedures were tightened'. The wife's company didn't get any more work but did at least carry out the work it had been paid to do and the Chief Executive was promoted to a non-executive post. Promoted! He was earning more money for doing less. Jo had almost been sick at the news. She couldn't carry on, doing the same old thing for even smaller wages because she was part-time now.

Not when totally corrupt men were being promoted into even more expensive posts to run the hospital into the ground.

She thought of Gayle often. Gayle who had phoned her with courtesy on the day before the story was to be printed to warn her what was in it and how to play it cool at work.

Gayle who had joked about her two ex-husbands, unruly teenage boys and unsuccessful dates, but took her work with an impressive, deadly seriousness. Gayle who obviously loved what she did and believed in it.

'You did a great job,' she had told Jo. 'Finding the documents, photocopying them. Ever thought about being a reporter?' It was probably banter, intended to make her smile.

But Jo had found herself saying: 'Yes. I have thought about it. How do you become a reporter? Do you have to go on a course?'

Gayle had laughed: 'I don't think so. Well, it's not compulsory yet anyway. Why don't you meet our health editor for a drink? Start with what you know best. Have a specialist subject and start writing about it. God knows, we could do with some good contacts up at the Royal. We could probably put you on the payroll for that alone.'

The health editor had advised a night course in shorthand; even better, the health editor was pregnant and planning a long maternity leave, so there was a temporary job coming up.

'Write me some sample stories,' the health editor had suggested, 'I'll see what you're like, give you some pointers and we can take it from there.'

Jo, who had gone along in a spirit of curiosity had suddenly found herself seriously considering a future job offer, a career change... before she'd even had the chance to breathe a word of it to her husband.

Well, OK, she'd decided not to mention a word of it to her husband – not even the Chief Executive and his wife story – because she knew exactly what her husband would say.

He would tell her she'd lost her mind.

He would remind her what a 'nice little job' she had. Emphasis on the words 'nice' and 'little'.

It was probably talk of her nice little job that had sent her whirling off in the direction of journalism in the first place.

She had eventually, after much debate with herself and her incredulous husband, gone on the shorthand course then taken the job, sealing the rumours that she'd tipped off the *Echo* about the Chief Executive and his wife, but not making it any harder to break many new stories kindly provided by the people she'd spent so many years working alongside.

When Simon had finally landed the plum London hospital post he'd been longing for, she and Mel had moved too.

She'd taken a pay cut to go and work for the *South London Press* with her eyes now firmly on the prize of making it as a national news reporter. Because she knew she was good. Despite all the cracks Simon had made about her 'joke' profession.

Just coincidence that when she finally got her national newspaper job Simon suddenly wanted to talk about more children? She wasn't so sure now. The pregnancy and post-natal time with Annette had been the busiest in Jo's life. She had worked ten and twelve-hour days, rushing around England in her car, flying abroad on foreign jobs, feeling like an important reporter, yes, feeling like a guilty, absent mother too. Her children had been in full-time nursery care until Jo's parents had decided to move down to help. Meanwhile Simon had worked very hard too.

Not difficult to see when the marriage started to fall to pieces. By the time Annette was six months old – where was Simon? Who was Simon? He was the increasingly distant Dr Daddy figure. The man who came home very late every night and spent the weekends he wasn't on call wanting sleep, peace and quiet, a round of golf or an evening in front of the TV. Slightly shocking to realise you've got a baby just a few months old who you adore and you can't stand her father. Jo hadn't known what to do with the feeling. She was in denial, hoping things would somehow improve.

But she didn't seem to have even a single opinion in common with him any more. Whatever she'd seen, whatever she'd been so in love with, it wasn't there. Who was this person? The father of the small baby in her arms and she didn't know him. It was usual to feel strange for months after giving birth, she knew that; maybe it was best to wait, not do anything drastic. Not do what she wanted to do – run from the house screaming – until at least a few more months had passed. She had to make sure this wasn't some hormonal hell she would recover from.

Simon still looked good: a well-proportioned handsome face, blondish hair in a collar-length cut, his rangy body kept trim with gym visits, tennis and golf. He was a grown-up grammar school boy. All doctors were though, weren't they? They were good at school, sensible, a bit sporty, dedicated hard workers. A little bit self-sacrificing and a great big chunk of smug.

OK, not all doctors, but Simon and most of Simon's colleagues. How had he seemed to her when she was twenty-three and in love with him? Handsome, charming, clever, energetic, in a hurry to do well, to make people better, to make love to her, to marry her. Their romance had been wrapped up with the hospital. It was about flirting on shifts, trying to keep their minds on the job, not on what they'd done to each other the night before, it was about joining the rest of the gang in the bar that night, at lunchtime... whenever they came off duty.

It hadn't been a private romance. It had been a group one. She remembered how oddly dislocating their honeymoon had been. Their first holiday alone together, the first time they'd spent hours and hours alone with each other. After only a few days, they'd made friends with two couples in the hotel and joined them for dinner and sightseeing trips. And Simon, who'd been so quiet and lethargic when it was just the two of them, had come back to life again in the group. That was when Jo had made her first entry in the 'T' for Troubling section of the marriage filing cabinet. He was the oldest son of a doctor father and traditional doctor's wife. He had some puzzling, old-fashioned ideas about how their married life was going to be. He didn't exactly say he wanted Jo to give up her job when they had children, in fact, he always seemed quite glad of her income, but he had an ingrained image that men worked hard, had the main job, had priority.

Women did the children thing. Jo, brought up by two egalitarian, lefty teachers, couldn't have come with more different perceptions. She'd thought they were two individuals together, both able to fulfil their own potential, both able to parent.

Nothing about splitting up from Simon had been easy. In the early days, she had agonised about whether they were doing the right thing, but now she was trying to make peace with her choice and focus on the good that had come from it. There was nothing wrong with Gwen, Jo tried to tell herself, apart from the fact that the woman had moved in with Simon, so had also moved into the lives of Jo's children three days a week. For that reason alone, Jo found it hard not to resent her.

She hated the way Gwen fussed over Simon, cosseted him, massaged his neck and his ego, doted on him, ironed his shirts and made his supper. She hated the way Gwen fussily kept house, all ironed tablecloths and daily vacuuming, and neatly folded rugs on the arms of the sofas. Even the girls, when she got them back on Sunday, seemed to have been Gwen-ed. Their hair was shiny, their tops had been ironed, their shoes polished. It was probably well intentioned, but supremely irritating.

Still, Jo couldn't help herself from thinking about Simon and Gwen's sex life. Did the silk blouses and sensible skirts clothe a simmering cauldron of passion? What was it exactly that her ex-husband saw in their rather frumpy friend? Jo was distracted from her thoughts by her mobile.

'Mum—?' Mel's voice filled the car. 'Where are you?'

'Hello, precious. I'm nearly there, just ten minutes away.'

'We need the cake. We've eaten everything apart from the disgusting pizza Gwen made.'

'Mel. Be nice to Gwen. No kind of pizza is disgusting! Just hang on for me. Ten more minutes, I promise.'

11

THURSDAY: 5.45 P.M.

'Mummy!!'

When Jo finally got to the door of Simon's flat, both daughters were there to greet her. She set the mountainous pink birthday cake, stored in a cool bag in her car all day, to the side and gave each girl a big hug before entering with a smile fixed firmly on her face. There, that was sure to hide the teeth gritted behind it.

'Hello, sorry I'm late. I did leave on time, but the traffic was terrible,' she announced to the room – the open-plan living space, all shiny wood, cream décor, careful display of possessions and floor-to-ceiling window over-looking a chink of riverside. She didn't think she should be apologising. Thursday was one of her busiest days, usually she didn't leave the office till 8 or 9 p.m. It was hugely inconvenient of Simon to arrange the party today even if it was Mel's actual birthday, but he'd ruled out earlier in the week and couldn't do Sunday.

Gwen, Simon and her parents, as well as a handful of Mel's 'best friends' from school, were all here, chorusing 'hello'.

Simon stood up to greet her. In immaculate blue and white check shirt, chinos with an ironed knife-edge, Simon looked even lighter and leaner than on Sunday when she'd seen him last, and he was still sporting the beard she hadn't got used to. In the months since their split, it was as if Jo and her ex-husband were trying to obliterate their marital selves and transform into different people. Make it clear there was no return. They'd gone through various forms of greeting over the years: passionate snog to start with, obviously, dutiful peck on the lips later on, then moving to frosty glares, disdainful handshakes. Now, in an attempt at being civilised, one kiss on the cheek was settling into the way they said hello.

Jo leaned over to peck at him quickly; there was no other contact, no hand on arm or back, or any of that.

His new beard prickled against her cheek and he wafted aftershave. The strength of the smell made the back of her throat contract. She went over to kiss and hug her parents and then had to kiss Gwen too because otherwise it would have been odd.

Her parents moved to opposite ends of the leather sofa, so she took the invitation to sit between them. They were so sweet; obviously they thought she needed protection here in husband territory.

'How's work?' her dad asked.

'Oh busy... the usual,' she told him. 'The children have been good as gold,' Jo's mum told her. 'Haven't they, Steve? No fights, no rampaging. Absolutely nothing like your and Matt's birthday parties. I'd be wiping cake off the ceiling by the end of the day.'

This made Jo smile as she remembered the year of the 'jelly bombs'.

'Are you OK?' Jo asked her mum, giving her hand a squeeze. 'I could come round on Monday with Nettie to see you. I've not had the chance to talk to you properly for weeks.'

'Yes, do that. Come for lunch, you'll still be back in time to get Mel from school.'

'OK.'

Jo looked up to see Gwen hovering with a plateful of sandwiches.

'The flat looks great, Gwen.' Jo waved an arm about, taking in the table set up with pretty pink glasses, printed napkins and platefuls of already decimated party snacks and leftover pizza.

'Oh, we're getting organised. Books on the shelves, things on the walls,' Gwen answered, holding out the sandwiches.

Paintings from Jo's marital home, so familiar she could close her eyes and visualise them, were on these walls alongside ones she recognised from a rare visit to Gwen's old flat. Jo registered the weirdness of this but tried not to dwell on it.

'Bet this is your first children's birthday party in years?' Jo ventured.

'Er, yes—' Gwen smiled. 'M&S seemed to have everything required, though – matching cups and napkins, that sort of thing.'

Jo was quite tempted to ask why Simon hadn't been the one out buying the birthday accessories. But she decided, in the interests of world peace, to leave that question unasked.

Mel and Nettie were to-ing and fro-ing, showing her the new birthday loot, and soon she was busy trying to keep several conversations going at once, with her children and the adults.

'Mummy, Mummy!' Nettie interrupted, 'I got a joke.'

'OK, you tell me your joke,' Jo replied.

'Knock knock.'

'Who's there?' Jo and her parents answered together.

Nettie scanned the room in search of inspiration; she looked up at the ceiling where a hairline plaster crack was visible in the snowy white paint.

'Crackie,' she answered.

Uh oh... Jo hesitated, this joke was a loose cannon now, it could go anywhere. 'Crackie who?' she dared.

'I like to pick my crack.'

Oh, good grief. What?! Time to hyperventilate.

Her dad's eyebrows shot up.

'Nettie, did you bring any toys with you today? Why don't you bring them over and show me,' Jo said.

'Let me get you a drink, Jo,' Gwen offered.

'Juice or something soft would be great,' was Jo's response. 'I've got the cake, by the way. Shall I put it on the table?'

'Yes, of course!' Gwen said.

When Jo took off the layers of foil wrapper, Mel and her friends crowded round for a look at Barbie plunged waist deep in the rippling cake waves of a vibrant pink flamenco outfit.

'Wow, she's amazing!' one of the little girls exclaimed.

Nettie gasped, open-mouthed, even though she had seen the cake on the kitchen table this morning.

'Mum's boyfriend made it. He's a chef,' Mel said matter-of-factly, which led Jo to adopt an expression not unlike Nettie's. How on earth did Mel know any of this?! Had she heard Marcus arriving last night... leaving this morning?

'Hey, it was mainly me,' she told her daughter, but then turned to see her parents' expression of surprise. Somehow, she hadn't quite got round to mentioning a boyfriend.

'Welcome to 21st-century family life,' she said, not really wanting to have the boyfriend conversation here or now.

'Nettie' – she scooped up her little daughter, needing to move swiftly on – 'how are you? Have you had lots of supper?'

Nettie shook her head.

'Well, what about you and Mummy have some tasty sausages.' Jo pulled out a chair, sat down with Nettie on her knee and picked up one of the three remaining cocktail sausages.

She popped it into her mouth, 'Mmmm.' She held another one out to her daughter, who bit off a big mouthful.

'Here's your drink.' Gwen came over and put a glass of orange juice down beside her.

Jo was halfway down the drink when she registered that the rhythmic rasping noise was coming from her daughter on her lap. She swivelled Nettie round so she could look at her face: she was bright red and gagging.

'Oh my God,' Jo cried, 'She's choking!'

Quickly she leaned Nettie forward and prepared to do back blows.

'Simon!' she shouted. Even wanker doctors had their uses.

But before Simon could make it over, Nettie turned to the plate on the table in front of her and half retched, half spat the mouthful of sausage out.

'Yuck!' she exclaimed, when her mouth was empty, 'So hot. So hot.' There was water squeezing from the corners of her eyes. 'Need a drink.'

Jo held out her orange juice, Nettie put her chubby hands round the glass and took a long drink.

'Don't know what that was,' Jo explained to Simon who was beside them now. 'Don't think it was a choke.'

Nettie took three more big gulps, set the glass down and said: 'Pepper.'

'Oh dear,' Jo sympathised, patting Nettie soothingly on the back.

'Was it?' Simon picked up the offending regurgitated mouthful and nibbled a piece of it. 'Hmm, I think she's right. Ooops. Must have been a mixed pack.'

'Never mind,' Jo said to Nettie, cuddling her tight.

'Ouch, my arm,' was Nettie's response.

'Oh dear, what's wrong with your arm?'

Nettie, wearing her short-sleeved plum party dress and matching velvet shoes, pushed her little chiffon cap sleeve up and revealed a small red welt.

'I had a jection.'

For a moment, Jo was stopped in her tracks. 'Ow,' she soothed and held Nettie close against her chest, where now she could feel a wave of annoyance. She did not need to ask what the injection was. Simon must have picked Nettie up early from nursery today and taken her to the doctor's for a Quintet shot. And it was true, she had said she would do it this week and she hadn't organised it. But she still felt furious. He should have at least told her. The feeling that now they were no longer a family, there were all these areas of her children's lives that she wouldn't know about, wouldn't be a part of, felt overwhelming. And he was just standing there, a piece of mashed sausage in his hand, looking at her in a way she could only interpret as defiant.

'She's my daughter too,' he said. 'This is the sensible thing to do.'

'But you could at least have told me, beforehand.'

'What and listen to some of the crack-pot scare stories you write up for that rag you work for?'

Jo glanced over her right shoulder and saw that Mel and her friends had retreated to the bedroom to play, then she did something she'd never done before in all the years she'd been married. She stood up – Nettie in one arm, chin hooked over her shoulder – and she slapped Simon so hard that his face swung round and a bright red palm print sprang up on his cheek.

The loud 'thwack' drew both her parents' and Gwen's attention immediately, but the strange thing was, although there was a stunned moment's silence as they realised what had happened, they quickly looked away and began talking to cover up.

Her father asked her mother loudly if her drink needed topping up and Gwen hurtled off in the direction of the kitchen.

Simon rubbed his cheek as he and Jo weighed up the pros and cons of screaming at each other, here at Mel's eighth birthday party right in front of her grandparents... friends... little sister...

'I don't think our lawyers will like that,' Simon said perfectly quietly and calmly to his former wife.

'How dare you,' Jo hissed back. 'If you want to start a custody battle, you're going the right way about it.'

Simon continued to rub his face: 'This is not the time or the place to talk about it,' he said.

'No. I'm too angry to talk to you.' Jo was actually shaking with rage. She was going to kill him, tear him limb from limb when she got the chance. How *dare* he?

'Why don't you bugger off into your kitchen and let me try to calm down?' she said in as low and controlled a voice as she could muster.

He turned on his heel and followed Gwen.

Although Jo might have liked a few moments to try to pull herself together, the opportunity was lost with the stampede of girls rushing to the table, back from whatever had been so urgent in the bedroom a few minutes ago, to demand cake, which meant candles, singing and all the adults round the table catching each other's eyes uneasily.

Still, slicing forcefully through Barbie's dress over and over again gave Jo the opportunity to vent some of her Simon rage, but the cake stuck in her throat and the party was well and truly spoiled for her.

As the adults sat quietly at the table letting the children make the noise and conversation for them, Jo was suddenly finding it difficult not to cry.

She stabbed her fork hard through the heart of the pink, spongy slice in front of her and hoped Simon was watching. And, *God, Marcus*, she thought as she put the piece into her mouth, *this was good cake.*

* * *

Jo was the last guest to leave the party, by quite some time. The teeny guests left soon after the cake, and her parents hung on for another half hour to help clear up and to be polite.

Once they'd gone, to avoid Simon and Gwen, Jo took her daughters to the bathroom – hi-spec, slate floored, yet somehow coldly bachelor – ran them a deep bath and washed cake icing, sweat, baby's first blusher and all the rest of the day from them.

She towelled her children carefully, anointed dry cheeks, arms and legs with baby cream, put them into their sweet little matching pyjamas, supervised teeth cleaning, then brushed out their hair, all the while listening to chit-chat and a barrage of corny jokes.

'What did the inflatable teacher say to the inflatable boy who brought a pin into the inflatable school?' Mel asked, head cocked to the side for an answer, eyes fixed on her mum, as if this was the most important question in the whole world.

'I don't know,' Jo complied.

'You've let me down, you've let the school down, but worst of all you've let yourself down.'

Oh, that was good. Jo began to laugh and all the tension of the day began to bubble up into the laugh, until she was giggling uncontrollably. She had to stop: if she carried on laughing like this, Mel would tell her this joke twenty times a day from now on until... forever.

Nettie held out a sparkly purple hairband: 'Put this in, please,' she asked.

'For bed?' Jo replied.

Nettie nodded solemnly and fished around in her little purple toilet bag for further accessories. She took out a raspberry lip salve and a compact mirror, then, with all the elegance of a mademoiselle on the Rive Gauche, she flipped open the mirror and dotted salve on with her pinkie.

'All ready for bed,' she said finally.

'I love you,' Jo said, squeezing her tight and pulling Mel in with her other arm, 'I love you both so much. It's time for me to say night-night. Daddy's going to tuck you in.' Jo managed to muster as much warmth for the word 'Daddy' as she could. 'It's time for Mummy to go off and do some work.'

She wondered why she was using work as an excuse. It just seemed less bald than saying 'Mummy has to go, because she doesn't live here.' Mel looked fine with this, but Jo could already see Nettie's face crumple. 'I want you to stay,' her youngest daughter said.

'Nettie, it's not for long,' Jo said and put an arm round her.

'It is, it's for three sleeps.' She held out three fingers to her mother. 'I'll miss you very much.'

'I'll miss you too. Will you promise to phone me?' Jo picked her up and they headed out of the bathroom to find Simon.

'Let's see what Daddy's going to read to you tonight, shall we?' Jo soothed, 'I bet he's got some really good stories.'

But Nettie's head was already buried in her shoulder and there wasn't much doubt that it was going to be one of those terrible, screaming handovers that would make Jo want to wail and scream with guilt and distress herself.

Despite the earlier row, both she and Simon tried to manage it as kindly as they could, but still Jo's last sight of Nettie as the bedroom door closed was of a distraught red face with tears streaming down the cheeks.

* * *

Once Jo had shut the door of Simon's flat behind her, she let several of the tears she'd been trying to stop all evening slip out. Hell. Hell. Hell. But she had to do it this way. Surely her children would thank her in the end? Surely it was better to have two equally caring parents rather than one fed-up, full-time totally harassed one and one hazily distant unknown one?

She could not look after her girls all week. That was the simple truth. Her hours were far too long on Fridays and Saturdays, and also, she feared sacrificing all of her time off to childcare and domesticity.

She'd seen enough divorced mothers do this. They were always at home, they were always with the kids, they were imprisoned; once the children were in bed, they couldn't even get out for a pint of milk. Whereas the dads swanned in on Sunday afternoons offering trips to the cinema, meals out and other treats and really it was so grossly unfair that it should be illegal.

Drudge Mum and Santa Dad was how it often went after the divorce. And hardly surprisingly, Santa Dad had so much time and freedom to himself – no washing-up, no laundry, no packed-lunch making, no school runs – that he was busy working out, going out, rediscovering himself, oh, and sleeping with everyone willing and able.

So no, although it was so hard to say goodnight and leave the girls here, she had to stick to her guns and make sure Simon took just as much responsibility for his children as she did. Otherwise, how would she ever move forwards?

12

THURSDAY: 8:45 P.M.

Jo had just walked through the door of her home when her mobile began to trill.

'Declan,' she greeted the voice on the other end of the line, almost pleased to hear from the night news editor, he was becoming as much of an evening ritual as brushing her teeth.

'Thought you should know, one of the children with whooping cough is reportedly in a coma and on life support. Just wondered if this is going to affect the copy I'm supposed to be getting from you tonight.'

'A child is in a coma?' she repeated, 'Jesus. Yes, I'd say that pretty well affects everything.'

'I'll get Jeff to call you, shall I?' Declan offered. 'He's phoning me back in five anyway.'

'Right, OK, I'll talk it through with him. How old is this child?'

'Eight.'

'Eight and... he? She?'

'She.'

'She's just got whooping cough, no other complications?' Jo asked.

'It's coming in on the PA newswire. No further info at the moment.'

'Which hospital is she in?'

'Northampton, I think. We're sending someone there tonight to keep us up to speed, try to speak to the family and all that.'

'OK.' Oh God... writing a piece about the possible dangers of Quintet when someone's child was possibly going to die of a disease that the vaccination supposedly prevented was possibly going to be too difficult.

'The techies are at your desk again,' Declan added. 'Two of them this time, been there all evening. Occasionally I go over and ask how they're getting on, but they're saying they've never seen anything like it.'

'Really?'

'Has your computer broken down?' Declan asked.

'No, it's just running really slowly. This is the first time I've asked them to come up and look at it, though.'

'But... I've seen the tech department at your desk before. They've been in a few times over the last couple of months.'

'No, Declan, this is the first time I've asked them to look at it—' Jo suddenly thought about the unfinished bag of peanuts in her desk drawer that had attracted the rat. What if someone *had* been there – at her desk, tampering with her computer?

'Jo, are you sure?' Declan asked. 'Because if no one's been asked to check out your computer, then who was—?'

'That's just what I'm thinking,' Jo broke in. 'Why don't you let me speak to the people who are there now?'

'OK.' There was the click of one receiver going down and a silent pause before a new voice picked up.

'Ms Randall,' came the voice at the other end. 'Hello, I'm Manzour Khan, we're running through some checks, but it looks like your computer's been set up to spy on you.' He waited a moment to let the implication of this settle on her. 'My colleague and I,' Manzour went on, 'think a program has been installed that forwards copies of your email and possibly other files on to another address.'

'What?!' she asked, trying to make sense of this. 'My computer is spying on me? But who—and where would it send—oh my God.' She suddenly realised what this meant. Someone was *spying* on her. Someone who could send technicians to her desk and do this properly. Was she at risk? Were her children at risk? What was going on?

'Well, we don't know that yet. It's all passworded up, very clever. Quite interesting, really.' Manzour sounded caught up in the technicalities. It didn't seem to have registered with him yet what this really meant: that either a member of his department was happy to take on extra-curricular spying activity, or someone was coming in and out of the newsroom to her computer on a faked id. Someone badly wanted to know what she was up to. Whatever explanation emerged, whichever way you looked at it, it couldn't be good.

Manzour added: 'You'll have to come to our department tomorrow and help us make a full report about it. Have you got a computer at home?'

'Yes, a laptop,' she answered.

'Well, we'll have to check that out, too, mate. It's quite possible that whatever this is on your work computer, it's got copied onto your home one.'

'Oh my god,' Jo exclaimed, beginning to feel properly shocked. 'How long do you think it's been going on for?' Manzour asked.

'The computer's been slow for... months.' Now when she thought about it, how stupid she'd been. 'And Declan says someone's been coming down from your department to look at it, although this is the first time I've put in a request.'

'We'll look into that, see what's on the logs,' Manzour replied.

'Good, because I really need to know what's going on.'

Her house phone began to ring. She told Manzour that she had to go but gave him her mobile number so he could keep in touch.

'Jo Randall,' she answered her other phone.

It was Jeff.

'We can't run your piece this week,' he began. 'This girl might be dead by Sunday. We can't be critical of the vaccination now; we'd be accused of reckless irresponsibility. We'd be child-killers.'

He wasn't wasting any time putting his side of the argument.

'Look, Jeff, it's Thursday night,' Jo reminded him. 'No need to rush this decision. I don't think we should just do like the government wants and ignore the issue. They know a very small category of children shouldn't have this injection and they need to make that public.'

'Well, we might just have to sit on this for a week or so. As you know, timing is everything.'

'It's always a mistake to sit on anything!' she said, realising how petulant she sounded.

'Oh, come on, Jo. You know it's not. Reporters can never bear to wait for stories to come out. But the *Mail* won't run the story about those twins they pinched from you tomorrow. I'm willing to bet my pension on that.'

'Don't talk about pensions,' Jo sighed. 'I think I just kissed my share of a juicy one away tonight.'

'So, all did not go well with the doctor?'

'No, not really. Tonight I surpassed myself... I smacked the doctor,' she confessed.

When this met with a stunned pause, Jo quickly jumped in to justify herself: 'Reasons, Jeff.'

'I'm sure. But be careful, Jo. Lawyers are involved. You don't want things to get nasty.'

It was Jo's turn to fall silent.

Then she remembered to ask, 'Did Declan tell you about my computer?'

'Yeah, I'm pretty concerned about that. I'll talk to Spikey in the morning and make sure it's investigated as a top priority.'

'Yup.'

'We have to keep your work secure and you safe,' he added.

'Oh, thanks,' she answered. 'Very reassuring. So, should I get bullet-proof glass for my car like Vincey, then?'

'Bulletproof glass!' Jeff laughed. 'I don't think they do that for family hatchbacks. But Jo, we'll make this a top priority. We'll find out what it's about.'

'Yeah... I am a bit worried,' she added. But honestly, that was an under-statement. This was horrible. Every journalist expected some hassle but industrial espionage and feeling unsafe... she had not signed up for that. But... her reporter brain was also thinking – *I've really rattled someone. There's a story here.* 'So, what are we going to do about the story?' she asked.

'I'm not sure yet.'

'Can't wait too long,' Jo reminded him. 'It's Friday tomorrow.'

'No, I know that. But don't bother writing up the Canadian stuff yet. Get to bed early, sleep on it, we'll brainstorm in the morning, see how this girl on life support is getting on, see what line the other papers are taking.'

'Fine, see you tomorrow.'

'Likewise. Goodnight, Jo.'

'Goodnight.' She stayed on the line to hear the click of Jeff hanging up, appreciating how much calmer she felt now that she'd spoken to him, and then she dialled the number of the friend who knew a lot more than she did about computers, viruses and internet espionage.

***

'Hello?' Bella said on picking up.

'Hello, you, it's Jo. Are you still up?'

'Of course I'm still up, it's not even 9.30 yet, what kind of a wuss do you think I am?'

'That's my girl. How's work and everything?'

'Everything's good. And with you?'

'Well, I've had better days: my exclusive for the week has gone tits up, I slapped Simon, oh, and my work computer is being bugged.'

'Your work computer's bugged?!' Jo loved her friend for immediately homing in on the most important thing.

'Simon deserved a slap,' Bella added. 'I'm surprised you haven't done it before now.'

'Yeah,' Jo agreed, 'that's what I was thinking.'

'Just maybe don't do it again, because lawyers, divorce etc etc. Now, tell me about the computer.'

'It's been slow for weeks, so finally I get the tech department in to take a look at it and they say my email's being forwarded somewhere else and, basically, I'm being spied on.' Jo was surprised to feel a lump press up in her throat as she said this. 'And that's quite scary really.'

'Bloody hell,' was Bella's reply. 'But look, don't feel too paranoid. It happens a lot. For a cheap day rate, you can hire out a technical assistant to do the work and if you've got access to someone's computer, bingo. Try not to get too freaked out, there's some poor noddy sitting in an office somewhere in Bombay, probably, who has a mountain of your spam to sort through for whatever it is he's after. He's only getting paid a few quid, so he probably won't look properly and may never find it anyway. But you know what?' Bella asked.

'What?'

'I'm quite impressed. You must have rattled somebody's cage. For a change,' she couldn't help adding. 'Am I allowed to tell Don? Or shall I get it leaked to *Media Guardian*?'

'Tell me what?' Jo could hear Bella's husband asking in the background.

'Oh, thanks, I'm so reassured,' Jo said huffily.

'No, honestly, keep me up to speed with what your techies are going to do and if I can think of anything better, I'll let you know... Any chance it's anything to do with the company... you know the one?'

It struck Jo as slightly strange that Bella didn't say the name out loud on the phone.

'Why aren't you saying who?' she asked.

'Well, just being ultra-cautious. You know, if your computer's being bugged—' she didn't end the sentence, but the implication was there. Her phone... why shouldn't they bug her phone as well? This thought gave Jo something of a jolt. There really was a story here and maybe she did have to be much more careful.

'Quite a lot of chance, I'd say,' was Jo's answer.

'Well, well.' There was a pause while Bella took this on board. 'Do you really think it's them?'

'I've reported before on this kind of injection, you know, and generally positively. But obviously, I'd be the person with a very big interest in a new one. Maybe they've been keeping an eye on me ever since it was launched, who knows?'

'That's not on, is it?' Bella replied. 'Maybe we will have to look into this. I'll call your mobile, Jo, is that OK?'

Abruptly Bella hung up and seconds later, Jo's mobile began to ring.

'Mobiles are harder to bug these days,' Bella explained.

'You don't think we're being a bit over the top?' Jo asked.

'Better safe than sorry.'

Before Jo could ask what on earth she was talking about, Bella added: 'But we should act sooner rather than later.'

'Act? And just how can we act? Call the police?'

'No, no, no,' Bella said. 'We act by calling a virus security review at their headquarters. I could let them know that there's a deadly new hard drive disease on the loose and that I need to get into their offices tomorrow night to update their systems and make sure they can be defended against it. You can obviously be my assistant and we'll have a little snoop around the files while we're there.'

'Bella, I thought you didn't want to get involved with stories on... er... this company?'

'I didn't, but they've bugged your computer!'

'I don't even know that yet.'

'It's pretty likely, though.'

'Suppose so... but isn't what you're suggesting... against the law?'

'The law? I'm not sure the law has really caught up with the technology in this area. OK, we have to hang up now. We mustn't be on for longer than forty seconds.'

'Really...? You're worrying me now.'

'I'll call you tomorrow with details. You can be my temp, OK? Everyone has temps these days, even the Houses of Parliament. The fact that there isn't more terrorism and industrial espionage carried out by temps is a mystery to me.'

'Scaremonger!' It was Don again, heckling. Bella was going to tell him all about this as soon as she put the phone down, Jo knew it.

'Don can't act on this info yet—' Jo said.

'No, no, of course not. I'll tell him my livelihood is at stake, that always shuts him up. Come with me tomorrow, we'll have a rake about and see what we can dig up.'

How could Jo refuse an offer like that? It would be Friday, Simon would have the girls, she'd be at work late, but then she could join Bella afterwards for a search of the Quintet files.

'All right, you send me the where and when. And I'll see you tomorrow. Now you get back to that nice husband of yours.'

'Oh, I will. Are you having an early night?'

'I *should* have an early night,' Jo admitted. 'But instead, I'm going to get changed and go out to meet my favourite chef.'

'Really? You do realise that us old ladies need our beauty sleep,' Bella teased.

'Oh shut up, Bella!' was Jo's reply. Although it was after ten on a Thursday, with a mountain of shit to shovel tomorrow, she wanted to see him. She wanted to have a little bit too much to drink and some distance from Simon, the birthday party and her worries about Annette.

'Rock on, girl,' said Bella, sounding more than a little jealous, which made Jo feel better.

She always knew she was doing the right thing if Bella was jealous.

* * *

Spiral-patterned, figure-flattering, knee-skimming: she loved the cheap dress she'd put on to go and meet Marcus. Just before she stepped into the nightclub he'd called from, Jo fluffed her hair and pressed her lips together to smooth out the latest application of lipstick. Even if it was the dark, 'ageing' one because she hadn't had a chance to get the flattering pink Tilly had recommended.

Jo bought a ticket at the door then paid to have her coat checked in. She hurried through a twisting wallpapered corridor and came out into the packed, smoky space of the dance floor. She'd never been here before, but she could appreciate immediately that it was nice: relaxed and groovy. Lots of young bodies swaying together to something... hip-hoppy? Jazzy? Soulish? She was far too old to know.

Slides were being projected onto the dancers and one of the walls. Images of trees, leaves, bubbles, sky, clouds made it feel all the more dreamy. She began to shuffle through the bodies, looking for Marcus. 'Sorry, excuse me...' But people made way without the slightest murmur. They smiled, they waved, they said 'hello there', and let her pass. This wasn't London. This wasn't a nightclub. She'd obviously landed in some bubble of happy hippie heaven. Or then again maybe everyone was on drugs.

Marcus couldn't be found, so she took sticky stairs up to the mezzanine that curved right around the dance floor. It was busy up there too, bodies packed into groups, both standing and seated in small booths. Jo made a circuit, not able to stop herself from noticing how young everyone was.

Boys in jeans and tight T-shirts with wispy beards, girls wearing the bare-shouldered tops and tight high-waisted skirts.

But down there, at the table near the small, raised stage, were three grey-haired men drinking bottles of beer. She leaned over the balcony a little further to see if she could spot anyone else older than her. Look at the barman! She could be that boy's mother! She felt a hand slide over her back and round her waist, so she turned, hoping it was Marcus and not someone she'd have to tick off for being so forward.

'Hiya,' Marcus said before kissing her hello.

'This is fun,' she told him, breaking off from the kiss. 'But I can't stay too late.'

'We better go dance then,' was his reply. He put arms round her back, pulled her in and began to sway. 'My friend, Jed's band is just about to come on.'

'Oh, you're friends of the band, are you? Were you on the list?' she teased. 'Did they have your name at the door? Did you get out of paying the 50p entry?'

'If the doorman only charged you 50p, then he must have fancied the pants off you,' Marcus teased back, offering her his bottle of beer.

'Fancied me? The old granny, when there are so many gorgeous young things here!'

'You're hardly the oldest person here.'

'You're right – I've spotted some grey-haired groovers down there.' She pointed and Marcus's eyes followed her finger.

'That's Jed's dad,' he explained.

'Jed's *dad*!' she groaned.

'Stop it,' he insisted. 'I'm taking you downstairs for a drink and a dance – to cheer you up.'

They went down hand in hand. Several bottles of beer later, she was pushed up close against him on the dance floor, beer in one hand, her chin resting on his shoulder, his hands round her waist, their hips bumping together. Vaccinations, Simon, work problems – they'd all drifted from her mind. She'd joined the forever young people in the happy, hippie bubble. Her eyes were fixed on the ever-changing slide show on the wall, and her body seemed to be following the jazzed-up samba music just as easily as if she'd been brought up in Brazil, which was kind of ridiculous as she was a late-thirties London working mum whose idea of a good night out before Marcus was a lively dinner party, hosted by somebody else.

Astrud Gilberto was singing something about needing someone to samba through life with her and Jo found herself humming along.

She let her eyes close as she danced, savouring the realisation that she hadn't felt so free, so careless and vaguely irresponsible for a very long time.

'You feel good,' Marcus whispered against her ear. Any moment now she was going to take her chin from his shoulder and kiss him on the mouth. Brush against his lips, push her tongue into his mouth and taste him once again. But she was enjoying the moment before that to the full.

13

FRIDAY: 8.50 A.M.

Jo switched on her computer as usual, but today she half expected it to explode or shrivel into a pile of dust.

But no, it ground lazily through the start-up procedure, just as normal. She wasn't going to send any emails, obviously, not if they were being snooped on, but she'd decided she would check through the inbox, in case something interesting had come in overnight.

She scanned through quickly: press releases, press releases, some notes from friends and colleagues. An email from her mother reminding her about lunch on Monday and hinting there was 'something' she wanted to talk about. Hmm, now what could that be? She'd Vacu-sacked Dad and packed him into the cupboard? She'd shrink-wrapped all her belongings and couldn't find them? Or maybe a full-on lecture about why ex-husbands should never be slapped? Yes, that was more likely, given the circumstances.

Oh, something from the anonymous emailer. Jo's curiosity wouldn't allow her to pass that one by without taking a peek inside.

She clicked it open to see another newspaper cutting. It was just a small paragraph from the *Evening Standard*, which had been scanned onto the page, about a generous donation six months ago by Wolff-Meyer to the historical pathology archive of the London and Middlesex Hospital. There was no further explanation and no accompanying message, so Jo failed to see what this could mean. Historical pathology? Pathology of the past?

Tissue samples, slices of infected brain... diseased corpses. It was a bit too early in the morning, especially after last night, to be thinking about this sort of thing. She closed it up and went on down her list. What did Green Tony want? Jo opened the email from him and read:

Urgent, urgent! Give us a call as soon as yr in. Will try yr mobile 9 a.m.

The next name on the list hadn't attracted her attention straight away but now that she was reading the sender's name properly, she scrambled to open it. An email from:

sav.tyler@hotmail.com

could only be a good thing, couldn't it?

Jo could hardly contain her rising excitement as she read:

Dear Jo Randall,

I try to read your paper every Sunday and I always pay close atten-tion to what you are writing about. You are always thorough, well-informed and don't hesitate to tackle the difficult stories other papers shy away from.

I know of your interest in an interview. I know I have taken a long time to make a decision, but I've decided I would like to speak to you. Tony will contact you to make the arrangements.

I look forward to meeting you,

Savannah Tyler

Jo resisted the temptation to throw both arms in the air and cheer. Finally, a break, a great big break! She punched Tony's mobile number into her phone. 'Hello, you know why I'm calling, don't you?' she said before he'd even got out his hello. She lived for moments like this. When all the other crap seemed to evaporate and something truly brilliant was about to come off. Spikey would wet himself with joy.

'Hello there, Jo,' Tony replied. 'Looks like it's all systems go, then.'

'I've only got one question for you, Tony,' she said. 'When? And hope-fully your answer is: "today".'

'Today we can do.' See? Sometimes it really was this simple, sometimes you didn't have to beg and scrape and whinge and plead and twist twenty different arms all at the same time.

'OK, is she at home? Am I going to do her at home in her lovely eco-house? Say yes and I will be there in the time it takes to U-turn my car and hightail it up to Oxford.'

'Yes, you are to meet her at her home,' Tony replied. 'She's there all day and is just waiting for me to call her back and tell her when you'll be there.'

'You are a wonderful, fabulous man who deserves to win hundreds of seats in the next election and I love you,' Jo gushed. 'OK, let's go through the details.'

Jo told him the ground she planned to cover with Savannah and gave him the name of the photographer who would probably be used.

Then Tony informed Jo of what Savannah wanted to talk about and was prepared to talk about. He also gave the warning: 'Nothing too personal, Jo, I just want to make that clear again. She will really back off. She's stormed out of telly interviews for that kind of thing, so she'll slam the door on you. She is a very private person.'

'Do we know anything about her personal life?' Jo coaxed. 'No partner? No kids? No immediate close family? Where was she born, brought up? What's her past?'

'The stuff on record is: no partner, no children. Savannah was born and brought up in Argentina,' Tony told Jo. 'Her mother was Argentinian, her father British, worked over there. I can't even tell you if they're still alive, because I don't know.'

'Brothers? Sisters?' Jo asked.

'No details on that.'

'Did she study in Britain?'

'No. Schooled in Argentina. Went on to study chemistry in Madrid. Her working life, mainly as a research chemist, has been divided between Britain and abroad. She now lectures at Oxford University part-time and is a party activist the rest of the time.'

'Hmm. Any company names she's worked for?'

Tony gave an emphatic 'no' to this. 'Look, this is still an interview,' Jo reminded him. 'Not a party-political broadcast. She's going to have to give us something.'

Tony uttered a deep sigh. 'Jo, just go and meet her,' he said. 'I'm not going to interfere any more. You're both big girls, perfectly capable of looking after yourselves and getting what you want from this. So, maybe you should just sort things out between you. She'll soon tell you which questions she doesn't want to answer and you're far too charming to be flung out of the door, aren't you?'

'Charming? *Moi*?' was Jo's smiled reply to this. 'OK. Stop worrying about me. I'll be fine. We'll get on like a house on fire. I'm going to send the photographer round right now, so we're not disturbed later... and, well, what can I say?'

'"Tony, I owe you a debt of undying gratitude"?' he answered.

'Tony, I owe you a debt of undying gratitude,' she repeated. 'Or at the very least, a fine dinner on my expense account.'

'I'll look forward to it.'

'Oh and you have to go by train to Oxford and by bus to her house. That's the deal.'

'W-what???' A reporter on assignment without her car... no, no, no. Her car was her mobile office. Tony just said goodbye and hung up.

'What's all this?' Jeff was hovering at her elbow. 'Photographers?' he asked. 'Being undisturbed? Aren't you aware your big story of the week is being scuppered as we speak?'

'I am fully aware of that. Good morning to you too, Jeff. But right now, I've no idea where to take that one next. I'm desperate for a flash of inspiration there. But...' She swivelled her chair round, taking an appreciative glance at the much higher than usual boots she was wearing under her boring old work suit. It was probably a mistake, as soon as she wore heels, she could guarantee she would get a job at the top of a mountain – in fact that was probably where Savannah lived... somewhere miles above sea level, inaccessible by car or suede high heels.

'But,' she repeated to Jeff, 'I didn't think I'd need to ask you whether or not to arrange a photo to go with our exclusive Savannah Tyler interview.'

'Really?' This was said quietly, eyebrows raised as Jeff pulled up a chair and drew it close.

Their knees bumped together for a moment, but they knew each other well enough not to have to apologise for that, he just moved slightly to the side. His large notepad came down on her desk, he pulled his pen from his shirt pocket and began to take notes. He was the only man she knew who could make writing look macho. He used a fat silver biro, with his work-man-like hands and pressed down hard.

'She's expecting me at her home just as soon as I can get there,' Jo said, finding it hard to rein in her enthusiasm. 'I'll send the snapper we use in Oxford to take pictures while I'm on my way, so the whole thing should be wrapped up by early afternoon.'

'This is really good, Jo. One nice thing to talk about at conference. Meanwhile everything else is going tits up. By the way, take a look at this.'

She clicked onto her email and scanned down to the anonymous message.

'I thought you weren't using your computer any more. In fact, I thought you had to go and make a report about all this to the tech department.'

'Ah yes, well I'm bit busy today and tomorrow. It'll have to wait till Tues-day. Anyway, I'm just looking at my email, I'm not sending anything.'

'So what's that all about?' He looked at the note: 'Pathology department benefactors?'

'Why would a pharmaceutical company be interested in a pathology lab?' she asked.

'Maybe they were just being charitable,' Jeff ventured.

'Charitable!? This lot? Who, by the way, are my number one computer bugging suspects.' Jeff raised his eyebrows at that, but Jo continued, 'There's something going on there. Are they checking up on samples from ill people? Are they monitoring samples? Are they trying to find out what people die of? There must be some sort of research going on. Is there anyone we know who can make some calls?'

'Who sent you the email?' Jeff asked. 'Don't they know more?'

'Ah well...' Jo maximised it so that the anonymous, no-reply address was revealed.

'An anonymous email? You want me to jump through hoops for someone who won't even leave you their name. Maybe it's a red herring sent by your computer spies. Maybe you should just delete it and concen-trate on the stories we do have, rather than worry about the ones we don't.'

'All right, all right.' He did have a point. 'Keep your hair on.' But Jo had every intention of following up this lead.

'What about the rest of your department?' Jeff asked. 'Have they managed to put anything together yet this week?'

Over Jeff's shoulder, Jo could see Dominique and Aidan coming in through the office double doors.

'They're getting on nicely, but you can ask them yourself,' she said.

Dominique gave a cool, upbeat appraisal of how her stories were going. Made it sound like she'd done as much research as a NASA scientist. The wind farms report was filed and when Jeff told them a double-page spread was likely, both Dominique and Aidan looked suitably pleased.

'I'll file the asthma and pollution story shortly,' Dominique added.

'Remind me of that one again,' Jeff said, which prompted an ever so slight sigh from Dominique: 'We've put asthma league tables, region by region, alongside air pollution league tables and got a lovely match.'

'Oh yes. Aidan? Anything else to add to the list?'

Aidan was hanging his jacket over the back of his chair in his usual way, but Jo thought there was something of a flush to his face this morning. He'd either run to get to the office on time or he had some good news.

'Well, I wasn't going to say anything until—' Aidan began.

'Oh, go on,' Jeff prompted him. 'Nothing a news editor hates more than being kept in suspense.'

'Well—' Aidan sat back in his chair and almost seemed to be enjoying his moment in the limelight, 'I might have something interesting on Savannah Tyler – but I won't know until this afternoon.'

'Something interesting like?' Jeff's pen was hovering above his notebook.

'I haven't been told. Just "something very interesting". My contact has promised to give me a call later.'

Jeff couldn't help shrugging his shoulders. He'd heard it all before. Junior reporters desperate for a scoop, talking up every tiny nugget of information they could glean. Nothing went on his list until it was more than a 'something'.

'OK, good stuff,' he encouraged Aidan. 'You keep in close touch about this. But try and hurry it along if you can, because Jo is interviewing Savannah today, which is a big story for us. Any added extras would be most welcome.'

Jo watched the slight eye-widening going on. Dominique and Aidan were a little in awe, and more than a little jealous that she had finally pulled this one out of the bag.

'She's agreed to a full chat?' Aidan asked.

'Well, I'll see when I get there,' was Jo's answer.

'At her house?' he added.

'Yeah.'

'Apparently, it's amazing. Totally eco, of course. Should be really interesting.' He sounded so enthusiastic that, for a moment, Jo considered inviting him along. It would be a kind, generous thing to do. Wouldn't it?

But no. Sorry. She wanted this one all to herself.

'I need to look up all the back stories on her, then I'll be off,' she told Jeff. 'What's the word on the girl in the coma?'

'Not in a good place, but stable. So verdict is, we can't do anything negative about vaccines unless we have a cast-iron story and even then it can't make people frightened of the vaccine. So, take your time. You'll work out how to play it, how to write it. Just try and do it by the end of the day.'

She shot him a sarcastic smile: 'Thanks. I'll have plenty of time to read the papers, do the research and make the calls on the train.'

'Train?!' he asked.

'Yup, that was part of the deal. I have to travel there and back by train. Savannah, as you might imagine, is just a teeny bit anti-car. And I have to take a bus to her house.'

'And you've agreed to this?' Jeff asked, smiling. 'Just take a cab and get it to drop you off on the corner,' he said. 'She'll never know.'

'That's hardly in the Green spirit, is it?'

'She's quite something, isn't she?' Aidan threw in.

'Savannah?' Jo asked.

When Aidan nodded a bit too dreamily, Jo couldn't help adding: 'Yes, certain men seem to fall quite helplessly under the spell of Savannah... and fortunately our editor is one of them.'

14

FRIDAY: 10.35 A.M.

The train to Oxford was peaceful, soothing even, after the obstacle race she'd endured to catch it. On board, Jo made calls as best she could. Anxious to make sure that Nettie was OK, she put in a call to Simon and was surprised to receive something of an apology from him. Annette was fine, he reassured her and he wouldn't do anything like this again, not without full consultation.

Once she'd offloaded a bit of her 'I should think so too' indignation, she decided to call a truce, so she could pump him for any useful pathology contacts. Then she'd phoned or left messages with all the medical people she could think of, worrying away at where the vaccination story should go next. She was also trying to find out if anyone could tell her more about the London and Middlesex Hospital pathology lab.

But as Jeff had warned: anonymous email was dodgy. If Wolff-Meyer was spying on her, couldn't they also be sending red herrings her way?

The three messages she'd had so far from this one source were printed out in a file in her bag. She took the pages out and spread them across the table. There was the cutting about the first whooping cough victim, Katie Theroux. Then there was the story about Dr Taylor almost struck off for giving single injections, then the snippet about the pathology lab donation.

Katie and Dr Taylor were both genuine. And the lab donation story checked out too. Someone was trying to guide her in a certain direction.

She folded the pages back into her file and turned to the other bundle of papers in her bag – printouts of all the available Savannah Tyler news stories. There wasn't much, considering how well known she was becoming. Some news coverage of early protests: 'Oxford Greens block roads to demand cuts in traffic,' 'Hands off our parks,' that kind of thing. Whatever Savannah was involved in, there was always a big photo of her – hardly surprising because she looked so striking.

Jo took several minutes to do the 'woman to woman' appraisal: Savannah was unusually tall, she had a slim figure and long, pale brown hair, rather radically streaked with white at the front, which she tended to wear tied back in a ponytail or up in a messy bun. She had a taste for floaty dresses, sturdy boots and exotic knitting. In all the photos, she was wearing long, elegant cardigans over dresses, or patterned woollen coats, everything buckled and belted, with scarves and chunky necklaces. Her face was one of those pale, sculpted wonders, which always looks fabulous in photos: high cheekbones, grey-ish eyes and a wide mouth. Apart from the white streak, she looked about five years younger than her newspaper-stated age of thirty-seven.

The later cuttings were all reports on speeches, events or appearances she'd made on TV. As Jo knew, she'd never given a personal interview.

Most of the articles were straight:

Greens call for huge investment in public transport.
A Greener way ahead for schools.

But there were mocking pieces as well:

The Barmy Tree Army

and the inevitable:

Will this Green Goddess lure the voters?

Jo had already discussed the 'Green Goddess' nickname with Jeff.
'Do we have to call her that?' she'd asked.
'Er, yes, I think you'll find that we do,' Jeff had replied.

'It's so tacky and so obvious.'

Jeff had just tilted his head to the side and said: 'Yeah, well, so are we.'

'No, we're not,' she'd insisted. 'We're a family newspaper.'

'Hmm, we still like to be tacky and obvious, though.'

'Please, couldn't we just try something a bit different? Green Queen? Green Dream?'

'Let's see what your angle on her is. That might give us a better head-line. Jo, I will look into it,' he promised. She must have looked unconvinced though, because he'd added, 'I will personally supervise the sub in charge of the headline if it makes you happy. How about that?' Then he'd shooed her out of the door to go and catch her train.

* * *

Once she was off the train, the bus took her efficiently through the centre of Oxford. The sun was out after a shower of rain so buildings and pavements were gleaming. Jo spotted ancient stone archways smothered in green and purple climbers, tiny leaded windowpanes, shop fronts which didn't look as if they'd changed since Victorian times, signs for cream teas on every corner, but soon the bus was moving to the other side of town where the buildings grew smaller in scale, then became two-storey houses lining the roads.

'This is it,' the driver told her, pulling up at what had to be the last bus stop in town where the houses ended and a wide, old-fashioned English common opened out.

Jo had already checked her directions and knew she had to take the first left turn, walk for five minutes, then third on the left and she would be there – at number 59.

Walking down a small road of single-storey cottages with bright doors, flowers and decorative pots in the front gardens, number 59 wasn't hard to spot. The cottage at the end of the lane was the most cheerful and the most bizarre. It was so close to the stile beside the grassy common that maybe it was once the gatekeeper's house.

Obviously, Oxford planners were open to new ideas, as she doubted that a home like this would be allowed in her patch of London where the regimented rows of terraced houses looked so exactly the same.

Her first impression was of rampant, overgrown greenery. The front garden was full of plants, bushes and two fruit trees. There were pea plants clambering up over the wooden fence, and the garden sloped down from the house in raised beds, densely planted, not just with flowers, but also with potatoes, runner beans, raspberry canes, and plants Jo couldn't identify. Two window boxes were filled with herbs.

But the most extraordinary thing about the little house was its roof. The other cottages in the street had dark slate tiles, but the whole roof area of number 59 was planted in grass that had grown long and tufted, apart from the area of sleek solar panels.

Jo had barely set her hand on the wooden gate when the front door opened and there was Savannah calling out a cheerful 'hello'.

From where Jo was standing, Savannah, at the top of her sloped garden and the two steps to her front door, looked enormous, completely out of scale with this dainty cottage. How could someone so tall live in such a small house?

'Jo Randall?' Savannah asked in a clear, unaccented voice. 'Come in. Have you had a good journey? Were my directions all right?'

Answering 'yes', smiling, doing the shaking hands thing in the cramped lobby at the top of the steps, Jo assessed this woman. She was even taller and more handsome in real life, with her striking face and dramatic flash of white hair, today partially tied back with a jewelled clasp.

She had dry brown hands and an assortment of silver rings that clanked against Jo's own when they shook hands.

'It's so good to meet you at last,' Jo said, and meant it. Savannah's dress of choice today was pale green and flowered, with a deep V-neck. Over it she wore a long pale green cardigan. The effect was casually glamorous. There was a flat seashell round her neck on a slim leather string and her face, bare of make-up but gleaming with moisturiser, was strong with a shapely nose, those soaring cheekbones and a friendly smile.

She held onto Jo's hand, warmly and told her, 'I've been wanting to meet you for a long time. I like what you do. I like the way you make complicated issues easy to understand and you always question everything.'

'Thank you.' Jo smiled at the compliment then followed Savannah into a bright sitting room, all white with big pot plants, a leather sofa, crammed bookcase and interesting things on the wall.

Dominating one entire side of the room was a huge, framed photograph of Earth taken from space.

'That's fantastic,' Jo commented, pointing to it.

'Get up close,' Savannah urged her. 'Everyone loves to look at it. It's amazing what you can see, so many colours and the brilliant blue. It's incredible. There's something about seeing Earth from space, which makes it overwhelming, impossible to understand. Planet Earth. My mission's to protect it, of course.' She delivered this line with a throaty giggle. Jo went over as instructed to take a closer look.

'It's wonderful. Where did you get it?' she asked, deciding that she had to have one. The girls would love it.

'A friend of mine's an astronaut.' Savannah laughed, as if slightly embarrassed by this revelation.

'Really? Who?' Jo asked.

'Er – I don't think I can tell you.'

'So soon into the interview and already you're not answering my questions,' was Jo's smiled response.

'Ha ha, very good. No, it's just I don't think he's meant to hand out prints. They're all property of NASA, or the CIA more likely.' More smiles. 'But he came back from his first mission a total convert to my cause. Because when you're in space you realise we're on a tiny blue planet filled with life in this vast, empty wilderness. No one can comprehend how. Or why. But anyway—' she stopped abruptly. 'Mysteries of the universe aside, how about a cup of tea? Whatever you'd like, I'm sure I'll have it. Come to the kitchen with me.'

Jo followed her through a doorway which had been extended to the height of the room.

'Was the photographer OK?' she asked, looking around. Fortunately, the ceilings in the cottage were higher than she'd expected, so Savannah, who must have been at least six foot two, didn't have to stoop. In fact, her posture was upright and graceful for such a tall person. She moved calmly, purposefully. Serene strength. Those were the words that sprang to Jo's mind. With the height, the face, the bright knitted clothes and the silver accessories, Jo was reminded of photographs of Native American chiefs.

'The photographer was fine,' Savannah said, opening a cupboard entirely filled with boxes of tea: green tea, black tea, herbal tea, loose tea, bagged tea. As she'd said, every taste in tea could be accommodated. 'He photographed me outside in the garden, then out on the common. He asked if I could wear something green...' she gestured to her outfit. 'So, all the usual, really.' She flicked a smile, lifted the cover from something that looked like a hi-tech version of an Aga and set a full kettle of water on the surface.

'What's that?' Jo asked.

'This is my electric stove, run off the panels on the roof.'

'Right. OK, let me get out my notebook and recorder,' Jo said. 'So, solar panels, a grass roof, an electric stove. What else is different about the house?'

'Oh, loads of things,' Savannah replied. 'You've got to come over here and see my eight-bin system for a start. This bin is for bottles, then there's newspaper, plastic, metal, compost, cardboard, batteries, bits and pieces I'd like to keep and use again... oh, and the last one... that's for rubbish, so I hardly ever use that.'

Jo looked at the row of four small metal bins on the floor and the four bins suspended above them on the wall.

'That's a lot of bins,' she said. 'Do you have to take everything to the recycling place yourself?'

'On my bike? Yeah, some things, but the collection service is getting better.'

'On your bike?!' Jo tried to picture this, wondered if she should get the photographer back to capture it.

'How are you going to convince people to have eight bins?' Jo asked. 'I haven't got room in my kitchen for eight bins.'

This elicited a deep sigh. 'Why are people always so put off by the *inconvenience* of sustainable living?' Savannah asked. 'When global warming really gets under way, that's going to be much more inconvenient: catastrophic floods, storms, heatwaves, the collapse of the rainforests and so on.'

'Right... well...' Jo didn't want to wade right into the environmental lecture yet. 'So, eight bins. Good. What else is different?' she asked again.

'There's lots of non-toxic paint and non-toxic varnish, although I'm quite into leaving surfaces bare: waxed wood, wax-sealed plaster, I like to think of it as Italian *palazzo* style.

'The insulation under the floors and in the loft is made of wool, plant fibres, even old newspaper articles,' she smiled at Jo. 'But it's not all back-to-nature. I've got lots of hi-tech stuff: triple glazing, solar panels, very efficient fridge-freezer and washing machine, a top-of-the-range computer... but generally, I like to use old stuff: reuse, recycle and all that. My sinks, my bath, my taps and most of my furniture are old instead of new. Or they're made of things that can be recycled: wood, metal and leather. I steer clear of plastic and that awful MDF stuff.'

Jo looked round the kitchen, trying to understand what was different about it. There was a square porcelain sink under the window with fat old-fashioned taps that caught her eye and the plants, and more plants, on the shelves, on the windowsills, on the kitchen table.

'You still haven't told me what tea you'd like,' Savannah said, reaching up to the mugs.

'What do you recommend?' Jo asked, pulling up a chair at the table. She had decided this should be a woman to woman, round the kitchen table kind of interview. Not a come to my study, sit at the other side of my desk and be intimidated by me thing.

'How about green tea with jasmine?' Savannah answered. 'Enough caffeine to give you a boost without getting buzzed.'

'Sounds good,' Jo said.

So, the tea was brewed in a chipped grey pottery teapot. And the two women sat down facing one another. Jo stacked fresh tapes beside her machine, primed it ready to go and opened with the words: 'So, Savannah, what turned you Green?'

Savannah couldn't help bursting into loud laughter in response to this, but she did finally reply: 'I grew up in the Argentinian countryside. It was a much simpler life, much more in tune with nature than the lives we live over here. My father was English,' she said.

'What did he do?' Jo asked, noting the past tense, picking up the implication that Savannah's father was dead.

'He was a cattle breeder. He had herds of beautiful blue-black animals and I ate steak and drank milk every single day. I think that's why I'm so tall. Like the Masai.'

Jo now recognised the lilt to Savannah's voice. It was a long-eroded Spanish accent.

'Does your mother still live in Argentina?' she asked.

'No,' Savannah said and there was a long pause before she added, 'My parents were both killed in a plane crash. My younger brother still lives in Argentina. He runs the family farm and I go to visit him every year, if I can. He has a wife, three children and never comes to England. He hates towns and he hates to leave his animals.' She gave a little smile at this.

Savannah's parents were killed in a plane crash. How absolutely awful. Dreadful. And, Jo hated herself for the thought, here was her exclusive, human-interest angle. 'I am so sorry to hear that... When were your parents killed?' Jo asked as gently as she could but still felt the uncomfortable harshness of the question. It sat badly with the warm tea, the shafts of sunlight falling onto the wooden table and the sweet pea petals in the vase beside her.

Savannah drew in a breath. For a moment, Jo thought that she wasn't going to answer, might even tell her off for asking.

But Savannah took a sip from her cup, set it down on the table and said steadily: 'It was eight years ago now. They were making a short internal flight in a small plane, they hit bad weather and the plane flew into a hillside. Everyone on board was killed. My mother always hated to fly, so I never like to think of what she must have gone through. It was a very difficult time for me. I was working in Alaska, I felt terribly alone. It was a very — difficult—' Savannah used the word again, while Jo was busy thinking: *difficult?* It must have been hell. Her admiration for Savannah growing by the minute. 'A very difficult time,' Savannah concluded. 'They were lovely people. I loved them so much and I've managed to make some kind of peace with what happened... but I think you can understand why I don't like to talk about it.' She folded her arms, turned her face slightly and Jo was reminded once again of Native American chiefs.

'No, I do understand that totally,' Jo said. 'I wasn't aware of your loss and I didn't mean to go there. It was just the sequence of questions— Why don't we get back to you?' But Jo knew she would have to probe the parents' deaths again later on – and ask for a photo of them. 'I left Argentina aged eighteen,' Savannah began, 'to go to university in Madrid and since graduating, I've divided my working life between Britain and abroad. That's the potted guide.'

'What do you work as?' Jo followed up.

'I'm a research chemist.'

'Erm... yes, that's what it says everywhere, but I wanted to find out more about that, especially as... it doesn't sound terribly—'

'Green?' Savannah offered.

'Well, no.'

'I do choose who I work for very carefully,' was Savannah's response. 'Also bear in mind, the information I learn is useful and I'm often telling my employers things they don't want to hear.'

'Right.'

'I've worked with oil companies, chemical companies, pharmaceuticals.'

'What's your area of expertise?' Jo asked.

'Well... how to put it simply? I'm often looking at reactions – how things react with each other. The short and medium-term effects. Personally, I've always been interested in the long-term effects. But no one's going to pay me to do that kind of work, because no one would make enough money out of it. The seventh generation from now – that's the one we should be thinking about. The Native Americans had a saying "How will this affect the seventh generation?" That's the kind of long-term view we should be taking.'

Jo felt a little flash of vindication. See! She was dealing with a chief. A chief who was skilled at turning the answer to every question into a party-political broadcast. 'When did you get involved with the Green Party?' she asked next.

'About ten years ago,' Savannah replied. 'It was something I'd been thinking about for a long time, then I met some people who really impressed me and I signed up.'

'Has it affected your job?'

'In some ways, yes, in other ways, no. I do less research work now anyway. I don't need the money because my parents left me some and I don't need the status. I like to spend as much time as I can on the cause. Furthering the political cause.'

'Furthering your political career?' was Jo's next question.

'Well...' Savannah graced this with a laugh, 'I don't see it like that. I would love there to be a Green MP. It's ridiculous that there isn't one, all to do with our antiquated voting system. But I'm not personally ambitious, I could make a much bigger salary, much bigger splash out there in my own line of work. But I'm very passionate about Green politics and if the best thing I can do to further the cause is stand as an MP, then that's what I'll do.'

'So, you don't think you'll enjoy it?'

Savannah smiled at this, wary of giving the wrong answer.

'I'm sure it will be an amazing opportunity. But it would be even better to be an MP in a Green parliament, we'd get a lot more done.'

'So, I bet you're dying to tell me what a Green parliament would do,' Jo said.

'Ha, well,' Savannah smiled, 'we're pretty radical, you know. We'd probably do the opposite to any other kind of government. We want a sustainable economy. We want local jobs, local food, local products. Not apples that have been flown by jumbo jet from the other side of the globe. We would encourage you to get rid of your car, but we'd give you great public transport, walkways and cycle paths. We'd tax pollution to the hilt but we would help people to use less oil, gas, electricity and produce less rubbish.'

'I'm a bit worried this means we'll all be working on an organic farm,' Jo told her.

'Would that be so bad?' Savannah asked with a smile. 'Think: clean air, clean water, clean food. Preserving what's left of the natural world for future generations. Finding a way of letting humans live well that doesn't destroy the one and only world we've got.'

'Sounds good but incredibly idealistic,' Jo said.

'You've probably got the Green Gloom,' Savannah smiled. 'People think about what's happening, know in their hearts it can't go on, but feel helpless and depressed. So, they stop thinking about it and carry on.

'But I'm determined to be optimistic. We *can* change. No one can imagine how the future will look. I'm sure if you'd told someone just thirty years ago about how things would be today, they wouldn't have believed you. They'd have thought you were being totally idealistic: everyone will have a mobile phone, houses will be worth hundreds of thousands of pounds, there'll be a huge supermarket in every single town, the internet will connect people all over the world in seconds—'

'Can't we have all the hi-tech stuff, all the convenience of modern life and still be Green?' Jo asked her.

'I think mainly yes with a bit of no,' was Savannah's answer. 'I mean, downloading music, films and information is much more environmentally sound than producing CDs, DVDs, textbooks, carting them all over the world, then dumping them in landfill.' She was gesturing so enthusiastically with her arms that her bangles were clanking: 'I do understand that people want progress and to make their lives better,' she said. 'But we've got to move forward in a clean, sustainable way.

'I'm a scientist,' she added. 'I hope science can make things better, not worse. There are a lot of green scientists because they're out on the front line, measuring the ice-melt, pollution, or the ways medicine could be harming as well as helping.'

'Hmm.' Jo was scribbling hurriedly, but thought she heard something pointed in that final remark.

'You've reported on vaccinations before, haven't you?' Savannah was asking her now.

'Yes. I'm looking into Quintet this week. As well as you,' Jo replied.

'Quintet should be interesting,' Savannah said.

'I'm hoping you'll be interesting too,' Jo added. 'Got any good vaccination contacts I should tap?'

'I'll think about that,' was Savannah's reply.

No one ever trusted a journalist all the way.

So often an interview was like a card game with the interviewee giving careful consideration to a question before setting strategic answers down on the table.

'So, how did you get over the Green Gloom?' Jo decided to pursue this line.

'Nature will have the last laugh,' Savannah said with a smile. 'If humans do too much harm, we'll wipe ourselves out and solve the problem. The Earth will carry on, for several billion more years anyway. I'm just hoping some eco-warriors up a nice clean mountain in New Zealand will survive and human life can start again in a better way.'

'This is supposed to cheer me up?!' Jo exclaimed. She drained the last of her green tea from the mug. 'Would you like to show me round your house and maybe the garden?' she suggested. 'Gives you a chance to talk about the Green lifestyle you've adopted.'

'Good idea.' Savannah seemed to draw a fresh burst of enthusiasm from this. 'But remember, no point having a nice house if you haven't got a decent planet to put it on.'

'No.' The Green Gloom was definitely descending on Jo.

* * *

The beauty of Savannah's home was not in any overall 'wow' factor, but in the details. It was comfortable and all the small things had been very well done. The floor was wooden and polished. The doors, skirting boards and window frames were bare wood, stripped back and waxed. In the sitting room was a small leather sofa, creased and well-worn, sheepskin rugs, a corduroy beanbag, a knitted blanket folded at the edge of the sofa. This was a place to be comfortable and cosy.

'I thought you'd be anti-sheepskin and leather?' Jo asked. 'You know, animal rights and all that.'

'I'm a cattleman's daughter, remember, I think a bit of organic, sustainable meat-eating is fine, and once it's killed, the entire animal should be put to good use. No waste. Waste is the crime.

'In New Zealand there's a zero-waste policy,' Savannah added. 'Everything in a household bin is sorted, separated and recycled. Plastic is being stored in underground mines as a resource for the future. I try to have faith that it will happen over here, eventually. I'm not sure why Britain is taking so long to catch on. Fishing, gardening, bird watching, hill walking are all great British traditions. Deep in their hearts, people love the countryside. But their souls have been suburbanised and they've forgotten.'

There was a faded colour snapshot on the mantelpiece in a frame. Jo guessed it was a photo of Savannah's family. Savannah saw what she was looking at and explained: 'My parents and my brother, Alfredo – Alfie. I think it's funny how my dad looks so Argentinian and my mum looks English.'

Jo picked the photo up and looked closely, wondering when was going to be a good moment to ask Savannah if she could borrow a snapshot of her parents. All three adults were squinting against the sun so it was hard to make out their features clearly. Savannah's father was a tall, strapping man in a pale blue shirt, with dark hair, a deeply tanned face and one arm across his son's shoulders.

Alfredo, even taller and more handsome, was grinning with his hand on the waist of his petite and delicate mother. What looked so English about her was the wide-brimmed floppy straw hat and the finely printed puff-sleeved dress.

'My mother was a wonderful gardener,' Savannah explained. 'She kept a fully stocked kitchen garden with vegetables, fruit trees, flowers and herbs. She always wore a gardening hat to keep the sun off her face, but in the summer, her shoulders, arms and legs would turn as brown as a nut. She was a small woman with a huge laugh, Mama. She—' but Savannah broke off. 'Well, anyway.'

'I'm so sorry,' Jo said and placed the photograph back on the mantelpiece. As she did, she saw a tiny frame up there, round and intricate, no bigger than a 50p piece, with a baby's sunny, smiling face inside.

She assumed it was one of handsome Alfredo's children and she would have asked, but Savannah was already at the front door, offering a tour: 'Organic vegetables first, then the compost heap, the insulation and the solar panels.'

* * *

It took almost an hour, and afterwards Savannah insisted Jo stay for lunch, even though it was Friday and Jo had nothing but endless work ahead of her.

Over a seventeen-ingredient salad – everything from the garden – and an organic, free-range, happy hen omelette, Jo turned her tape recorder off, put away her notebook, with the spare snap of Savannah's parents inside, and chatted with something approaching normality.

'Have you given much thought to what it will be like to be an MP?' Jo asked.

'Some days,' was Savannah's answer. 'I don't take it for granted... but we'll know if it's going to happen soon. Obviously, I'll be the only Green and I'll be very busy. But then Finlay might join me soon afterwards. You've heard about him?'

Jo nodded.

'So how Green are you?' Savannah put to her. 'Am I allowed to ask that? Or is it like therapy and only you get to ask the questions?'

'Well, I suppose it is like therapy. I like to at least pretend I'm neutral,' was Jo's reply.

'But are you really? The things you write about every week indicate a certain sympathy with us, surely?'

'You could say that,' Jo admitted with a smile.

'Ooh... a politician-like answer.'

'Sorry, am I being cagey? I don't want you to think you're getting an easy ride.'

'But I'm not! Look how severely you've twisted my arm to get that picture out of me.'

Jo laughed.

'I'd just like to know if you've ever thought of going Green, politically.'

'I'm very impressed with what you're trying to do. OK?' Jo decided on finally. 'That's all you're going to get out of me and that's strictly off-the-record!'

When lunch was over, Jo ordered a taxi to take her to the station, despite Savannah's pained expression.

'I've got to rush if I'm going to make the 2.30 p.m.,' Jo told her, justifying the decision.

The women shook hands on the doorstep and Jo wished Savannah well. 'I really hope you do it,' she said. 'It'll make the House of Commons much more interesting. I'll be watching on the night.'

'Thank you,' Savannah said and held her hand. 'I look forward to reading your article... I hope!'

* * *

As soon as Jo was in the taxi, she rang the news desk. Jeff's deputy, Mike, picked up and, not caring if it was bad form, insubordination or whatever, she said a pleasant hello and asked if she could talk to Jeff. It was simpler this way. She didn't want any of the Chinese whispers or misunderstandings that speaking to Mike often resulted in.

'So, what have we got? Anything interesting?' Jeff asked as if she'd been to some rubbish press conference that might make a paragraph on page 22.

'Anything interesting?!' she retaliated. 'More like everything interesting.

Her parents were killed in a plane crash, she was devastated, never got over the loss. She's full of radical ideas: taxing rubbish, building mines to store all our waste plastic in, paying everyone in the county a "citizen's income"—'

Jeff interrupted with: 'Yes, but have you found out about her love life?'

'Jeff! Please, can't we try and stay just a tiny bit on the highbrow side with this?'

'Maybe, Jo, but I've got some very interesting information for you. I've just had a call from your little protégé, Aidan.'

'Oh, yeah?'

The taxi was making good time. She was being whizzed through side streets and would easily catch the train.

'He has some names and dates you might like to write down if you've got a free hand. Are you in a cab?' Jeff asked.

'Yes.'

'Well, you might want to tell the cab to turn around and take you straight back to Savannah's house.'

'Aha.' Why did she have a sinking feeling about this? A feeling that it was going to get messy. Had Aidan unearthed some boyfriend who had moaned about what a terrible lover she was and now she was going to have to go back and ask Savannah about it? How horrible.

'Stop your cab,' Jeff reminded her.

'Just a sec then.'

The driver was grumpy about the request and complained that he already had another job lined up in the centre of town.

'Look I'm sorry—' She took the few moments necessary to promise him extra money on top of the fare.

'Right,' she resumed the conversation with Jeff. 'What have you got for me?'

'A birth certificate,' he replied: 'Felix Martin Teyhan. Father, Philippe Teyhan, engineer, mother—'

He didn't need to say it, she already knew: 'Savannah Tyler, scientist.' Oh God. She felt the lurch in her stomach as she guessed what was coming next.

'And a death certificate,' Jeff said, but with understanding, not any sort of 'wow what a great scoop' note of triumph in his voice: 'Just twenty months later. Felix Martin Teyhan, respiratory failure. Post-mortem and toxicology report, no abnormal indications.'

'Jesus. Not even two years old. Where and when did this happen?'

'Felix was born in Wainwright, Alaska. His death took place there as well,' Jeff said, adding the dates. 'She said she'd worked in Alaska.' Jo was doing the maths. Eight years ago... Savannah's parents had died earlier in the same year. How absolutely dreadful, no wonder Savannah never talked about any personal stuff. Presumably she and the baby's father had split up as well. There hadn't been any photos... any indication... and that was when Jo recalled the tiny picture frame. The small smiling face was Felix: Savannah's dead son.

15

FRIDAY: 2.30 P.M.

When the taxi pulled back up in front of Savannah's house, Jo took a moment to collect herself. She had done this hundreds of times before, knocked on someone's door hoping to be granted an interview about something very difficult. But it never got any easier. In fact, she sometimes thought it got harder. When she was younger, she had been hungrier for the story, less concerned about how her interviewees might feel. Now, she cared a lot more about people, she worried about doing the right thing and about trying to tread the fine line between public interest and the right to privacy.

As she paid the taxi driver, she could feel the thud of her heart in her chest and the dryness of her mouth.

She tried to run the words of one of her very first news mentors through her mind: *'People always think they don't want to talk about difficult things, but they do. They really do. You've just got to make them realise that.'*

She knocked on the door and waited for it to open.

Savannah's face registered surprise to see Jo there again. 'You could have phoned,' Savannah said, 'I'd have answered any follow-up questions on the phone, you know.'

'I'm sorry. I'm really sorry to be here again like this. But I just took a call from my office and they've sent me back to see you. Someone has spoken to another one of our reporters and passed on some information...' Jo took a deep breath and broke the news: 'Savannah, I know this is really hard. Awful. But would it be possible to speak to you about Felix?'

Savannah was still looking Jo directly in the eyes; she didn't break the look, so Jo saw the change in expression take place. The friendliness, the colour and the relaxed happiness left Savannah's face almost immediately, to be replaced by a look of shock and hostility.

'I am so sorry,' Jo added. 'I can't imagine anything worse.' Jo was a journalist, yes, but she really, really liked this woman and as a mother, had absolute sympathy for her. Also, Jo understood that Felix was the clue to Savannah. The unreachable, untouchable part that had been missing before. Before this revelation, there was a whole side of this woman that Jo and presumably the public didn't really understand. How could someone so striking be single? Someone so motherly be childless? How could someone so nurturing be alone? Now it all fell into place.

Savannah was a mother who'd lost her child: the worst kind of bereaved, someone living every day with a hurt that would not heal.

Savannah took her eyes from Jo's face and looked up to see the taxi making a three-point turn in the narrow street and heading off, as instructed by Jo. Best to make it look as if she was sure Savannah would invite her in again, she'd decided.

'You're going to miss your train,' Savannah said in a voice that sounded dry and strained.

'I know. I've already missed it. But I couldn't possibly have spoken to you about this on the phone.'

'No.'

For a long moment, Savannah stood on the doorstep looking lost. She gazed past Jo into the distance and seemed to slump, shrink up inside her vibrant outfit. Jo waited, realised she was holding her breath.

'OK,' Savannah said finally. 'Maybe you should come in again.'

Jo didn't dare make a reply, she knew from experience that even the wrong tone of 'thank you' might land her back outside again on the wrong side of a slammed door.

Savannah stood in her sitting room, still looking dazed. Jo kept a distance, didn't presume to take a seat.

'How did you find out about this?' Savannah asked, but not harshly, with some genuine curiosity mixed in with her obvious shock.

'One of my juniors has a contact in Oxford, I think. The news desk has acted on his tip and done a records search in Alaska. They've found the certificates relating to Felix. I didn't know this was happening and I'm so sorry,' Jo added. 'You've been very open and honest with me about the things you wanted to discuss. I don't like the way I'm forcing your hand here. But you're standing for election and everyone's interested in you. Look,' she went on, gently, 'I can totally understand why you didn't want this public, but stories like this have a habit of coming to light.'

'He's not a story,' Savannah said, voice strained to the verge of tears now. 'He was my son.'

'Savannah, I'm so sorry...' Jo repeated. She was within reach of the little picture on the mantelpiece. 'Is this him?' she risked.

Savannah nodded.

'He's beautiful.' Jo looked at the picture more closely and saw that what she'd taken for bright rosy cheeks were in fact cheeks covered with a vibrant rash. She put the frame down gently.

'Why don't you sit down... can I make you some tea?' Jo offered.

'Maybe—' Savannah wiped a tear from her cheek with the back of her hand. 'I've no idea how to play this— This wasn't part of the plan.'

'The interview plan?' Jo asked and Savannah nodded.

'Why don't you tell me a little bit about Felix and what happened and we'll work out together how to fit it in with the rest of the interview.' Jo wasn't being dishonest. 'I promise I will treat you the way you deserve to be treated about this.'

Green Queen's dead baby heartache

was, yes, probably going to be the headline and top item of the story, but there were ways of playing it, nuances, other elements she and Savannah had control over. This great big revelation didn't have to run away with them or be the only story.

'What tea would you like?' Jo asked.

'Just a glass of water, please.'

* * *

When they were seated on comfortable chairs in the sunny sitting room, facing one another, Jo gently coaxed the story from her. Savannah took regular sips of water, as if that made it any easier.

She told Jo about moving to Alaska for an important research job, meeting Philippe there, then deciding to have a baby together and succeeding surprisingly quickly.

'Felix was beautiful to us. Of course he was.' Savannah couldn't meet Jo's eyes very often as she talked. She preferred to settle on the middle distance, on the little picture of her baby, anywhere but on the person asking her these hard questions.

'But soon after his birth,' Savannah continued, 'it was obvious that he wasn't in good health. He had terrible eczema, he had bouts of wheeziness, his face would puff up and we couldn't work out what was causing all these problems. I know much more about it now: multiple allergy syndrome. But I didn't know anything then, and the doctors we took him to, time and time again, weren't much better.'

'Eczema is hell on earth for a small child,' she explained. Jo, once a nurse, knew this. 'As soon as he could co-ordinate himself to scratch, that's what he did. He would rub his hands up and down against all the sore, weeping patches of skin, rub his legs against the seams of his clothes, zips, cot bars, whatever would give him some relief from that terrible itching. He would wake up howling with frustration three or four times a night and we'd find him in blood-stained Babygros. There were open sores on the back of his knees and other folds of his skin that never healed.

'He had this scary look about him – puffed-up eyes, dry, dry skin; he looked middle-aged. Not like a baby. There was the awful knowledge of pain in his eyes. And something else, something I interpreted as: "why can't you help me?" That was what I read every time I looked into his eyes.' Savannah took another sip to steady herself.

'He was in and out of hospital,' she continued. 'Wet wraps, overnight bandaging. His little hands tied to his bed so scabs would have a chance to form. Dear God, it was inhumane. Not just for him, for me and for Philippe too.

'I would have done anything, given anything to make him better.'

She took a long drink from the glass, leaving just an inch of water at the bottom.

'You're a mother,' she directed at Jo. 'You know. You know how much you love and sympathise, empathise, and how much you worry.'

Jo gave a nod.

'My skin broke out in sympathy. I never got a full night's sleep, because Felix didn't. I was barely rational. Of course I couldn't go back to my job, Philippe was struggling to cope with his. Maybe if I'd had some peace of mind, I'd have been able to find out more, do some research, understand what caused his condition, what was making it worse and what might have helped to make him better. But instead, I was busy all day and most of the night trying to cope with him. Just trying to exist from one week to the next. We had good doctors, but they ran out of ideas, which made me feel helpless.'

Jo heard the gasp in Savannah's voice, as if she was struggling now to hold back tears.

'It's OK,' she soothed. 'Just take your time. Shall I bring you more water?'

Savannah nodded.

When Jo was in the kitchen, above the sound of water rushing from the tap, she heard Savannah blow her nose. Not for the first time, Jo wrestled with misgivings about the ethics of her job. There was no doubt this was a great story, but it was also a private misery. A misery she felt uncomfortable intruding on.

But real good did come out of tragic and terrible stories. She knew that it did. Changes were made, actions were taken – a powerful story had a way of exposing uncomfortable truths. Savannah would make a great MP, Jo was certain of that. Maybe this story – harrowing though it would be for Savannah to tell it, for her to see it printed in a paper – would help to get her elected. She brought the glass through to Savannah, who took a drink and continued.

'There's so much more help now about allergies. Now, I'd be told about a special diet, cutting out high-allergy food, I'd get advice on washing powders, anti-allergy clothing, bedding, non-toxic household cleaners. There are even special cotton padded pyjamas with built-in mittens and feet you can buy to soothe eczema. All this sort of thing might have given him a chance... But then again, maybe not. Maybe he was over-exposed to toxins in the womb. The job I was doing when I was pregnant, the chemicals I was in daily contact with. Looking back, it was utter stupidity.' Tears were falling down her cheeks, hanging from her chin and then dripping noiselessly onto her shoulders, but she managed to carry on talking in an almost normal voice.

'It's what's known as the cocktail effect. No single exposure that someone can point a finger at and say "it was the lead", "it was the mercury" or whatever. But both Philippe and I were working with all kinds of *slightly toxic* things all the time. We were living in a brand-new apartment with new carpeting, new kitchen, new furniture, lots of electrical equipment. I mean, it seems so obvious now that this was totally the wrong environment for a hyper-allergic baby, but I didn't know any of that and neither did Felix's doctors.'

'Did your parents have the chance to see Felix?' Jo asked.

'Luckily, yes,' Savannah managed. 'We were in Argentina for the two Christmases we had with Felix. Philippe's family came over to meet him as well.

'The plane crash happened in April and we took Felix to Argentina for a third time for the funeral. Philippe went back to work and I stayed on for many weeks because Felix seemed to improve there. I thought it was the sunshine, the drier climate, but you know, maybe it was because we were outside a lot and we weren't living in a brand-new box laced with chemicals.

'Felix was walking,' she went on. 'He was talking well for a one-and-a-half-year-old. He loved the cows. He loved his uncle; he had two little cousins to play with. The fact that Felix finally seemed to be getting better was the thing that I held onto, that kept me going through that terrible time.

'But of course Philippe missed us and we missed Philippe.' Savannah was twisting the paper tissue between her fingers into a tight strand. 'So, after eight weeks or so, we packed our bags and went back to Alaska.'

Without much of a pause, in as steady and matter-of-fact a tone as she could manage, Savannah delivered the words: 'We'd been back five days when Felix had a fatal asthma attack.'

Jo felt a shudder pass over her at those words. She didn't like to think of what that meant: watching your baby suffocate to death.

'In the hospital?' she asked, almost not wanting to know.

'He died at home, before the ambulance could get to us,' came the steady reply. 'We were in a remote place and it was on another call fifty miles away.' Savannah wasn't crying any longer. Her eyes had taken on something of a glaze as she fixed them onto the photo of her son on the mantelpiece.

'At night?' Jo probed.

'No. On an ordinary Tuesday morning. An ordinary, sunny Tuesday morning. Philippe was at work. Felix was with me... And you should understand that I fought to save him.' Savannah was rocking slightly, eyes still fixed to the mantelpiece: 'I did everything our doctor had taught us, everything the ambulance operator talking at me down the line calmly, over my screams, could recommend. But when I saw—' and here her voice faltered, seemed to dry up for a moment, before she managed: 'When I saw he was going, he was really going— I had to stop. I had to put the phone down, stop battling and just hold him for one moment longer. Let him go in some sort of peace.'

Jo felt tears of her own slip down her cheeks. 'I'm so, so sorry,' she whispered. Her instinct was to go over to Savannah and put an arm round her. But she worried about whether it would be welcomed. And then her mobile intruded on the moment.

Jo fumbled in her bag and didn't even look at the number before switching it off. No matter if Spikey himself was on the line, he would have to wait.

Once Savannah had taken another drink and wiped at her face again, Jo asked about the years that followed. Savannah described it as just managing to survive, although her relationship with Philippe hadn't. 'It was too tough,' Savannah tried to explain. 'I felt as if I had a right to grieve for longer than him, to grieve more than him because I'd lost more people.

'I blamed myself and I thought Philippe blamed me. I couldn't comfort him and he couldn't begin to comfort me. I'd lost my child and I'd lost my parents. I'd lost my past and my future all at the same time. I don't think it's an exaggeration to say I was out of my mind with grief.' Something of a challenging look came with this explanation. Jo read it as 'but don't you even dare to suggest in any way at all that I'm out of my mind now'.

'In the end, part of getting better was to move on from each other. Move on from the daily reminder of what we could have had... and didn't,' Savannah explained.

'Is that when you came to Britain?' Jo asked, wondering how long it must take after this kind of grief, before a person could even begin to function normally again.

'I got here eventually. A sort of roundabout way... over years,' Savannah said with a little smile. 'Lots of different jobs and some interesting people on the way. It was quite hard to be taken seriously again. After you've been out of the industry for some time, and you've been treated for – big surprise – depression. People can recover. They don't "get over it" but there's room in the mind for all this. It just needs to find its place. I did finally come to terms with my new world order.'

Savannah's phone began to ring, as it had done every so often throughout the afternoon, but this time the answering machine in her bedroom didn't click on automatically, so she apologised and went through to the other room to answer.

When she returned, they were both conscious of the time. It was approaching four o'clock. Jo had to get back, although she hated to break this talk off now.

'You probably need to go, don't you?' Savannah asked her.

'Well, you know, yes, I do,' Jo admitted, 'but I don't want to rush off from you like this. It's important to me to know how you'd like me to play this interview.'

'Ha,' Savannah smiled. 'I don't suppose I can get you not to mention Felix at all though, can I?'

Jo shook her head.

'I'd rather you'd not known anything about this. That was the way I wanted to play it, that's why I've avoided interviews, so I haven't had to deny anything or lie to anyone, I feel as if I've been hijacked by you.'

There was a prickle in her voice that Jo was immediately alert to.

'Savannah,' Jo began, 'you're standing for election, you're probably going to win and become Britain's first Green MP, every news editor in London is digging about in your past, inviting old contacts out for drinks, trying to squeeze some little nugget out about you. This was going to come out, believe me. I'm glad it's me who's found out about this first. And I hope you'll be glad too.'

But Savannah sighed and added: 'I know what you're going to write. The whole, secret heartbreak/tragedy of Green Queen... Goddess... whatever,' she snorted at the thought. 'What I actually stand for, the changes I'd like to see, the revolution in the way we live, will be squeezed down to two paragraphs right at the bottom of the page.'

'It won't. I absolutely promise you, it won't,' Jo insisted. 'In fact, I'll use those very words: that you didn't want people to know about Felix because you thought it would only take away from the message you're trying to get across. That you only spoke about it because we found out.'

'And you know what,' Savannah added, 'I think it's sexist. That somehow what I do, what I stand for isn't nearly as important to your paper as the fact that I've lost a child. I mean, obviously that's hugely important for me... but for people who don't know me, how is it relevant? Why should it matter? Would you put such emphasis on this if I'd been a man? Felix's father?'

This was a fair question. Most papers were sexist, some less so, some more so. But they were reflective of a society that was still sexist. Jo and Bella had once done a survey of two newspapers for a month to find out how many negative stories there were about modern mothers versus fathers. It had come out as twenty-eight to three.

'Savannah,' Jo spoke slowly, choosing every word with care, 'the public doesn't know you. You're single, you're childless, you live alone, you're a scientist politician. It's hard for people to place you into any sort of context. This is about your human side. This is the part that will help people to really get you, connect with you. They'll have great sympathy for what you've gone through and respect that you've tried to keep it private. And they'll understand that your son's allergies are an important part of your commitment to make the world a cleaner, safer place. It'll work out fine,' Jo insisted.

'Well, OK, it will probably be over-important for a few days and then something else will happen, you'll fall off the news pages and people will remember your story, but back in the right context. The other important things about you will come back into focus. Trust me just a bit,' she added with a smile, 'I've been doing this job for a long time. I know how it works. Well, some of it anyway.

'And don't think your interview will be the only thing in the paper on

Sunday. I've got a whole whooping cough/vaccine story to investigate and some celebrity is bound to have done something incredibly scandalous that will take all the attention away from you,' Jo said with a smile.

Savannah glanced at her wristwatch, then told Jo: 'It's 4 p.m. on Friday afternoon. How the hell are you going to get in a whooping cough investigation between now and tomorrow afternoon?'

'I have the feeling I'm going to be up all night,' was Jo's reply.

16

FRIDAY: 5.48 P.M.

As soon as Jo had passed through the double doors into her newsroom, she sensed a strange atmosphere.

There was the slightly hushed, heads down, every desk filled, hard-working Friday evening feeling, but also something else, something bubbling under. Everyone was so smartly dressed, for one thing. The news desk were all in white shirts. She saw Jeff's best suit jacket hanging over his chair.

It wasn't until the features editor crossed her path, thirty yards ahead in a red silk dress, that Jo twigged.

'Director's drinks... 6.30 p.m. onwards, Jo. Something tells me you've forgotten,' came Mike's voice as she walked past his desk.

'F-u-c-k,' she spelled out to him. 'I've got to write the whole Tyler interview up now. Then I'm going out on something important tonight. I can't do director bloody drinks. Why the bloody hell have they picked a Friday anyway? It's our busiest night.'

'Number one reason: it's drinks with the whole group, not just us. Number two reason: you think they give an arse? So long as we're bringing home the bacon, who cares what our office hours are.'

'Jo?' Jeff walked up to his chair, having heard most of this exchange, 'I know you're snowed under, but you have to come for half an hour, shake the relevant hands.'

'Why didn't you remind me?'

The answer to this question was too obvious: 'Would you have come back in here if I'd reminded you?'

'No.'

'Well then.'

'Jesus, I've not got anything to change into—'

'Go and speak to Tilly. She'll have something,' was Jeff's suggestion.

'You think I can just slink into something from the fashion department's rail?!' she spluttered, but still, the compliment was nice.

'Go and ask her... she did a piece on fat birds last week. There might still be something left from that,' he teased.

'Your charm, sir, knows no bounds.'

'Go away!' He flapped his arms at her. 'Sort this out. We're both far too busy to even talk about this. But Savannah's good stuff, is it?' he asked just once again. They'd already spoken about it on the train.

'Top of your list, matey, unless you've got anything better.'

'No. Good, good.'

She had turned to walk away but still caught Rod's teasing: 'Jeff! Jeff! There's a beetle in my drawer... Please can you come over here and stun it with your big strong arms?' which provoked some raucous giggles.

Oh ha, bloody ha.

* * *

Tilly was at her desk in something diaphanous, pale grey, chiffon and perfect.

'You look fab,' was Jo's opener.

'Oh dear and you look like you've just got off the bus,' Tilly said back.

'Train, actually. Four-twenty from Oxford. I've got a whole interview to write up for the front page tonight, plus some late-night detective work. Somehow, I'm supposed to do cocktails in between... and no one reminded me.'

'Oh dear, oh dear, and have you come to me in the hope of a rescue remedy?'

'Well, I mean, if you had something I could dress this suit up with a bit?'

But Jo looked down at her boxy navy-blue jacket and matching trousers without much inspiration. Even if she took off her shirt, added jewellery, a lacy bra and strappy heels, she wasn't going to transform into Kate Moss.

'No. I can't rescue that suit, Jo,' was Tilly's verdict. 'But don't worry, There might be something in the storeroom for you. We did "best dresses on the high street" last week, as modelled by our readers, and I don't think they've gone back yet.'

Jo followed Tilly into the little room, kept locked at all times, from which the fashion pages were created.

'Over here in the bags.' Tilly summoned Jo to a pile of carrier bags, taped up and labelled, ready to be returned to the shops that had lent the clothing.

'Open those up, we're bound to find something,' Tilly instructed.

Everything that Jo got her hands on was hideous: clingy, satiny – there was even a dress in pea-green and mushroom.

'Look, I don't know about this,' she told Tilly. 'Is it so bad if I turn up in my suit? I'm working, I'm at work, for Christ's sake. Isn't it enough that I'm going to be working till God knows when – without any overtime, by the way – without having to dress up in cocktail gear as well?'

'I agree with what you're saying,' Tilly replied. 'Yes, it is ridiculous, yes, it is a pantomime, yes, they should pay us overtime... But... it's a *free* drinks party with our bosses' bosses, you're there to meet and be met, to impress everyone with your charm. Plus, you're single now and you should be allowed to enjoy these rare treats to the full. Now what about this? This was my favourite of the whole shoot.'

With a flourish, Tilly lifted a shimmery pink and gold number from its carrier bag resting place and shook it out.

'Size 12,' she added with a degree of practicality. 'Most of us are paying the nanny overtime so we can stay on for this bloody party for free,' Tilly threw in. 'Welcome to free market economics! If our bosses treated us the way we treat our nannies, we'd all be a lot happier. Wouldn't we?'

'That's really very nice,' Jo took a closer look at the dress, reaching out to touch the fabric.

'Careful,' Tilly warned. 'There's a reason it costs £54.99 and not £540.99.'

'Ah.' The pale pink dress was synthetic satin, the kind nighties had been made of when she was a child. The stuff that made your hair stand on end when you whipped it on and off. If you did it in the dark, you could even see sparks.

Over the pink was a clever golden layer made of a coarse, striped nylon mesh. It felt horrible but still, the dress looked lovely.

'And we've got the shoes.' Tilly dangled pale pink strappy sandals from one hand. 'And somewhere in here, the coat that we photographed with it. Go on, try it on. It looks lovely.'

Jo got out of her suit and shirt, not minding that Tilly would be able to appraise her workaday white bra and shorts.

'At least you're shaved, that's all I'm going to say.'

'Ha. Well, I was out on Wednesday night.'

'And not going to get out much again, if you carry on wearing pre-pubescent underwear.'

'I thought it was back in fashion. I'm sure I've read all about "the new modesty" on your bloody pages.'

'Yes, well, that's fine if you're eighteen. Not if you're thirty-eight.'

'Thirty-five!' Jo exclaimed. 'I don't look thirty-eight. Do I?'

'Yes, darling,' Tilly trilled, 'Of course you look thirty-eight. You wrinkled old crone!'

Once Jo was in the dress, Tilly was delighted with the effect.

'Your fairy godmother has triumphed again. Now shove your feet into these shoes, let me give you some of my free sample Dior apricot lipstick, since you still insist on wearing that purple gunk, and we shall be off to the ball.'

'What size are these shoes?' Jo asked, scrunching her toes hard against the unyielding pointy ends.

'A five, unfortunately, but you can do it for half an hour, can't you?'

'Maybe,' Jo replied, very uncertain.

* * *

The room, spread out over the penthouse of the building with a wall of windows overlooking sparkling city lights and London's most exclusive marina, was already packed by the time Jo and Tilly arrived.

Jo was trying to squeeze through to the long table laid out with food and drink but she knew almost everyone in the room, so it was impossible not to keep getting drawn into those irritating mini-conversations an event like this was all about.

'Yes, we think the redesign is working well, ah, here's Jo. Her pages have a much more unified feel to them now, don't they, Jo?'

'Um, er yes... hello, Floyd, how are you?'

Several minutes of listening to the chief sub, aka most boring man on the planet, and his ideas for the sport pages followed, before she could politely say: 'Look, I'm just on my way to the bar. I'll catch up with you later.'

But before she made it there, a champagne glass was nudged into her hand, then a hand at the small of her back began to steer her towards the circle of frighteningly important looking bigwigs in the centre of the room. 'Nice dress,' Jeff said.

'Yeah, watch it though, it's pretty scratchy and if I get too near a naked flame – *whoosh*, I'm going to be toast.'

He gave an amused smile then added: 'The directors want to be introduced to you.'

'Oh, joy. Let me just have a few sips of this first.' She gulped at her champagne, despite the difficulty of rapidly swallowing the small, sharp bubbles.

'I wouldn't do that,' Jeff warned, 'or else you're going to burp at the Chief Executive.'

'OK,' she told him, when her glass was half drained. 'Lead me to my execution.'

* * *

The little party drinks and little party snacks were so deceiving. You thought you'd eaten, when in fact you'd only had twelve beads of fish egg on a Ritz cracker, and you thought you'd only had a drink or two, when in fact you'd necked down four cocktails with the alcoholic equivalent of a bottle of vodka.

Meeting the paper's Chief Executive, which she had done several times before, provided just the sort of panic-inducing situation where all the drinks party disasters could happen at once.

She gulped hard at the champagne and tried not to actually pant with fear as Jeff led her over.

'Jo Randall, how do you do?' The steely-haired, immaculately dressed *über*-boss was holding out his hand at her. 'You're much prettier than in your byline photo.'

'Oh n-n-n-no, not really,' she stammered.

'Get a new photo taken of her immediately,' he said to the assorted execs standing in the circle around him, in his inimitable: 'Am I joking? No one can be sure, so rush to do what I'm asking anyway' power trip.

Jo was now in the inner circle, the boss opposite her, various executives, the Finance Director and Spikey all crowded around.

'Busy week?' Boss was asking her. *Terror, terror.*

'Yes, as always,' she smiled, winningly she hoped, praying he wouldn't ask the follow-up.

'So, what are you working on?' No luck, he'd asked it.

'Oh well, I'm not sure if Mr Skinner would want me to breathe a word,' she said with a smile. And look, she'd managed to refer to her editor publicly as Mr Skinner, not Spikey. That was a good thing.

'Feel free,' Spikey volunteered. 'I'm sure Mr de Groote isn't going to tell our rivals.'

Oh, thanks a lot.

'Well,' she began. 'The whooping cough story. We'll have some new angles on that. Also, the prospective Green MP, Savannah Tyler, we've got a cracking first ever, up close and personal interview with her.'

Spikey chipped in with: 'A real team effort. Great story.'

Team effort?! Crap! Her effort and a tip, a mere tip, from Aidan.

'Oh God, I hate that woman,' was de Groote's magnanimous reply to this. 'Bleating on about recycling and taking the train. She just doesn't live in the real world, does she? I'm not giving up my car for anyone. Took delivery of the classic Aston Martin DB-7 the other day. Probably does about two miles to the gallon.' He gave a cheery guffaw. Did he expect them to agree? Did he expect them to politely join in dissing their week's exclusive? There was her own editor nodding in agreement. Savannah was sliding right off the front page as they spoke.

'So whooping cough,' de Groote added. 'Tell me what you're doing on that. No, I'll tell you—' he gave a big grin: 'Inform every parent in the country to go out and get their child vaccinated with the new injection made by Wolff-Meyer. I've got a lot of shares in that company.'

A tray of canapés swung in front of them and she picked the one nearest to her and bit in, hoping he would go away and pick on someone else.

What the hell was this? She'd attempted to bite the canapé in half, but now she realised she had a piece of crumbly oatcake in her mouth and between her teeth was the stringiest bit of ancient smoked venison, or maybe even smoked deer hide, she'd ever encountered. She was trapped. If she let go with her teeth, the remains of the strip of venison would be hanging from her mouth. She couldn't bite it in half, but nor could she hoover the whole thing into her mouth. She would suffocate, not to mention spend an hour trying to chew the bloody thing down.

She was frozen, hand at her mouth, teeth clamped down on this monster, when, of course, the boss asked her another question.

'So where do your ambitions lie, Jo? Going to stay on the news floor for ever, or do you think you'd like to join us up in the stratosphere one day?'

No one needed to tell her that this was an important question. She suspected that she probably would not like to join the stratosphere, she probably wouldn't fit in. But it was bloody nice to be asked and it deserved a careful, well chosen, ambitious kind of answer. Not silence as she wrestled with Grampa Roe Deer.

She moved the oatcake away and sort of coughed the offending sliver of smoked venison into her hand. 'Excuse me, so sorry about that... The stratosphere... I haven't thought about it, Mr de Groote. I enjoy my reporter's job. But the newspaper needs to grow, develop, and I hope I can help with that.' See? Great answer, situation rescued... victory.

Except, the boss smiled, held out a hand to her and said: 'Good, good, well it's been a pleasure to meet you, Ms Randall.'

Oh God! She transferred the oaty reindeer remains to her left hand, which was also holding her glass, making a clumsy mash of things, wiped her right hand hastily and gave it to her boss's boss to shake.

'Well... it's been...' Jo stumbled over her excuse, 'been a p-pleasure to meet you, but I've got a mountain of work to get through tonight... that front-page exclusive isn't going to write itself!'

De Groote made a curt nod.

Come and work in the upper echelons?! Jeeeez, no thanks, can you imagine working for a bunch of arseholes like de Groote every day of your life? She'd rather poke her eyes out with a spoon.

'How did that go then?' Jeff was at her side.

She snorted at him: 'Don't think you have to worry about me being summoned from the news floor just yet.'

'Good,' was his verdict. 'Are you heading back to the office?'

'What do you think? I've got to knock the Savannah piece into some sort of shape. Then, as I explained to you in great detail yesterday, I'm meeting my friend at the Wolff-Meyer headquarters.'

'Maybe you should leave that till next week,' Jeff suggested, possibly feeling guilty at how much work seemed to have piled on to Jo's shoulders.

'But she's already there. This is the best chance I've got to do some serious research,' Jo said.

'Well, just go and join her. Do the Savannah write-up tomorrow. We'll wait for you.'

'Thanks, I appreciate it.' And she really did. 'Is your wife here tonight?' she asked.

'No, I have to talk to you about that—'

'Really? Is she OK?' Jo suddenly worried.

'She's fine. We'll talk tomorrow, post-deadline. After work drinks? Are you staying on tomorrow night?'

'Am I staying on?! I'll probably still be filing,' she replied.

She waved him goodbye and slipped out of the party.

* * *

'You stupid, bloody, fluff-headed fashion twit!' It was no use swearing at the door, it was no use jiggling the handle up and down a hundred times, and it didn't even help to kick the door hard with her size five torture shoes.

The door had been locked. The key was in Tilly's handbag and Tilly was already halfway to Battersea. But Jo's clothes were on the other side of that door. Jo knew this, Tilly had now been informed of it, too, but there was nothing either of them could do about it.

'Just go home in the dress, your clothes are totally safe,' Tilly had told her on the mobile.

'But I'm not going home, that's the freaking point,' Jo had pointed out,

'I'm going to do some subtle undercover work in a freaking pink lamé dress from freaking H&M. Unless you know of a 24-hour suit shop, I'm absolutely stuffed!'

'Oh, just shut up now, Jo, it's not the end of the world,' Tilly had told her. 'Button up the coat, take your disgusting old handbag with you and I'm sure no one will bat an eyelid.'

'Disgusting old handbag?!' She couldn't believe what she was hearing. 'My handbag is a Mulberry bag. It cost nearly a month's wages and *you* told me it would be an investment purchase.'

'I told you to get it in any colour apart from russet,' Tilly snapped.

'Oh, did you? Well... well... so what? I liked the russet,' But she felt winded. All that money and it was the wrong bloody colour! That was bloody fashion for you. It was a game with so many tortuous and complicated rules, she should never even try to play. 'I have to go,' she added.

'I'm sorry about your suit,' Tilly said. 'And it's not really a disgusting bag... I just said that because I was annoyed.'

'Thank you. I like the flipping bag.'

'It's great, really,' Tilly added. But it was no use, Jo didn't believe her. Investment bloody purchase. Who was she trying to kid? It had been in fashion for five minutes, well no, apparently it had been the wrong colour for even those five minutes. And what about all those other investments she was supposed to be making? The pensions plan, the savings account, the rainy-day fund? She had 'invested' in the stupid handbag. Maybe she could resell it on eBay? Just the thought of that made her feel sad. She was joined at the hip to this bag and to the big, battered leather wallet inside it. Jeff had given her the wallet last year.

'Jo, do you realise you've been here four years to the day?' he'd said, casually leaning over her desk.

'Have I?' She'd felt horrified that the time had passed so quickly but it had also occurred to her that generally, she loved her job, and Jeff would probably be celebrating her 20th anniversary here one day. 'Let me go and see what I can find in my freebie drawer to mark the occasion,' he'd added.

'Oh, you're too kind! Yes, I could really do with another baseball cap with the crappy logo of a kids' film that went straight-to-video.'

'I'll look out for one of those, then.'

But he'd returned to her desk with the wallet. 'You're in luck,' he'd said, handing it over.

'You get freebies from Mulberry?' she'd asked.

He had tapped his nose in reply.

'Look, it has room for all the receipts you're supposed to hand in to me slightly more often than twice a year, please,' he'd added.

'Thanks. This is very nice.' She'd looked it over appreciatively.

It matched her bag exactly. Same colour, same leather, same design. What were the chances of that?

17

STILL FRIDAY: 9.15 P.M.

'So, what do I say at the door?' Jo was on the phone to Bella getting the story straight before she turned up at Wolff-Meyer and risked giving anything away.

'Oh, Jo, hello,' Bella gushed with quite unusual enthusiasm, 'I'm so glad you got my message. I could really do with an assistant tonight, there's much more work to do here than I was expecting. There's corruption cropping up all over the interface and we'll be running test drives all night long at this rate.' Ah, this talk was obviously being made for the benefit of someone else in the room with her. Or, who knows, maybe someone else on the line?

'There won't be any problem getting into the building, I'm assured,' Bella added. 'Security have been told to expect Jo Dundas with ID, obviously' – something of a little growl on 'obviously' – 'and they'll bring you up to where I'm working.'

'Right, that's fine. You've caught me on my way out, I'm afraid. Shall I just come like this? Or is there time for me to go home and change?'

There was a pause as Bella digested this. Of course, Jo was supposed to have known she would be here tonight.

'I'd rather you just came straight over, but I suppose it depends what you're wearing, Jo.'

'A pink dress and heels,' Jo replied. 'I'm not even wearing the heels any more because they're such damn agony.'

'A pink dress and heels?' There was something so trilly about Bella's voice that there had to be someone else in the room listening. 'Will we allow that, Mr Mortimer? Yes, Jo – a pink dress and heels will be fine.'

Mr Mortimer? Jo wondered who he was. Bella wasn't bringing anyone. He had to be from Wolff-Meyer. Maybe they were going to have a babysitter all night long. Maybe their plan to snoop round the computer system wouldn't work out at all.

* * *

When Jo arrived at the drug company's glittering headquarters, she was escorted smoothly through reception and down one of the many long marble-floored corridors, then up in a glass elevator to the computer-packed nerve centre, where Bella was already ensconced.

'Hello, nice to see you, glad you could make it at such short notice,' were Bella's words of greeting. Once the security guard was out of earshot, Jo asked: 'What about Mr Mortimer, is he still around?'

'No, no. We're all alone.'

'Look at you,' Jo smiled at her friend. 'And I worried that I was over-dressed for this job.'

'I had a meeting thing before I came here,' Bella told her.

'Aha.'

There she was, the woman determined to take the corporate-computer-systems world by storm, in her latest 'my career is going stellar' purchase: a pale blue-grey tightly nipped-in suit. Vivienne Westwood? Yves St Laurent? Something astronomical anyway. Complicated lilac heels, three inches high, completed the look, along with the two other items of career-girl slick: vibrant red, I'm-here-for-business lipstick and a white blouse so well pressed you could hurt yourself on the edges. The handiwork, surely, of Helinka, the world's most fabulous nanny-slash-housekeeper. Bella ran a hand through her thick brown bob, one of those soft, on-the-shoulder rumpled ones that only very expensive hairdressers can cut, undid the buttons of her jacket and flung her high-heeled feet up onto the desktop.

'It's *Desperate Housewives* meets *Mission Impossible*,' Jo couldn't resist.

'OK, here's the plan,' Bella began, ignoring the teasing. 'Most of the virus checking and software updating is going on over here,' she gestured to two large screens grouped on her left. 'It's mainly automatic, it'll alert me when anything needs to be supervised. So over here' – this meant the two computers on her right – 'we can start looking around. We can run searches for key words, we might be able to find a log of meetings, minutes of issues discussed, that sort of thing. 'But I warn you it's going to take ages because the system is on total go-slow because of the check-up in progress. So, you might as well pull up a chair beside me and I bet you'd like some of my supper.'

With this, Bella unzipped the large, insulated bag at her feet and began putting metal tins up on the desktop, then two proper plates, cutlery and glasses.

'What is all this?' Jo asked, amazed at her friend's forethought.

'This is Helinka's idea of a meal for one. Maybe she thinks I'm pregnant – or maybe she's hoping to get me pregnant, so she has a baby to look after as well as my boys and my household and my hob.'

Bella began to take the lids off the dishes and the tins, releasing appetising aromas into the room. There was even a half-bottle of red, which had been carefully uncorked and then had the cork pushed back in.

'I have died and gone to heaven,' Jo said as she leaned over one of the dishes and inhaled. 'I'm starving, I've had one roe deer canapé since lunch.'

'Well now you can have bortsch, latkes, blinis with smoked salmon, red cabbage casserole, lamb stew with dumplings – just your standard Eastern European evening fare.'

'This is unbelievable.' Jo settled down into the chair beside Bella and began to help herself to some of the food. 'I can't believe you have a nanny who cleans your house to palace standard *and* cooks you amazing takeaway dinners. That is just so unfair.'

'The children go to school and nursery, you know, Helinka needs something to fill her day,' Bella reminded her, spooning creamy pale purple perfection into her mouth.

'I know, but this is gorgeous. And she's such a brilliant cleaner. I totally hate you. How dare you have all the things that every woman wants? My cleaner can't be trusted not to use the toilet cloth to wipe down the cooker and last week she cleaned the bathroom with an entire bottle of £25 shampoo.'

Bella snorted at this: 'Get a new one then.'

'Bottle of shampoo?'

'No, cleaner!'

'You say that – but how do I know a new one won't be worse? And anyway, I like Angelica as a person. She's having a hard time. Her son's in borstal, she's being moved out of her flat by the council...'

'Oh God. Get a new one,' Bella interrupted. 'Helinka might know someone. If you're really lucky, she might know someone like herself: fifty-five years old, fantastic cook, wonderful house-cleaner, grandmother of fifteen, sends half her pay home to her family in Serbia every month.'

'Is Helinka legal?' Jo had to ask.

'Of course she's legal,' Bella tried not to splutter. 'I pay every penny of her taxes. Out of my *net* income, thank you very much, chancellor of the bloody exchequer. Do you know, if she was my groom, I could put her entirely through the books as a business expense?'

'Bastards,' Jo spoke through a mouthful of stew and dumpling. It was delicious, best thing she'd tasted in weeks.

Bella was making a start on the tiny blinis.

'And are you pregnant?' Jo asked. 'Because if you are, I think I should be at least one of the first to know.'

At this, Bella began to laugh: 'Oh my God, no. Three children! Do you think I'm insane?! You know I did do that thing... that probably everyone does at least once. Where I thought to myself "oh, three... three would be nice... a little baby again... it would be so lovely", and I dropped the contraception for a month only to snap out of it in horror. Three!!! What am I thinking?! Have I gone stark, raving mad? Total panic until my period arrived. You've done that too, haven't you?'

'No. I've never done that. I don't recall having sex at all with Simon once Nettie was born. If I did, I've obviously blanked it out,' Jo said.

'Poor old you.'

'And no, two is plenty,' Jo added, in between mouthfuls. If she did very occasionally have just the slightest of pangs when she saw some chubby new baby wrapped up in a buggy, she certainly wasn't going to admit to it.

'Why is everything in tins, by the way?' Jo asked.

'I never eat or drink out of plastic. It gives you cancer, makes your breasts go lumpy or something.' Bella turned to Jo: 'I read it in your paper... in fact, *you* wrote it!'

'Oh yes. But don't believe everything you read in the papers,' she joked.

'I don't... but I generally believe you.'

'Why is that?'

'I dunno, maybe it's the fact you do genuinely seem to have a conscience.'

'Oh, that. It's such a pain.'

'Look,' Bella leaned forwards and pointed to the screen, 'here's our chance to make a little search. What words do you think we should look for?'

'Er, well, whooping cough – or its proper name, *pertussis*?'

'Any refinements on that? The word *pertussis* might give us the kind of archive it will take all night to download.'

'Erm... *pertussis* outbreak? Yes. Let's see what comes up for *pertussis* outbreak.'

'Anything else? We can fit a few words in.'

'I know, give me a sec.' Jo began to unpack the file from her bag. 'Let's put in the name of the first whooping cough victim, because, who knows, maybe they held a meeting about it. We should also put in "Quintet trials" so we can find out what sort of data they have on that. Also, there's this funny message I got...'

She retrieved the anonymous email with the name of the London hospital pathology lab that had puzzled her so much. Although she'd phoned all the medical contacts she could think of, only one had been able to shed a little further light on it, informing her that the hospital had one of the oldest pathology departments in the country and there were samples stored there dating from as far back as the 1800s.

'OK,' Bella began typing:

pertussis outbreak
Quintet trials
Katie Theroux

and

London and Middlesex Pathology Dept

'And we'll confine the date to the last few months or so and "search"...'

Bella hit the final key with a flourish as the screen on her left began to flash.

'Oh, just a minute, something over here needs attention.' She typed for several seconds, then the screen cleared.

'Is this how simple your job really is?' Jo wondered.

'No! This is how good I am at it,' was Bella's retort. 'I'm scanning the entire Wolff-Meyer house system for new viruses and making it invulnerable to everything that we have on our files at the moment.'

'We? Who exactly is "we"?'

'I have contractors, people I use on a regular basis.'

'How is business going anyway?' Jo asked.

'Business is fantastic. I can hardly say yes to everything I'm offered.'

'So why don't you say no?'

'It's against my rules. Why do you think I'm sitting here at 10 p.m. doing this?'

'To do me a favour?'

'Well, yes, there's that, but also, it needed to be done at some point before my big meeting in New York next month. Companies are so wonderfully gullible about computers,' she confided, 'You just put the call in telling them: "we've heard about a systems breach, we'll have to come over and run some extra maintenance," and the business is yours. Nice, long-running, reliable contracts is what I'm after and this one is a beauty.'

'So why risk it for me?'

Bella considered for a moment before replying. 'Your computer being bugged got up my nose, I want to know if they're doing it.' Then she added, 'Plus, I want to find out if this company is as sinister as you think it is. And, it'll really annoy Don if I help you get some amazing scoop he wishes his paper could have had. Why don't you go and work for Don, by the way?'

'On a daily? I'd be mad. I can barely put in the hours and keep my family together on a Sunday paper. Anyway, what's happening in New York?' Jo asked, watching the screen in front of her flicker, the words 'still searching' in a corner box.

'I'm about to be offered some really good work over there, that's what's happening in New York,' Bella told her.

'But you're not going to move, are you?'

'Why not?'

'Well... Don, his job, your work here, your fabulous home, your children in school... all the usual reasons.'

'And if Don had been offered the spectacular New York career? Would you be saying the same things? Or would you be saying, "how wonderful, well done, you, when are you going?"'

'You know I wouldn't.'

'No, I know you wouldn't but other people would.'

'So, you are going?'

'I don't know. We're thinking about it – we being Don, me, and the children. But I'm in that ambitious woman's dilemma: if I take the opportunity, I'll be working flat out and although it will be great, I'll hardly see my family. A big part of me will hate that, and they'll resent it... but if I don't, I'll always wish I had. But why do we do things? Or think we want to do things? I'm questioning my motivation all the time.'

'Are you?' Jo couldn't help smiling. 'You don't strike me as the type of person who spends much time questioning herself.'

'Don't I?' Bella seemed a little hurt at this. 'I spend a lot of time questioning my motives. I wonder: do I want the work over there for the sake of the work alone? Or to impress people? What makes me happy? You know what I always say: *behind every successful woman is a dad who's not that impressed.*'

'And what did you conclude?' Jo was smiling at her.

'We probably won't do it.'

'But you're going for a meeting there next week.'

'Ye-e-e-s,' Bella paused, then confided, 'Don's coming too and we're going to see some schools, but... who knows.'

Jo's smile broadened: *'You're* going, you total liar. You're even lying to yourself.'

Bella seemed to be trying not to grin.

Meanwhile, Jo was trying to bat away the sudden sadness that even thinking about Bella moving away was bringing on. 'Couldn't you train Don up to work for you?' she asked her.

'I'm thinking about that. We might murder each other, though. I mean living together is one thing, working together is quite another.'

'I suppose. How long is this thing going to take?' Jo looked over to the screen again: it was still showing the 'searching' box.

'Depends how much it finds. If there's a lot of info on those subjects, it will take a while. Have a sip of wine, tell me how it's going with you.'

'It's OK, life continues,' Jo said. 'The girls are really well; I spoke to them on the way over here. It's turning into a quite an interesting week at work.'

'Ah ah... about to get more interesting, hopefully. Now, remember, we're on closed circuit TV, so don't do anything too attention grabbing.' Bella's eyes were on the screen behind Jo, where a small box announced:

Pertussis outbreak: 164 items
Quintet trials: 467 items
Katie Theroux: 26 items
London and Middlesex Pathology Dept: 77 items

'You're going to be busy looking through all that,' Bella said.

'So how do I do this?' Jo asked. 'Click on the ones I'm interested in and see what comes up?'

'Yeah, if a restricted access notice flashes up, tell me and I'll see what I can do to circumnavigate.' Bella's voice had dropped low although they were certain the camera was visually spying on them only.

After trawling for a long time through the 'Quintet trials' files and not finding one single shred of anything she could even make sense of, Jo decided to try a different tack. She would scan through the smallest group of files, the Theroux ones. A list of 26 headings appeared before her.

They mainly seemed to concern the employment of a Joan Theroux. She scrolled on down. This didn't relate to the first case of whooping cough at all. None of this seemed relevant.

Instruction of solicitors in employment tribunal brought against Ms J. Theroux

Hmm... obviously Joan had not had a happy time working for Wolff-

Meyer. Sheer journalistic nosiness caused Jo to drag the mouse to the heading and click.

Immediately the words:

restricted access file. Password protected

flashed across the screen. Jo wouldn't have bothered asking for help, she would have moved on down the list of results, except that Bella glanced over and told her: 'Here, let me on for a few moments, I'll try and open it.'

And Jo's curiosity to watch how Bella did it took over.

Bella moved her chair in front of the screen and began working. It seemed to be a long and tortuous process.

'What are you doing, exactly?' Jo wanted to know.

'Temporarily dismantling the restricted access program across as much of the network as I can.'

'Can you do that?'

'Of course, and it's something I'd legitimately need to do if I was checking the spread of a virus.'

It occurred to Jo that there was something a little unsettling about using a computer virus as an excuse to find out about a human virus.

'Right.'

'Here we go... should open up for us now.'

And Jo was back in front of the screen scanning down the page.

Illness leave...

Blah, blah, blah. Joan was obviously fighting the company for the way she'd been treated when she was off. But this was so recent. Why were solic-itors involved already? Blah, blah—

counterclaim...

she was accusing them of negligence... they were accusing her of negli-gence... Jo's eyes hit on the words:

contamination with a laboratory-modified virus

She scrolled the paragraph up slowly to the top of the page.

hazardous working conditions… unsafe working practices

A few more moments' reading and Jo realised what this was all about. Joan Theroux seemed to have become infected with one of the viruses she was working on in the company's research lab in Bedford. But Wolff-Meyer was threatening her with legal proceedings, claiming that she had breached their health and safety guidelines. Her lawyer was arguing that she had complied with all the guidelines but that lab practices weren't safe and had caused her to become infected.

What the hell was the virus? Jo scrolled on through the paragraphs and paragraphs of information but it didn't seem to be listed.

She brought out a notebook, to jot down some of the most important information: Joan's name, address, all the dates she could find. Joan Theroux lived in the village of Lower Stenton in Bedfordshire. Jo knew with conviction she'd seen that address before, not so long ago. With her heart thumping, she delved in her bag for her file of anonymous emails. She took out the printout of the first email, the one about the first whooping cough case.

Katie Theroux – of Lower Stenton, Bedfordshire

The house and the street name were different. But this wasn't a coincidence, was it?

It didn't look like Joan was the girl's mother, but she surely had to be a relative. What if Joan had been infected with a laboratory-modified strain of whooping cough, and had then gone on to infect Katie? Obviously, the strain was different enough to infect children even if they had been vaccinated.

'That must be it,' she said in a quiet voice, feeling the hair rise on the back of her neck.

'Oh, good,' Bella said, but Jo didn't even hear her.

The anonymous emailer who had sent her the first name, who had told her to look into that first case, who had warned her not all whooping coughs were the same, had also given the hospital pathology lab as a clue.

And here, next in her queue were files on that lab. Obviously, she had to look there next.

All seventy-seven headings on the lab were in front of her now. She might as well start at the top and read her way down.

There was just a slight problem: 'It's still saying restricted access, Bella.'

'Really? Must be under a different program.'

Bella battled for some time with settings.

'Maybe I'll have to go round there,' Jo wondered out loud.

'To the hospital? Jo, it's coming up to midnight.'

'Is it?' This was something of a surprise to both of them. 'Well... it's a hospital, there's always someone about in a hospital,' Jo said hopefully.

'Yeah, but it probably won't be someone who knows anything much. Hang on, there must be a way in here somewhere. We could see if something's been copied on to someone and stored in files that aren't so high security. That happens a lot. People copy stuff, paste it, send it on, someone else files it. Let's try that.'

Jo could see this was a game Bella didn't want to lose.

'I didn't really think your hi-tech computer business was all about you sitting in offices late at night, surrounded by supper tins, grappling with restricted access settings.'

'Not sure I thought it was going to be about this, but then your glamorous journalism job is about sitting outside people's houses waiting for them to let you in, isn't it?'

'Not so much these days.'

'I'm going to train up lots of minions,' Bella added. 'Have an empire... but of course I'll be brought in for the really tough cases, just like Red Adair.' When Jo made a quizzical face, Bella explained, 'He ran an oil well fire-fighting business, but still fought some of the fires personally, even in his sixties. Now shut up and let me concentrate. And can you go and pretend to check those screens over there, so we don't look too suspicious for the cameras.'

Long minutes went past. Jo watched the seconds at the corner of the screen stack up to midnight. It was already Saturday. She still had two potentially front-page exclusives to write. Well, make that, she had one to write and one to bloody well find.

Why wasn't she getting this? Katie Theroux has had Quintet, but nevertheless, she catches this different strain of whooping cough from Joan Theroux – her aunt maybe – who caught it in the lab. So, it's something being investigated in the lab – maybe for vaccination development?

And this somehow relates to a pathology department in London that has been given a large donation by Wolff-Meyer.

Pathology, post-mortems, tissue samples – the hospital couldn't have given old samples to Wolff-Meyer, could they? Wouldn't it have needed consent from patients? Relatives? But then, the samples were really old, weren't they? Some from the nineteenth century. They were out of copyright, as it were.

Jo did not like the thought taking root in her mind that if some old diseases could be revived, wouldn't that be an exciting new market for vaccinations? Or maybe it wasn't so sinister, maybe old diseases were simply being studied and used to help formulate new vaccinations?

'Here we go, here we are,' she heard Bella say, 'I've found a copy... Look at this. It's an inventory of everything that the hospital sold to Wolff-Meyer. It includes "a unique selection of brain tissue samples removed from corpses and preserved in wax in the 1800s".' Bella continued to quietly read from the document as Jo came and peered at the screen with her: '"Each comes with full annotations, causes of death, symptoms of illness, age and medical history of the patient. This is a unique medical record of infectious illnesses and other causes of death in London in the latter half of the nineteenth century."'

'Jesus. I thought they just made a donation. I didn't realise they'd bought the contents of the department. How the bloody hell can the hospital be allowed to sell this?' Jo exclaimed. 'Shouldn't it be preserved for the nation?'

'You'll probably find it was a private hospital at the time the collection was made, so now it's the private property of the trust. Probably someone from Wolff-Meyer sits on the board of the trust. Maybe they want to set some old diseases on the loose and sell a few new drugs.'

'I'm trying not to think that,' Jo admitted. 'I'm trying to believe there is a good explanation, that it's good science to look into what was bumping people off in the 1800s and learn from it. Maybe they were hoping to pick up some variations which they could make more effective vaccinations from.'

'Hopefully,' Bella said. 'But I don't think you're going to find out tonight. Look at this,' she pointed.

The words on the screen were transforming into an unreadable numeral code and computer hieroglyphics. 'I think maybe, Jo, as a precaution,' Bella was clicking, dragging, typing rapidly on the screen, 'you should get your things together, but slowly and naturally as if it's all part of the plan and leave the building. Just in case anyone arrives to chat to us.'

'You're joking? What about all that juicy stuff on the *pertussis* outbreak I was hoping to look at?'

'Not tonight, I'm afraid. We'll have to come back another time. I have to be on the safe side, here, I don't think an arrest for breaching security protocol would look so great on my CV.'

'OK, look, I'm packing, I'm smiling casually for the camera. And now I'm all set to go. Glad to have been of help to you tonight, Mizz Browning.'

'Glad you could make it too. We must break into some top security files again soon.'

'Can I ask them to call me a cab, down at reception?' Jo wanted to know.

Bella shook her head: 'Best not. Just leave without a trace.'

'I will phone you, very soon.'

'If I can get this to calm down, I'll see what else I can find for you, OK?' Bella said.

'Thank you, Bella.' And with that Jo headed out of the room in the iron grip of the size five shoes and down the long corridor to the lift.

* * *

Two streets away from the building, Jo had to take the shoes off again. Her feet were already shredded and bleeding, she was going to cause permanent damage if she went any further. It was ridiculous to walk the pavements of London in bare feet, she was risking much more than bleeding blisters doing this, but she knew that just two streets down was an all-night caff frequented by cabbies where you could almost always get a taxi.

There was a damp chill in the air she recognised as the temperature drop that happened just before dawn. She felt so tired, achingly, bone tired. She wanted a hot bath, lavender oil, to sneak into her daughters' bedroom, smooth down their covers, kiss them and run a hand over their silky hair, followed by ten uninterrupted hours of sleep in a clean bed. And absolutely not a single one of those things was coming her way. For a passing moment she wondered if she was still up to this job. If she still had the energy for the office politics, the hours, the travel, the stress. Then the jab of adrenalin at the details scribbled on notepaper in the inside of her handbag revived her.

The faintest sliver of light was visible behind the tall buildings ahead of her. The sky would soon turn pale pink, and when she finally landed a cab, she would be driven home through the cool quiet of a London dawn.

At home, she would wash, change, make herself a cup of tea, then get into her car and set off on the final phase of this adventure.

18

SATURDAY: 6.20 A.M.

Jo had once explained it to someone like this: if you want to catch an interviewee at home, then these are the journalist rules: you must leave your house at daybreak, with an address and a map. You must head out of London, passing a petrol station to fill the tank, jamming the fuel receipt into the bulging section of wallet dedicated to work receipts.

At the petrol station, you must buy a large coffee that tastes of almost entirely nothing and an apple pie which does not count as a nutritious breakfast and the filling is guaranteed to squish out and scald the roof of your mouth so badly that for the next three days, you'll have a rough patch there.

You must then drive, paying close attention to the road map, road signs and motorway turn-offs while listening intently to the radio news because today is the day we go to press and everything that happens today is important. You must also, because you've had no sleep the night before, try very hard to stay awake.

According to the rules, you must be in your car parked outside a potential interviewee's house before seven o'clock. This way, should they be leaving early that day, perhaps to avoid the attentions of the press, they are not likely to have left until you've had a chance to try and speak to them. But if, when you arrive at 7 a.m., a car is parked in the driveway and the curtains drawn, then the rules are that you must not knock the door until after 8 a.m. Any earlier would be considered bad manners. Not something you could be reported to the Press Complaints Commission for exactly, but bad manners nevertheless.

Jo followed the rules to the letter and pulled up in the dinky little village of Lower Stenton shortly after 7 a.m. The address she was looking for turned out to be a sweet white house right on the village green. A car was parked on the other side of the white gate and curtains were pulled over each of the windows.

She would have to sit tight and wait for an hour or so. She had plenty to do: a stack of the day's newspapers to plough through and her Savannah interview to write. By 7.42 a.m., it was time to call Jeff, because she shouldn't really be out here without news desk approval.

'Have you beaten me to the office?' were the words Jeff used instead of 'hello'.

'No, I'm in Bedfordshire.'

'What the hell are you doing there? I need you to write up the Savannah piece and give me something fresh on whooping cough.'

'I'm out here trying to get you something very fresh,' was her slightly snappy reply. 'I've been up all night on this, Jeff,' she added. 'I would love to be in my bed, I wouldn't have driven out here if it wasn't for a very good reason.'

'No, I suppose not,' he answered and there was something soothing to his voice, which for a moment made her close her eyes and think with longing about sleep.

'I'm too old to stay up all night,' she told him, 'not without major pharmaceuticals.'

'So why did you?' he asked.

'I've got this great lead on Wolff-Meyer.'

'Well, that's a major pharmaceutical.'

'Oh, ha ha. I'm not going through it all on the phone, but there's another reason for this whooping cough outbreak. I'm waiting to doorstep the person with the grudge who might like to tell me all about it.'

'I see.' He didn't ask any more, and Jo knew this was because he trusted her. If she thought this was important enough to be doing on a Saturday morning, when there was so much other stuff still unwritten, then it almost certainly was important enough.

'Keep in touch,' he added. 'You know you need to start filing soon. By the way, Dominique phoned in yesterday evening to say she's quit. Gone to the *Mail* as a feature writer. Did you know about this?'

'No!' was Jo's reaction, 'the *Mail*? God—' Something that had puzzled Jo for days was suddenly clear. 'She probably put them onto the twins' family. But they've still not run that story, have they? So we could potentially go back to the Townells if we wanted to.'

'We can... if it fits with the fresh and convincing new line we're still waiting to hear from you.'

'Yup, yup, I know, I'm getting onto this as soon as I can. OK?' She was distracted by the departure of Dominique. Ambitious, clever girl...

Aidan's triumph in the Savannah story had probably been the final straw. Dominique could never stand it when he got a better story than her. Maybe she'd had an offer she was considering and she'd finally decided to jump. Jo had been mentoring Dominique for almost a year and she hadn't even called to tell her first.

'We have to get her back,' Jo told Jeff.

'Who?'

'Dominique! She won't start till Monday, I'll call her tomorrow.'

'Are you serious? She's sold your story from under your nose, been in secret talks to leave, is obviously far more ambitious than we even guessed—'

'Exactly,' Jo said. 'We need her back. She and Aidan have to get a pay rise and work in my crack team. The Health and Environment SAS.'

There was a pause at the other end of the line.

'Oh, go on,' Jo urged, 'I know you think of us all as family.'

'Family?' he sighed. 'Some bloody, psychotic, dysfunctional *bloody* family,' he answered. 'How much of a pay rise are you expecting me to find them?'

When she told him, all he could say was: 'Don't hold your breath.'

'I'll call her later,' Jo said.

'OK, speak soon.'

'Bye.'

As soon as she'd hung up, her phone rang again and she saw Simon's number. She hoped this meant her children, rather than her ex-husband, were up early.

'Hi, Mum,' Mel's voice came on the line.

'Hello, darling! How are you?'

'Fine, fine. Daddy's going to make us pancakes when he gets up.'

'How nice. You go and get him up, then.'

'He said we can wake him at eight o'clock and not before, he's busy kissing Gwen in there or something, eeeeugh… yuck.'

Jo would have liked to agree, but instead said: 'Tell me a joke instead.'

'Oh, I know, I know! If you're American when you go into the toilet and you're American when you come out of the toilet, what are you when you're in the toilet?'

'I have no idea. And I thought I told you I don't like toilet jokes.'

'This is not rude, I promise, Mum.'

'OK, then, what are you?'

'European. Geddit? You're a peeing.'

'Very good. How's Netts? Is she with you?'

'Yes, I'm reading her a story.'

'That's very nice of you. What are you doing today?'

'I dunno yet. Bicycles in the park maybe.'

'Good. Shall I say hello to Nettie?'

'Yeah, speak to you later.'

'Bye-bye, big kiss.'

A silly, smoochy kissing noise came back and then Nettie's voice was on the line.

'Hello, Mummy.'

'Hello, big pumpkin. How are you?'

'I got a joke too.'

'Have you?'

'What are you in the toilet?'

'Ermm, I don't know.'

'A fish.' This was followed by raucous laughter.

'Very funny,' Jo replied.

'Bye-bye then,' and with that Nettie hung up.

'Bye,' Jo was left to say into the receiver. Some days she wondered if she would make it through another twenty-four hours without them. She missed them even physically: the squishy soft weight of Nettie in her lap, the bony, angular cuddle of Mel. Missed them, missed them, but realised that no solution was going to be perfect and at the moment, this was the best they could all do.

The dashboard clock was crawling towards 8 a.m. Her daughters would get Simon out of bed and she would go to the white house and knock on the door. It was a bit early for a Saturday. She would probably find Joan in a dressing gown. But too bad, this was going to be a very busy day, she had to get it started. And then there was the bladder situation. The early morning coffee would have to go somewhere, soon. And this didn't look like the kind of village to have a public toilet.

OK, 8 a.m. was now registered on the dashboard. Time to gather herself together and go and knock on Joan Theroux's door. Jo switched off her mobile, no time for interruptions now, shoved her computer underneath the passenger seat, slipped her handbag over her shoulder and stepped out onto the pavement.

She wondered how many people were at their windows watching her go down the street. In a little village like this, people noticed. Through the white gate and up to the low red door, which she already knew was number 15, she went. The front curtains were still drawn, but she put her finger on the brass bell and gave her practised ring – counting to five slowly – so that it was long, but not too long. A definite ring.

Jo waited for forty seconds or so, listening carefully for any sounds of movement, then rang again.

She was certain someone was home, because the upstairs curtains had been opened in the hour she'd sat in the car and she'd already driven right round the house, making sure there wasn't a gate at the back. She uncrossed her arms, took a step back from the doorstep and prepared to give her friendliest smile.

Now she could hear footsteps – maybe Joan had gone to get her dressing gown – then the door opened and sure enough, a dressing-gowned woman stood in front of her.

Gingerish hair, streaked with grey and up on end, a pale, early morning face without make-up. Jo put her at late forties, which was consistent with all that she knew about her so far.

'Ms Theroux?' Jo asked with the smile, but trying not to sound too door-to-door saleswomanish.

'Yes,' Ms Theroux replied, looking totally confused.

'I'm sorry to disturb you so early on a Saturday. But it's important. My name's Jo Randall, I'm a journalist, I'm with the—'

But Ms Theroux had already let out a gasp which, Jo knew, was never a good sign. 'You're from the paper,' she said, 'I thought I recognised you.'

'I know that you and Wolff-Meyer are involved in legal proceedings and I'm here because I was hoping to talk to you about that.'

'No. No. I can't say anything. Please go away.'

And then with an embarrassed fumble, Joan shut the door and Jo – not for the first time in her career, or indeed the last – found herself staring at a small brass bell.

Drat.

As a reporter, you always lived in the over-optimistic hope that someone, somewhere wasn't going to make it this hard for you. That someone really did want to talk about something interesting.

She turned from the door and walked slowly down to the end of the street, turned left and took deep calming breaths as she carried on walking. Finally, she doubled back and was at the door again.

She pressed the buzzer firmly.

It didn't take long for Joan to come back. She'd got dressed in the five minutes or so since Jo had left her and now stood in her doorway in jeans and a baggy grey top.

She looked taken aback to see Jo there again. Maybe she'd been expecting someone else.

'This is really important, Ms Theroux,' Jo got in straight away. 'An eight-year-old girl is in a coma, someone might lose their child over this. We've got to know more about this strain of whooping cough.'

The woman's face seemed to pale even further.

'I can't talk about it, I just can't,' she said, agitated now.

'I don't have to bring you into this by name,' Jo was talking quickly, trying to say as much as she could before the door closed on her again, 'I know a lot about this already and I just need to ask you for some more background information.'

'Please,' Joan looked genuinely frightened now, 'leave me alone.'

The door shut with a bit more force this time.

Jo walked slowly back to her car. She suspected someone like Joan would usually talk by the second or third day you came back to them. But there was no time for that. She would have to give it an hour and try again. Sometimes people just needed a bit of time to come to terms with the fact that the press was onto it and the inevitable was going to happen, before they could make the decision to speak.

Climbing back into the passenger seat, Jo took out her computer. At least she could start writing up the Savannah story. The whooping cough situation was trickier: she had enough information to write a story, but it was all from a dodgy source... er, well, computer hacking? Make that an *illegal* one... She needed Joan in person backing it all up.

She connected her mobile phone to the laptop so she could check this morning's emails.

There was an email from the Wolff-Meyer press officer.

In line with latest recommendation from the government, we would urge parents to have their children protected with the Quintet five-in-one vaccination. This injection has been extensively trialled and found to be overwhelmingly safe.

There is no significant evidence to suggest that Quintet can cause whooping cough or is linked to brain damage, epilepsy or seizures.

Jo flipped on the car radio and kept one ear out for the news. There was a name and mobile phone number at the bottom of the statement, so she unplugged her phone from the computer and punched in the number.

It rang for a long time, and finally a woman's voice answered.

'Hello, is that Nicola Stoppes?' Jo asked.

'Yes, can I help you?'

Jo introduced herself.

'Right, yes, I'm duty press officer, what can I do for you?'

'Hang on a sec,' Jo told her. The beeps announcing the on-the-hour news headlines had just sounded on her car radio.

A deep male newsreader voice began to go through the headline news. Whooping cough was the third item on the agenda. The coma girl was 'showing signs of improvement' but a second child in hospital was now judged to be 'critically ill'. No new cases of the illness had been reported for a second day.

Jo turned her attention back to the phone call.

'Nicola, I want you to get a response from Wolff-Meyer for me on this question. Did a rogue strain of whooping cough from the Wolff-Meyer lab in Bedford escape and cause the current outbreak, which is proving extremely serious? Two children are critically ill. OK, that's the question.

'Now just to underline it: we have good reason to believe that the Wolff-Meyer research lab is the sole cause of this outbreak. Not the Quintet vaccinations, but the lab itself. Have you got that? And please, Nicola,' Jo added, 'don't mess me around on this. Get the question to the person who needs to see it. I don't want to hear that you couldn't contact anyone, because I'll know that's rubbish. My deadline is 12 noon. All clear?'

It certainly seemed to be clear to Nicola, but not altogether welcome. When Jo clicked off the phone, she had several decisions to make.

First of all, she called Jeff back.

'You have got someone at this hospital, haven't you?' she asked him as soon as he answered.

'Where the whooping cough children are?' was his response.

'Yeah.'

'Aidan's there. He's briefed to phone both of us if there's any word.'

'Oh, good.'

'Take it you're not having any luck.'

'No. Not yet. But I'll sit in the car. Trying her again later.'

'Better get writing.'

'Yeah. Don't worry, I was coming to that.'

'Were you? Nice of you to think of us back here in the office getting our arses chewed off by Spikey.'

'Now there's an image.'

It felt cosily private holding his voice to her ear. 'What did you want to talk to me about, Jeff?'

'We'll save it for tonight, if you're still on for that.'

She'd missed an entire night's sleep but somehow still seemed to be functioning, and now Jo heard herself agreeing to join him for the Saturday night post-office drinks.

After a brief catch-up chat with Aidan, she put her phone to the side, opened a new file on the computer and finally began typing:

* * *

Savannah Tyler, the woman who hopes to become Britain's first ever Green MP next week, has spoken for the first time about the death of her only child and how the tragedy has inspired her fight for a cleaner, Greener Britain.

Ms Tyler, now 44, watched her severely allergic baby son, Felix, die in her arms of an asthma attack eight years ago.

With the emergency services on the line, Ms Tyler fought to save 19-month-old Felix but she tearfully admitted: 'When I saw he was really going... I had to stop. I had to put the phone down, stop battling and just hold him for one moment longer. Let him go in some sort of peace.'

Jo didn't need to double-check that quote, like many other words from interviews done over the years, it had been imprinted on her mind.

Just months before her son's death, Ms Tyler had lost both of her beloved parents in an airplane crash. The combination of the two tragedies sent her into a depression that ruined her relationship with Felix's father, Philippe Teyhan, and led to many dark years.

Baby Felix suffered from multiple allergy syndrome, a condition not widely understood when he was alive. He was allergic to most of the common chemicals found in every household and suffered chronic eczema and asthma. Ms Tyler who, if the polls are right, will take a seat in parliament for Oxford North in next week's by-election said: 'I'm a scientist by profession but my special interest in the far-reaching and long-term effects of chemicals on our planet is inspired by Felix. I think about him every single day and about the kind of world I would have liked to hand on to him. I suppose you could describe what I do as a tribute to my beautiful baby boy.'

It was hard to repress both the tearfulness and the buzz of excitement Jo felt as she wrote this. It was true that some stories just wrote themselves.

A half-glimpsed movement made Jo lift her head, just in time to see Joan stepping out of her house. Bugger!

She moved the laptop to the driver's seat, grabbed her keys and scrambled out of the car door. Slamming it shut, she started to run down the road.

Joan heard the slam, saw her and began to speed up to get away from her. 'Ms Theroux!' Jo called out as she was almost level with her. 'I don't want to follow you about all day, but I'd really like to talk to you.'

Joan continued walking briskly with her head tucked down.

Jo walked beside her. 'There's another child critically ill in hospital today, did you know that?' she asked.

This seemed to slow Joan for a moment, but then she carried on walking.

'I know this is in the hands of the lawyers. I know you are taking Wolff-Meyer to tribunal and that they are accusing you of negligence. But I still think there are ways you can safely talk to us about this.'

Joan looked round at her with something close to amazed fear on her face.

'How do you know this? Have they been talking to you?'

'No, not the people in charge of Wolff-Meyer, but some other people down the line, like yourself,' Jo lied. Well, what else could she do? Admit to spending a whole night hacking into files?

'Who?' Joan asked, but at least she had stopped walking now.

'Look, I have to respect their request for anonymity.'

'Would you respect my anonymity?' Joan said breathlessly.

'I'd prefer to use your name, use your picture and let everyone know that you've nothing to be ashamed of,' was Jo's response to this.

There was a pause. Joan was obviously thinking hard.

'You've already spoken to someone else?' Joan asked.

'Yes.' Jo hoped the God of White Lies wouldn't strike her down on the spot. It was far from ideal to not tell the truth, but if it helped bring important truths to the surface, she was willing to do it occasionally and for the right reasons.

'You already know what's happened?' Joan asked.

'Yes.' Same prayer to the same god.

Joan's shoulders sank a little. Jo took this as a sign of something she'd observed in other reluctant interviewees: Joan had probably been living and worrying about this for weeks, maybe it would be a relief to finally talk.

Slowly Joan turned and began to walk back towards her house without saying anything. She pushed open the gate and said the four words Jo had been praying to hear.

'You'd better come in.'

19

SATURDAY: 11.58 A.M.

Just before noon, Jeff caught the call he'd been waiting for all morning. 'Even my back-up computer battery's dead,' were Jo's first words. 'Either I'll have to spend two hours dictating this on the phone to someone or I'll have to come back in. Can you wait that long?'

'We can probably wait,' was Jeff's verdict. 'Just get back quickly. I take it you've got it all from this woman. I mean, you can imagine how twitchy the lawyers are. They will need to pore over your copy before we go accusing major drug companies of spreading death and destruction – in fact there's talk about holding this till next week to make sure it's done properly.'

'And what have you said to that?' she asked, feeling a wave of anxiety.

'I've said bollocks. Although we've got another cracker to share the front page with you: someone rather famous was arrested first thing this morning for downloading child porn.'

'Who?'

When he told her, she could only give the expected: 'No way!' response that their readers would make.

'The police are going to make the arrest public by the afternoon, but only Vince has the full details,' Jeff added. 'Just so you know who you're up against.'

'I love a front-page battle with Vince,' Jo said, but she could feel her heart sink. 'I still think "Quintet Lab Releases Killer Whooping Cough" is better,' she said, 'It's more important.'

'Provided we get a snappier headline than that, yes, it is better. It's a proper scandal – the latest in the long line of "Randall scandals" our paper is proud to print. Do we have a statement from Wolff-Meyer yet?' he added.

'Their duty press officer was briefed first thing this morning. I await a reply. Although they might try to delay coming back to us, in the hope that without their say on it, we won't print.'

'Too bad,' Jeff said. She glowed with the knowledge that he had absolute 100 per cent faith in her. 'Really? You'll go ahead without hearing from them? I mean, it's a serious allegation. Is Spikey fine with it? And the people above Spikey?' She remembered de Groote and his Wolff-Meyer shares remark.

'I think it's going to be OK. It's an important story, Jo. A cover up uncovered. That's always good.'

'I can't name this woman I've been talking to, Joan Theroux. She won't go on the record,' Jo began her explanation. 'What she said comes anonymously and without pictures.'

Jeff winced. No news editor liked to hear that the source of a major story was going to be just that, 'a source'. Almost every other reporter in the newsroom would now have been told, nicely but firmly, to get back on the doorstep and knock again. But he didn't need to ask Jo, he knew she would have tried hard enough.

'Nothing else we can do?' he asked anyway.

'No.'

Jo had been invited into Joan's neat and floral house, where she had been told in no uncertain terms, by a woman who seemed genuinely scared, that the tribunal case was being dropped and she had decided to take the settlement offered by Wolff-Meyer.

'It's the only way I can leave all this behind with my professional reputation intact,' she had confided. 'If I take them to court, they'll accuse me of bad practice, negligence, they'll throw the book at me. They'll blame me for infecting my sister, Monique's daughter, as if I'd ever risk something like that.' Joan had looked at once defiant and tearful. 'I wasn't well, but I had no idea I was ill with a virus from the lab. I'd never have risked contact with Katie or anyone else if I'd known.'

'So, don't you want to argue your case in public?' Jo had asked, but at the same time wondered if she'd ever have the nerve to do something like that herself.

Joan had almost laughed: 'Even if I could afford the best lawyer in the world, they'd be able to afford ten of them. I would leave a tribunal looking like dirt. They've told me that.'

'In writing?'

'What do you think?' Joan had asked straight back.

'Do you think your home is bugged?' was Jo's next question.

'No, I'm pretty sure it's not. My brother is a police officer, he's come and checked. He's also told me to walk away and not try to take them on.'

They were sitting in a bright sitting room with pink sofas, green and white patterned walls, accessorised cushions and a coffee table with house and gardening books stacked on top.

A strange setting to be discussing industrial espionage, Jo couldn't help thinking. But she had believed Joan. Wasn't the fact that her own email was being intercepted proof enough that they were up against a powerful corporation that would go to considerable lengths to protect its own interests?

'You can't take the truth away from people.' Jo had argued, but Joan had just turned her head and looked out into her garden. The rims of her eyes were pink; she'd been crying this morning.

'Of course you can,' she'd said in a quiet voice, almost a whisper. 'If the company counterclaims loud enough, it will be believed. I mean what is proof? Line up enough scientists, enough scientific evidence on your side and you will be believed.'

'But people are more cynical than that. They will listen to the person speaking out against the system. They will,' Jo had argued, trying her hardest to persuade this woman to change her mind.

But Joan's head had remained turned to the window, looking out over her flowerbeds, her deep green lawn, a white wrought-iron table and a single matching chair. 'What do you know?' Joan had asked finally.

Carefully, putting in as much authenticating detail as she could, Jo told her everything she had been able to glean from her late-night session at the computer with Bella.

'Well, you have all the essential details,' Joan had said when the spiel was over. 'If you write that, you won't be wrong. The information you've got is good. We were working on new vaccine development,' she'd explained.

'Some "older" strains of whooping cough, like the ones recovered from the historic samples still exist in different parts of the world,' she'd continued. 'We're always inventing and investigating new vaccines and more efficient versions of existing vaccines. To know that I might somehow cause the death of a child... that's unbearable.'

* * *

As Jo headed back down the motorway to London, she took a revealing phone call from Bella, on the hands-free, obviously.

'Are you finally awake then?' Jo greeted her friend's still groggy voice.

'Am I finally awake? If this is the kind of thanks I'm going to get after staying up most of the night looking at hundreds of tedious computer files for you, you can get yourself another hacking assistant,' Bella replied.

'Were you able to go through more?' Jo asked with a burst of excitement.

'Yes, I was. Things calmed right down again once you'd gone. I've always suspected that you're one of those people with high personal static who has a strange effect on hard drives. But anyway, I'm phoning to give you three important nuggets of information.'

'Yes?' Jo moved into the slow lane so that she could concentrate.

'Number one thing,' Bella began: 'In certain rare cases, with susceptible children, the Wolff-Meyer safety investigation team *suspects* that Quintet can be linked to seizures and brain damage.'

'Oh my God!' Jo exclaimed.

'They are paying for research work. They are also keeping this extremely confidential. I only found out because someone had emailed a document to their home computer, so it was on the email system, which wasn't so highly protected.'

'You are a genius.'

'I know. Now, a company called Bexley Computing Systems Ltd is being paid a monthly retainer for unspecified "maintenance". My suspicion is that this is where your email is going and probably many other people's, judging by the size of the retainer. So, see what your tech department can unearth. Now finally, the news you may not want to hear...'

'OK. I'm listening.'

'Let's hope not too many other people are,' Bella joked, then said, 'The Joan Theroux situation may not be quite as straightforward as you thought.'

'Oh?'

'Wolff-Meyer is investigating the possibility that she was stealing material from the lab and selling it on to a competitor.'

'Oh.' Jo thought of Joan's pink eyes and frightened face, her sincere-sounding words, and felt a bubble of anger.

'The whooping cough strain, which dates from the 1830s by the way, and is making these children so ill, almost certainly comes from the lab, but it may be entirely Joan's fault that she caught it and let it out.'

No wonder Joan was so upset. No wonder the thought of children possibly dying as a result of her greed felt so 'unbearable'. Jo couldn't respond for a moment or two, because this was such a surprise.

Then she asked Bella: 'But they've no proof?'

'Well, according to one report I saw, they know she did on several occasions remove material from the lab without authorisation and she's never given satisfactory explanations for this, which is why they threatened her with a negligence charge.'

'Bella, you've gone to so much trouble for me.' Jo was moved by her friend's exhaustive efforts.

'Not just for you, Jo, I had to find out for myself. However much of a hard-nosed capitalist you may take me for, I don't want to make my money from a bunch of evil baby-killers. And I think I've now come to the conclusion that they're not as bad as you maybe believe. Mistakes get made, but they seem to be doing what they can to rectify them.'

'They still need to make public that certain children can be harmed by this vaccine and they know it. That's important too,' was Jo's reply to this. 'But it looks like they didn't release the whooping cough and they've tried to do everything they can to track down the leak and stamp out this outbreak.'

'Yup,' Bella confirmed. Jo was already thinking about how to write up her story around this new information.

'I'm going now. You need to work and I need to get outside and see some daylight.' Bella wound up. 'See you tomorrow for lunch, OK?'

'OK.' Jo was roused from her thoughts. 'Thank you, Bella, I owe you big time. Bye-bye.'

20

SATURDAY: 7.20 P.M.

The small and shabby old Swan pub, a world away from the glossy wine bars and other drinking 'venues' that surrounded the newspaper offices, was the bolthole of choice for newsroom refugees on Saturday night.

The Swan had a sticky floor, gloss paint on the walls and a fierce landlady. The pub was probably kept in business by the Friday and Saturday night drinking habits of the entire news group.

In the course of a long and frantic afternoon at her desk, Jo had filed her Savannah Tyler exclusive, her Quintet damage warning story for children with family history who were at risk – which came complete with the Townells' interview and one other – and, perhaps most important of all to her, her story about the leak of an antiquated whooping cough strain from the Wolff-Meyer laboratory, which had made a cluster of already vaccinated children dangerously ill.

It counted as one of the best weeks of her career, but she didn't feel happy or elated. In fact, she was so wound up that she was seeking solace in a series of vodka and tonics in the rowdy bar, which was already filling up with other reporters.

The only story that was absolutely 100 per cent running was the Savannah piece. She'd seen that laid out, headline, picture and all. The other stories were still, after 7 p.m. on press day, 'with the lawyers' both from the newspaper and Wolff-Meyer.

Wolff-Meyer had finally contacted her to say they would only make a response via their legal team to the newspaper's legal team. Spikey and possibly the group editor were both involved. She'd seen them bobbing in and out of the lawyers' office all evening.

'It's out of your hands,' Jeff had told her. 'Go to the Swan, have a drink, calm down, I'll come and tell you when I know what's happening.' That had been over an hour ago now. She could see Vince coming back in holding printouts of the first edition front page in his hands. He handed them out magnanimously around the bar.

'No!' The Swan's landlady was gawping at the main headline. It was Vince's child abuse allegation.

'Not him! I don't believe it. He's got kids of his own. That's terrible!'

'You can go ahead and believe it... every single word. He'll be officially charged next week.'

'No!'

Unfortunately, Vince was coming over to stand beside Jo and she was going to have to force herself to take a look at the printout.

'Savannah's here,' he told her. 'Sidebar obviously,' which meant it was the garnish at the side of the page, the words on the side of his brilliant scoop.

'Another drink?' he asked.

'Why not?' she replied, knowing perfectly well how many reasons there were not to. She wasn't far away from being sloshed; she had already forfeited the right to drive her car home, so would have to come back to work tomorrow to pick it up... She might need to have another conversation with the lawyers or her editor and she wasn't going to be in a fit state to do it. Not to mention the fact that she'd used up her week's entire alcohol unit allowance round about Tuesday: 'Vodka and tonic, please.'

She heard him ordering it and adding: 'Double please, it's Saturday night after all.'

Turning back to Aidan and Declan, she tried to remember what they were all talking about before Vince and his front page appeared.

'I really miss her, I really do. No one in newspapers is happily married, I can tell you that for free,' Declan was informing Aidan sadly.

Oh yes – Declan's divorce. How could she forget?

'Are they, Jo?' Declan added, putting an arm around her shoulder. 'Jo's just like me. Divorced. Husband couldn't take the paper pressure any more, could he?'

'Erm, I think it was maybe a little more complicated than that. Anyway, don't scare Aidan. He's not even interested in marriage yet; he certainly doesn't want to talk about divorce.'

'And then there's Jeff—' Declan added.

'Jeff's been married for twenty-odd years,' Jo smiled. 'He's the exception to your rule.'

Declan shook his head vigorously, causing the Guinness level to swing dangerously in his glass.

'He's moved out. The missus as well. They're putting the house on the market.'

Jo couldn't believe what she was hearing: 'Jeff's splitting up from his wife?' She wanted to be sure she'd heard this right.

Declan nodded.

'What's happened?' she asked.

'Don't know.'

'When did it happen? He hasn't said a thing.' Although obviously he had; he just hadn't said a thing to her. Clearly this was what he had been planning to talk to her about tonight. Maybe he wanted to ask advice or have her shoulder to cry on.

'I think it all came to a head a month ago. He's been staying in a hotel since then anyway.'

'In a *hotel*?! I can't believe it,' she said.

'So has your mystery techie been revealed?' Declan wanted to know.

Jo, head still reeling with the Jeff news, nevertheless had an answer for this question: 'Bexley Computing Systems Ltd. I had a tip, the tech department followed it up and it checked out. Don't ask me how. The company won't admit anything and apparently the program that was shuttling my emails about has been dismantled, but I'm getting a new super-secure desktop and laptop, courtesy of Mr de Groote.'

Jo didn't mention the other mystery that the techies had solved for her: the anonymous emailer.

'Got any good friends at the Green Party?' head technician, Manzour, had asked her.

'Lots,' she'd told him.

'The noreply@yahoo messages are generated by subsidiary of a Green Party chat list. Someone's been quite clever to suss this out and get messages to you through it.'

Savannah? Jo had wondered. Had Savannah led her directly to the Wolff-Meyer story?

'What's the news on your stories this week?' Declan asked next. 'Are they all going in?'

Jo double-checked the time on her watch then fished in her handbag for her mobile. They really should know by now.

As she speed-dialled the news desk, she glanced round the bar and saw Jeff walking in. She clicked the phone off and waved him over.

'How much have you had?' was his first question.

'Never mind that. Just tell me what's happening.'

'I just want to know if I should get you another, or if you're already dangerous.'

She pulled a face.

'Look—' he glanced at Declan, Aidan, Vince and the other professional nosy parkers all subtly pretending they weren't trying to overhear this conversation. 'Let's go to a quiet corner.'

She picked up her bag, slid off the bar stool and followed Jeff to the decidedly unglamorous space at the top of the stairs leading to the toilets, where they stood to talk. She had a bad feeling. Jeff jangled at the loose change in his trouser pocket.

'So, we're going to run the Quintet damage stories: the twin and the other baby. OK? That's all running,' he began. 'Even better, it's running with a full admission from Wolff-Meyer that Quintet has the potential to harm children with certain family or medical histories and both the public and the medical profession need to be made fully aware of this possibility. So, I think you'll agree that's a major breakthrough. Well done.'

She managed a smile at this, despite the horrible sinking feeling building in the pit of her stomach.

Jeff was handed a pint by a passing journalist which he accepted with a grateful nod. 'In the Wolff-Meyer statement which now accompanies your story – headlined on the second edition front page, by the way, and all over pages six and seven – Savannah's a full page three,' he went on, 'Vince's is one, four and five. But anyway, in the statement, Wolff-Meyer say they are rushing out a screening questionnaire to be given to every parent bringing their child for vaccination to try and pinpoint the rare children who could be damaged and prevent them from having the injection. They have asked for full information about your cases—'

'Well, they can buy the bloody paper then,' she interrupted.

'And they insist they will enter into talks with any concerned families.'

As Jeff paused to take a long sip at his drink, she was shocked to see that his wedding ring, the fat gold band which was as much a part of his hand as his solid fingers, was gone. Since when?! How had she not noticed this crisis going on in his life?

'But—' he began.

'But?' she repeated. 'There's a very big but, isn't there? You've struck a deal? The old whooping cough variant story gets spiked, in return for all this, doesn't it?'

He nodded slowly and took another long sip.

'They are not prepared to admit to any liability for the current whooping cough outbreak. They are extremely pissed off about that. They have promised severe litigation action against the slightest suggestion that this is their fault or in any way to do with them. They are *overly* interested in where our information comes from...'

'I bet they are. Didn't you tell them to have a look through the emails they've stolen from my computer?'

'Our lawyers did put to their lawyers that we had evidence of espionage.' Jo suddenly felt her heart squeeze. What if Wolff-Meyer likewise had evidence of espionage?

'They said they would conduct an internal inquiry into the matter. We helpfully provided them with the name of Bexley Computer Systems Ltd, as provided by our technical department.'

'Oh good,' she tried to relax a little. Bella was excellent at her job. She would have covered her tracks.

'The Department of Health has been issued with guidelines to quarantine cases, and all those in contact with those cases have been given a 'special' vaccine by Wolff-Meyer. There haven't been any fresh cases for two days, so they are hoping the illness has been contained. But there's no way we can run that virus variant story,' he said. 'We don't have the evidence in black and white. So, we can't go with it unless we want to feel the force of a multi-million-dollar lawsuit.' He added.

For a long minute, Jo couldn't reply. This was how it was sometimes. The best ones got away. The paper lived to fight another day. Didn't mean it didn't hurt like hell. Didn't mean that she wasn't burning with a furious sense of injustice, tears pricking at the back of her eyes. But then, that was just a bit of selfish pride really, wasn't it? All the vaccine-damaged and whooping cough families would be cared for and compensated privately.

Maybe the rest of the story would come out in the end, despite the best fire-fighting efforts of the pharmaceutical company.

And meanwhile, wasn't the Quintet promise a victory? Parents would be fully informed and children would be screened. There would be much less chance of this happening to anyone else's precious child.

She squeezed at her nose to try and make the tears that were threatening go away.

'We all fought your corner,' Jeff told her. 'Spikey's very proud of you. Obviously, he doesn't know anything about your Friday night computer hacking mission and never will.'

'Thanks,' she said finally, tears successfully squeezed. 'I think maybe I will have another drink. What about you?'

'Yes please and don't let the buggers get you down.'

'Your wedding ring?' she asked. 'I can't believe I didn't notice... and you didn't say anything—'

'Yup,' he broke in, then drained the last of his beer. 'Come and sit down with me in a nicer spot. I've been wanting to talk to you about that.'

At a small table in one of the quieter corners of the bar, Jeff lined up two drinks for them.

'Something soft, orange juice for me,' Jo had changed her mind. She wanted to listen to this story with a slightly clearer head. Then he began to explain how he and Frances, his wife of nineteen years, the mother of his two teenage sons, had come to the decision to separate. 'I think it had a lot to do with the fact that it would have been our twentieth wedding anniversary this summer,' was one of his admissions. 'Every so often we'd talk about the anniversary and have these open-ended discussions about what we'd do to celebrate it. Were we going to have a big party? Go on a second honeymoon?

'The more we talked about it, the more time we seemed to spend wondering if we were happy, wondering where all the years had gone, wondering if just another twenty years of the same was ahead for us.

'I don't think I was as bothered about it as Frances. She's been really down for months. She went off to Majorca on her own in April, said she was looking into property over there, started talking about selling up, moving... early retirement!' Jeff spluttered at this. 'Early retirement,' he repeated. 'I'm forty-five, not sixty! I know my hours are long, I know I've never spent as much time with my family as they would like me to have – but does anyone?'

Jo had to shake her head.

'I've been as good a dad and as good a husband as I could have been but I am a bloody great news editor.'

Emphatically he added, 'I am not leaving my job.' He picked up his beer glass and took a drink. 'Anyway,' he went on, 'if Frances had me with her retired in Majorca twenty-four hours a day, we'd be divorced within a week.'

Jo's image of Frances filled her head. She'd met Jeff's wife at office parties and for the occasional chat in the car park when Frances had arrived to collect a three-drinks-down Jeff from the pub and drive him home to what Jo had always imagined would be a big, comfortable, conservatory-clad home in the outer reaches of north London. Jeff's wife was a glamorous forty-something with long blonde hair, a tan, a taste for suede, heels and pink nails. She worked in interior design, drove a stonking big suburb-mobile, smelled exotic, joked, gossiped and chatted constantly, doted on her teenage boys and had always seemed to be warm, loving, caring and super-tolerant of Jeff and his all-demanding job.

But what could you ever know about other people's marriages?

'This doesn't sound like anything too serious,' Jo reassured him. 'It's just a... mild mid-marriage crisis or something. Sounds like it will all blow over.'

'Ha, well, I don't think so. She's told me she's met an English estate agent over in Majorca and they've had what she describes as a "brief affair" but she's now gone back out there to "see what happens".' Jeff made the collar-loosening move that Jo recognised from some of their most stressful working moments together. His eyes met hers briefly but then wandered off around the room, failing to find anything to settle on.

'You're joking,' was her response.

'No, no...' he was looking at her again. 'I've known about this for exactly two weeks and we're already talking about selling the house,' he confided. 'That's how out of touch I've been with her. Not exactly a good sign.'

Jo wondered how Jeff had managed to keep up such an amazing imper- sonation of normality at work, while this was going on. 'You should have taken some time off,' she told him. 'This is terrible.'

'God, no,' was Jeff's verdict. 'We've spent entire evenings ranting at each other – work has been a nice escape. I've heard all the "you never appreci- ated me," "you take me for granted," "we're in a total rut" stuff every single night. It's been like living in a bloody soap,' he couldn't help smiling. 'I drove her to the airport first thing on Tuesday and it was a bloody relief to leave her there.'

He stopped for another swig, while Jo struggled to summon up words of comfort. It was just so surprising.

Jeff was a fixed point in her life, a constant, her support system. A man who'd never been to her home, who'd never met her children or her friends. In fact, she'd only seen him in the Swan or in and around the office, but over the last four years he'd become one of the most important men in her life. The fact that his marriage and maybe his state of mind were about to unravel around her was deeply unsettling.

'Has she been in touch from Majorca?' Jo asked.

'She's phoned the boys,' Jeff replied. 'Doesn't want to talk to me.'

'Bloody hell, Jeff. I can't believe it! Do you think you'll get divorced?'

'Well, what do you think? It's looking pretty likely to me.'

'Do you *want* to get divorced?' she asked him, registering the shadows under his eyes for the first time.

He propped his chin up with his hands and made the tongue-clicking sound she associated with moments of hard concentration and big-deci- sion-making on the news desk.

'I don't know,' he said finally, 'I don't know her any more. How did that happen? I know you... I know Declan over there, Vince, Aidan, Mike, Rod, Spikey, Binah... I know just about every single person in my office better than I know my own wife. How did that happen?'

21

SUNDAY: 00:31 A.M.

Jo fumbled in her wallet to find the notes to pay the grumpy taxi driver. She'd drunk at least two more than she should have, but the effect was already wearing off: she'd travelled home with the window down, clear cold evening air rushing onto her face, sobering her up.

There, in the welter of receipts, were the £10 notes. The ink on those receipts would fade soon and she'd have sheet after sheet of illegible paper with no idea of what to claim money back on. Oh well, *mañana, mañana*.

She folded the wallet closed again and suddenly thought of Mike Madell, the deputy news editor up at the bar much earlier in the evening. He'd seen her hauling out the wallet and he'd asked: 'You still using that old thing? That's nice. Jeff went to a lot of trouble to find that for you... phoning round shops all over London: did they have the right make? The right colour? Did they have the right style? Was it going to be big enough? I'm lucky to get a pint out of him on *my* birthday.'

Now wasn't that bizarre? Jeff had told her it was from the freebie drawer. Why?! Her fixed point seemed to be on the loose suddenly and it was... unsettling.

She paid the driver, hauled herself out of the cab, slung her bag and her computer carry-case over her shoulder and stepped towards her house.

Beautiful night. She stopped for a minute to look up at the clear sky. She could see stars and that didn't happen in London much, the lights were usually too bright for all but the most determined stars. But tonight, the sky looked a deep, vibrant blue pinpricked with more stars than she remembered seeing for ages. Must be some sort of freak atmospheric condition. Savannah would know... or her astronaut friend. The cab rolled out of the street and it was very quiet, house lights out all along the neat little row. Jo walked towards her gate, still glancing at the stars, and felt for the latch.

'Boo!' said a voice coming at her out of the darkness.

'Aaargh!!!' was her instinctive response.

'Sorry.' The shadow stepped towards her and she saw that it was Marcus. Hair loose, curling on top of his shoulders.

'What the hell are you doing here?' Jo said, but she wasn't cross with him. No, no, not at all.

'I biked over.' Now she saw the shiny cycle against her wall, wondered how she hadn't noticed it before.

'Have you been waiting long?'

'No, just twenty minutes or so. Been stargazing – like you.'

She walked towards him, close enough to feel the heat radiating from his body. She put her hands on his shoulders. Felt the collarbone, the warm, slightly damp T-shirt beneath her fingers. He moved his face towards her but stopped short when he was an inch or so away.

'Hello,' he said. She could feel his warm breath on her face; the tip of his nose was almost touching her.

Her lips were pricking with an anticipatory tingle but she held back from him just for one moment longer.

He put a warm finger up against her lips and smoothed over them. The prickle did not abate. She could hear her heart thud in her chest. Blood pound in her ears. All this just for the thought of a kiss with him.

His arms were round her waist, pulling her against him. Then he was against her mouth, pushing past her teeth with his tongue. And she was gone, all his. How did he do this?

Her elbows were on top of his shoulders, her body pushed into his. As close as they could be with their clothes on. Impossible not to think about the hard-on pressed firmly against her.

Her heart hammering so rapidly she was sure he must be able to feel it, Jo broke away, to be able to breathe, needing a long lungful of the night air.

'Shall we go in?' she asked, wishing her voice didn't sound as shaken as she felt. It didn't feel right to be so bowled over by a kiss. She should have outgrown this, be more adult, better able to cope. Be more cool about it. It took several moments to find the lock with her key because her hand was trembling. Inside the hall she turned on the light and this seemed to break the spell. She hung up her coat and dropped her bags.

Marcus was walking ahead of her to the kitchen. He didn't seem to like any other room in her house, always made a beeline for the kitchen or the shower. The shudder took hold of her again at the thought of him in the shower.

'Are you hungry?' she asked.

'Nope.' He stood, hands half jammed into his jeans pockets.

'D'you want a drink?' she tried.

'Just a glass of water, maybe... No worries, I'll get it.' He turned to the sink and began to run the tap. 'How about you?' he asked.

'Water would be good.'

'How's your day been?' he asked, opening the right cupboard, taking out two glasses.

She could only give a little laugh in reply to this: 'Interesting,' she settled on finally.

'Got a good scoop?' he teased.

'Not bad... there's a better one "on the spike" in newspaper terms. But that, as they say, is another story. Shall we go next door? You know, if you don't want food.'

Marcus flung himself across the sofa and she sank into the armchair opposite. His T-shirt slipped and she saw the smooth, honey-coloured hipbone jutting out from the top of his loose jeans.

She slid her eyes along his broad bare forearms, noticing the black plastic watch and the boy bracelets tied to his wrist on either side of it. His face was tilted up to the ceiling and she just wanted to go over there, ruffle him all up and throw her body on top of his.

He turned to look at her and she asked how his work had been.

'Busy, busy,' he said. 'We were one short in the kitchen, so the rest of us were flat out. Saturday night always frantic—'

He added a little anecdote and ended with: 'So there we are. That's about it.' But it wasn't. They were speaking simple, straightforward sentences. But everything in this room was complicated. Why was he over there? Keeping a distance? Maybe he didn't want to do this any more. But then, did she? How interesting would she find him in a few more weeks' time? All this heady adrenalin-hit stuff was going to wear off. She'd be left making small talk about Marcus's favourite topics: cooking, shopping for cooking, CD *burning*, vodka and cycling.

'Marcus, Marcus...' she said.

'Jo, Jo,' he answered, which made her snort with laugher. It sounded so Primary Four.

'What are we doing?' she asked.

'Hangin' out,' was his answer. 'I've got two things to tell you.' He sat up and opened the flaps of his bag: 'I'm going to South Africa for the summer and I've bought you a present.'

She felt somewhere between relief and deflation with those words. This was probably it. This was where they drew the line and said goodbye. Jo found herself surprisingly touched by the handbag. It was caramel coloured leather and small, but not too small, decorated with brass studs, a scattering of orange and pink appliquéd flowers with a tassel on the zip. She slid open the brass zip and saw a bright pink silk lining. With a smile, she told him, 'I'll hardly be able to get any of my stuff into this little bag.'

'Maybe that's a good thing,' he replied. 'When you have this bag, you can just take what matters... and come dancing with me.'

Oh, that was perfect.

His turn to smile now.

She thanked him profusely but from something of a distance. In her mind was the thought that this should be goodbye, this was a good moment. End on an up.

And he seemed to feel the same. After a little more talk, he stood up and told her: 'I should go. You've had a really long day and...'

And... well... he didn't need to say the rest.

But in the hallway, in the semi-darkness, she made the mistake – or was that, had the good idea? – of kissing him goodbye and found she was lost and disorientated. All that heart hammering and blood rush. It wasn't exactly nice, wasn't comfortable. She had no idea what to expect next. Why did this feel like a rollercoaster? All of a sudden, she wasn't in the slightest bit drunk, wasn't even tired. She was wide awake, minutely conscious of every tiny movement. His lips were soft, his mouth was a little dry, despite the glass of water. He tasted of garlic and cigarettes. Something a little stale and unbrushed, un-minty. Real. She realised her want for him was unbridled. Unstoppable. There was no way she could let him out of the door. He was pulling her skirt up. She didn't want him to, not in her head. Meanwhile, her hands were pulling the skirt up too.

Tights. Of course she was wearing tights. Was she expecting her twenty-something lover to be waiting at her door? They pulled them clumsily down too. 'I can't do this,' she said, but it was in between kisses, in between feeling his tongue curl against hers, letting it fill up her mouth.

'I don't mind,' was his answer, gasped out. 'You just let me know— know what you want—' Her hand was in his trousers feeling for him. And still she didn't think they should be doing this. In her head.

Her fingers on the velveteen folds at the top. The fingers of her other hand between his teeth now, touching his teeth and tongue.

She put her lips down onto the soft, warm skin pulled tight over his collarbone. She didn't even know why his collar and hip bones were such a turn-on for her. Maybe because these were the things she caught glimpses of when she talked to him, when she watched him.

'Can we talk about this upstairs?' he was asking.

In the bedroom, they took each other's clothes off, kissing frantically. Landing on the chill of the bedspread naked, they started to tangle together. One of his hands was held tightly around her back and the other... the other moved gently but deliberately against her, inside her, while his mouth stayed up at her ear, whispering against her lobe. 'Here? Just here? OK? Move me to the right place...'

She closed her eyes, curled an arm around him and pushed her face into his hair. Fell into a rhythm. At last, she felt in a private, enclosed space with him. This was just about them. It didn't matter what anyone else thought, didn't matter what she thought, what Simon thought, or her mother, or Bella or... anyone. It didn't matter what anyone thought. It didn't even matter what she was *supposed* to think.

This was her, alone with him. Private and alone. His fingertips on minuscule parts of her. In a room, in a house, in a street, in a city, in a country, in the world, in the universe. Who cared? It was a tiny insignificant stiffening of muscles, blood rush, and tingling.

He was hard again and moved into her, kept a finger expertly in place; she moved to get a better grip on him.

Just one tiny, insignificant stiffening of muscles, blood rush, pulse and tingling. Tiny— insignificant— unimportant, abandoned, but— just— yes — that's— yes—

She'd forgotten how real this was, how alive you were when this happened, how it could make colours explode in your head, behind your closed eyes. The pit of the stomach excitement, the feeling of falling, plummeting. She held onto him tightly, to keep afloat, to keep her bearings. He came with a quiet gasp and gripped her tightly until they were both so hot and sweaty that he had to move off and sink face first onto the bed. All quiet in the moment of exposure. She put her hand on his back.

'It's OK,' she said.

'Yeah... Who knows—?' he murmured.

Who knows— It was just coming back to her that she hadn't had any sleep. Hadn't slept for two days. Suddenly she didn't think she even had the strength to get in under the covers, she was so tired.

22

THE FOLLOWING FRIDAY: 3.25 A.M.

Jo's bedside phone had a soft, muted ring tone. The volume control was always turned down low deliberately, to save her from being thrown out of bed in the middle of the night by a blaring bell.

When the phone began to purr gently beside her, she picked up, suspecting she knew who this was. Who else would be awake on a Thursday night, make that, Friday morning, watching the results of a by-election on the TV?

'Hello, is that you?' she said into the receiver.

'Don't know. Which "you" do you think it is?'

'See, it is you.'

'So, you're awake then?'

'Of course I'm awake! This is exciting.'

'They're just about to declare.' Jeff's low voice on the other end of the line sounded tired, but conspiratorially close to her ear.

'I know,' she said.

'I thought you might like someone to keep you company for it.'

'Did you? That was nice of you. But we're going to regret this tomorrow morning, aren't we? Industrial strength coffee all round.'

'Never mind, it's only Friday.'

'Ha.'

Then there was silence, but it was comfortable. No need to say anything else. They were silent because the returning officer was stepping up to the microphone. The candidates standing for election in Oxford North lined up beside him: seven of them, twitching, adjusting collars, flicking their hair, all looking tense, even Savannah, whose hands were twisting together in a way that Jo wished she didn't recognise.

Savannah was taller than everyone else in the line-up and looked... well, 'extraordinary' would be the right word. Everyone else was in office wear: suits and shirts. But she'd chosen a soft, multicoloured, although mainly green dress, worn with high-heeled boots. No wonder she towered over everyone. Her hair was tied back and as well as the nervous hand twitching there was something else that set her apart: she looked ready. The returning officer leaned over the microphone and began to give details of the vote count. He named the candidates from the big parties and their tallies, which seemed high... too high. When he came to Savannah's name he gave a number, which Jo didn't think was high enough.

'Has she—?' she began, heart in her mouth. But then the whooping noises, claps and cheers started up and the camera, after a swoop of the disappointed faces, closed in on Savannah's huge, relieved smile. She started to shake the hands of the candidates standing beside her, then she waved out into the crowd and for a moment it looked as if she was moved to the verge of tears. But someone rushed up to hug her and a grin split across her face again.

'Green Party candidate, Savannah Tyler, takes the seat for Oxford North,' the BBC commentator's voice was cutting across the noise in the hall. 'This is something of a historic moment for the Green Party. Their first ever Westminster MP—' then commentator-spiel took over. Some blurb he'd no doubt spent all day rehearsing.

'Get us an interview then, you prat,' Jo directed at the TV, momentarily forgetting she was still on the phone.

'That's not me you're talking to?' Jeff said.

'No. No—' she was taken aback to hear his voice again, realised she was much happier about Savannah's success than she'd even guessed she would be. It felt important. 'This is amazing,' she exclaimed. 'She is amazing.'

'Really?' Jeff asked. 'Sounds to me like you're undergoing some sort of political conversion. Well, don't,' he added. 'They're all bastards. A year from now you'll be looking into Savannah's murky expenses fiddle or uncovering the fact that she's secretly on the payroll of an oil company.'

'Stop it!' she interrupted him. 'She's not like that. Nothing like that at all!'

'Jo Randall! You've been spun!' was Jeff's response. 'I'm sorry but all politicians, if they don't start out bastards, end up bastards. I'm much older and more cynical than you, so I know. But she's got to you, hasn't she?'

'Just to you, Jeff, I am going to admit to a great big girl-crush on Savannah Tyler,' was how Jo tried to express it. 'And you know what? She phoned me on Sunday, when the paper came out, and said if she got elected, she'd like to offer me a job.'

Now, she'd gone and said it. Four years of working for Jeff and she'd never once breathed a word about going anywhere else, although there were occasional offers. 'Obviously, as an MP, I'll have money for support staff,' Savannah had told her. 'I want to employ an excellent communicator to help spread the message.'

'Well, your party must be full of those kinds of people,' Jo had said, sure that Savannah couldn't possibly mean what, for a moment, Jo had thought she meant.

'Yes. There are good people here,' Savannah had agreed, 'but I'll be a lone Green voice, I'll need someone really exceptional... Jo, I realise this will come as a surprise, but if I become an MP, will you consider coming to work for me?'

'Me!?' And into Jo's mind had jumped all the reasons why she couldn't possibly... wasn't at all... had never even...

But Savannah hadn't wanted to hear, hadn't even wanted to have a big discussion about it, she'd simply said: 'Give it some thought. Sometimes it's best when an idea grows.'

'And what did you say to that?' Jeff asked, not missing a beat, not even sounding particularly surprised. 'I said I'd think about it.'

'Aha.' There was a pause before Jeff said: 'And what about your newly pay-risen SAS team?'

'I know.'

'I don't need to tell you that, as your news editor, I wouldn't want you to go. Can't imagine working without you.'

'No, but it's nice to hear. Maybe you should tell me anyway – and more often,' she said, suddenly aware of a squeeze in her throat.

'As your news editor,' he repeated, 'I don't want you to ever consider leaving the paper or else I'll have to send Vince in his bulletproof car to bring you back.'

She laughed at this.

'But,' he went on, 'not speaking as your news editor, speaking as your— umm— friend, maybe I should tell you to think about it.'

'Really? Why?'

'Because, you know... change is...' he considered for a moment and decided on, 'interesting.'

'Yup. It's also bloody stressful and kind of sad.'

'Yes, kind of sad,' he agreed.

'Yeah,' was all she could manage, because suddenly the thought in her head was: What's going on? Is Jeff asking me to leave? Doesn't he want to work with me any more? And now, she couldn't imagine being without her job.

'And maybe— if you didn't work at the paper, other things would be possible—' and here he stopped to clear his throat in an entirely uncharacteristic way. 'You know,' he went on, 'if you were working somewhere else.'

'Other things?' she asked. Now what? She found herself doing the throat-clearing thing. What was going on? What was the matter with them?

'Yes, other things,' he repeated and coughed.

If she worked somewhere else, it was occurring to her, like wiping mist off a window, then the unspoken boundary that, like their marriages, had stopped them from even thinking about exploring the *something*, which was only just the beginning of a feeling... well, that barrier would be gone.

Now, she allowed herself to remember in full detail, the very end of the Christmas party a year and a half ago. A year and a half ago! When she'd made her way through a packed, noisy crowd to seek Jeff out, intent on a mission to say goodnight to him, even though they'd see each other again in the office in the morning.

She'd got to him. The crowd had squeezed her in closer to him than she'd meant and he'd turned from the person he was talking to, not anyone she recognised, who'd excused himself.

Then they were there, facing one another, an island of two for a moment in this busy throng.

'Came to say goodnight,' she'd said as lightly as she could.

'Oh,' he'd given his quizzical smile. 'Goodnight then.'

Then the strange thing. The emboldened by too much champagne moment, maybe. Their heads had moved towards each other, intending a friendly kiss on the cheek, perhaps. But still something they'd never done before.

She'd got to his cheek but had felt drawn to turn so that her lips were on his. And he'd reacted by pressing his lips against hers, putting his arms tight around her back.

She'd noticed a flurry of things: how he'd smelled of aftershave, smoke, the dry-cleaning fluid on his best suit. The solid bulk of him, the strength in his grip, the want in that kiss.

And then she'd pulled back, met his eye, read there something of the confusion, bearings lost, that she was feeling herself.

'G'night,' she'd mumbled and turned to go and find her husband. To let Jeff return to his wife. To both return to normal.

And that's how the next day in the office had been. Normal. Absolutely nothing out of the ordinary in the way he spoke to her, related to her. Normal service was resumed. And she hadn't thought since then about how she could possibly feel about Jeff... if they weren't married to other people... and if he wasn't her news editor.

'And here she is,' Jeff interrupted her thoughts. 'Your leader,' he teased. 'Your girl crush.'

'Ha ha,' was Jo's response but she leaned forward as Savannah's face filled the screen.

Oxford's newest MP may have looked somewhat shell-shocked and flushed, but she spoke with collected calm. She had replaced the bright green rosette pinned to her dress earlier in the evening with a large green flower – surprisingly *Sex and the City* but probably biodegradable.

'This is a fantastic result for us,' she was saying into the microphones thrust into her face. 'This is the start of the Green revolution.'

Then she stumbled up the steps to the stage again, high heels obviously not quite her thing, to make her acceptance speech.

'I'd like to thank everyone who made this possible—'

'Here we go, the Oscars moment,' Jeff interrupted.

Jo didn't reply. Her eye had fallen on her two handbags. They were propped up, side by side on the chair at the side of the room.

One was the heavyweight, expensive label that could accommodate her whole life, everything about her. It was dependable, solid, strong. A lifelong companion that came with history. It came with a wallet from Jeff... in fact, it was the handbag version of Jeff. A little bit jowly, heavy set, ten years older, gym strong, a man who made writing macho, who came with a lifetime of experiences. Who came post-marriage, with his own children. Who would understand everything about her and her work. Who was married to the paper, married to the job. Who had an older, well worn, somewhat weary world view.

And then there was that dainty little Marcus bag. Fun, frivolous, futuristic. Lightweight. Everything was still ahead for him. Everything was new. He wasn't a long-term commitment. But neither was she, right now. She was newly freed. She was uncommitted. The Jeff. The Marcus. Heavyweight Italian leather for keeps, or appliquéd girlie glamour for the moment.

Which to choose?

She watched Savannah on the dais thanking everyone who'd helped her to run her campaign.

'Why rush the decision?' was the thought that sprang to Jo's mind. Why even make it a decision? She was in between. And being in between choices was just fine.

There was far too much emphasis on quick decisions, quick gratifications, quick solutions.

Maybe there was no quick remedy here. What about a long, slow, elaborate romance? Slow, simmering of years of unconsummated devotion.

The kind of wonderful, complicated mental creation that would have existed in the past. An unspoken romance that lasted and lasted and shaped the course of two lifetimes. She could wait until she was ready. Until she knew what she was ready for.

There was another more important decision to make first. Would she leave the paper at the pinnacle of her career, and work for Savannah? Again, she didn't need to decide today. The right decision would come.

'So, what do you think... might be possible?' she asked Jeff, clearing her throat, 'You know – if I were to leave the paper?'

'I'd probably ask you out to dinner,' was his answer.

'Is that it? Dinner! But maybe I'd say no,' she replied.

'I'll have to take that risk,' was his calm answer. As if he too was prepared to wait this out.

'I might not need dinner... I'm currently seeing a chef,' she risked.

'I know.' Still the same calm, steadying voice she knew so well. The voice she really did like to have pressed up against her ear, listening to her thoughts. No denying the lurch in her stomach that this conversation was provoking. But really, she wasn't sure if she even wanted him to suggest anything like this... it was too soon. She didn't know if she had anything to offer him yet... The delicious smell of Marcus was on her sheets, was on her skin, erasing her past, her mistakes and making her look to the future, like him. To better things ahead.

'So, what's next?' Jo asked, wondering how Jeff would reply. Wondering if any more of him or his intentions would be revealed.

'What's next?' he repeated. 'It's Friday morning. Time to get busy.'

No more secret sharing now, just the usual hint of friendly tease evident in all their daily conversations.

'The Savannah victory interview, obviously,' he said. 'I'm expecting you to do that for us. *Exclusive.* And then what the hell else have you got for this week?'

'A lot more,' she answered him. 'I might even surprise you.'

* * *

MORE FROM CARMEN REID

Another book from Carmen Reid, is available to order now here:
https://mybook.to/BrandCarmenBackAd

ABOUT THE AUTHOR

Carmen Reid is the bestselling author of numerous women's fiction titles including the Personal Shopper series starring Annie Valentine. She lives in Glasgow with her husband and children.

Download your exclusive bonus content from Carmen Reid here:

Visit Carmen's website: www.carmenreid.com

Follow Carmen on social media:

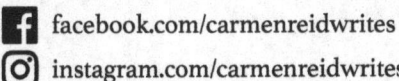

facebook.com/carmenreidwrites

instagram.com/carmenreidwrites

ALSO BY CARMEN REID

Worn Out Wife Seeks New Life

New Family Required

The Woman Who Ran For The Hills

Three in a Bed

Stuck in Second Gear

The Mum Who Got Away

Mum on a Mission

The Annie Valentine Series

The Personal Shopper

Late Night Shopping

How Not To Shop

Celebrity Shopper

New York Valentine

Shopping With The Enemy

Annie in Paris

Boldwood

Boldwood Books is an award-winning fiction publishing company seeking out the best stories from around the world.

Find out more at www.boldwoodbooks.com

Join our reader community for brilliant books, competitions and offers!

Follow us
@BoldwoodBooks
@TheBoldBookClub

Sign up to our weekly deals newsletter

https://bit.ly/BoldwoodBNewsletter

www.ingramcontent.com/pod-product-compliance
Lightning Source LLC
Chambersburg PA
CBHW011800010726
47497CB00012B/3221

* 9 7 8 1 8 0 6 5 6 0 4 2 4 *